The Peasant's Scroll

The Peasant's Scroll

R. J. Williams

CONTENTS

"Some of the more ancient [texts] have been discovered only in recent times by trained archeologists... including Gospels allegedly written by Jesus' close disciple... and his female companion, Mary Magdalene. For the most part, [texts] were suppressed, forgotten, or destroyed – in one way or another lost..."

–New Testament scholar, Bart Ehrman, *Lost Scriptures: Books That Did Not Make It Into the New Testament*

PROLOGUE

The Logan Nightly Examiner
The Voice of Logan County, Illinois
Wednesday Evening, August 16, 1972

Air Force Veteran Returns Home to New Pastor Assignment
By Charles Saunders, Staff Writer

STONEFORD — After two tours as an Air Force chaplain in Vietnam, Reverend Thomas McGarvey has returned to Logan County to take up a new assignment at Great Witness Community Church in Stoneford.

McGarvey, son of the late James and Catherine McGarvey of Springfield, served five years with the Air Force, four of them alongside combat troops. He was awarded the Air Force Legion of Merit and the Air Force Commendation Medal with Valor.

McGarvey, who appears younger than his thirty-six years despite the silver beginning to show in his sandy hair, spoke with characteristic humility about his service. "Just being home from Vietnam is a blessing," McGarvey said this week. "To be able to serve a church so close to where I grew up — that's more than I could ask for."

Ordained in October 1965, McGarvey's first post was Associate Pastor at St. Peter's in the Field Church outside Springfield. After hearing reports of heavy casualties in the Battle of Dak To in 1967, he felt a strong call to minister to soldiers overseas. With encouragement from a friend at the 183rd Tactical Fighter Group, he entered the Air Force chaplaincy.

"Looking back, I know my time in Vietnam was where I was meant to be. I wasn't carrying a rifle like the others," McGarvey recalled, "but I carried their fears, their prayers... and sometimes their last words. That was my duty."

"Now I want to take some of the lessons I learned there and bring hope to folks here at home."

McGarvey says he does not plan immediate changes as the church's new pastor, but believes churches must adapt to a changing society. "If not, I'm afraid the church may risk becoming irrelevant in generations to come."

A celebration of installation will be held this Sunday in Fellowship Hall following morning worship. The public is invited to welcome Reverend McGarvey home. Coffee, pop, and homemade pies will be served.

PART ONE
Stoneford

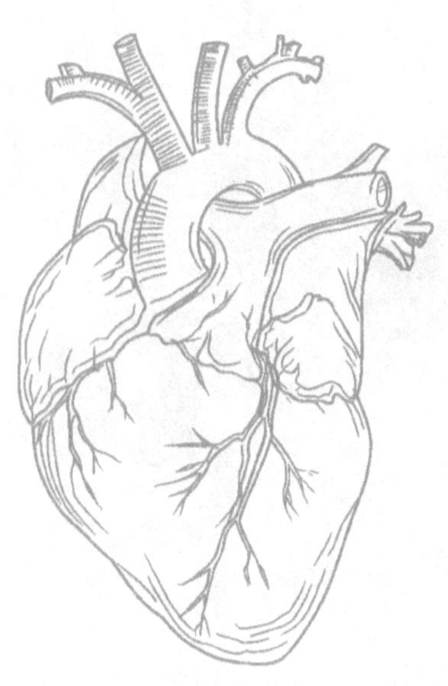

CHAPTER ONE

"Why do these damn elevators always take so long?"

Tom jabbed the down button again, then pulled his hand back and stared at his fingers. The same fingers that had just clasped together in prayer over Gladys Peterson's bed, assuring her that God was listening. Promising her that God cared... that everything would work out according to His plan.

He shoved his hands deep into his pockets.

Years of standing beside hospital beds, speaking words that were supposed to matter. Ten years of watching hope drain from faces when the prayers didn't change a damn thing. And Gladys... sweet Gladys, who'd brought him casseroles when he first arrived at Great Witness three years ago, who never missed a Sunday service. She deserved better than a pastor who doubted his own prayers.

A small plush toy in his coat pocket rubbed against his knuckles. He'd grabbed a couple from the church supply closet before leaving. Toys for the pediatric floor, just in case. At least those he could count on. Five-and-ten-cent toys that brought smiles to children's faces. Tangible. Real. Unlike whatever he'd just offered Gladys.

He loosened his tie. *Am I a hypocrite?*

The fifth-floor hallway stretched empty behind him. No one had seen him leave Gladys's room wearing the expression he couldn't quite hide—the one that said he'd just gone through the motions. Again.

The elevator dinged somewhere below. Tom exhaled and rolled his shoulders back. This was the job. This was what he'd signed up for. Comfort the sick. Pray with the dying. Offer hope even when—

His chest tightened. Not now. Not here.

He pressed his palm against his sternum and focused on breathing slowly. In through the nose, out through the mouth. The episodes had gotten more frequent lately, showing up at the worst possible times. Another thing he'd been putting off.

He hit the button again. Harder this time. "Come on!"

"No matter how many times you push it, it's not going to make the elevator appear any faster."

Tom turned quickly. His chest was still tight, and the sudden movement made his head swim. A young woman stood a few feet back, holding the hand of a little girl whose dark ponytail swayed as she peered around her mother's leg.

"Sorry." He forced a practiced smile. "Didn't know anyone else was up here."

The little girl pressed closer to her mother's side.

Tom stepped back, giving them space. He recognized that look. It was the look of caution. *Smart kid. Smart mom, teaching her to be careful.*

"It's okay, honey," the woman said, squeezing her daughter's hand. Her voice was gentle but tired—the kind that came from too many hospital visits. "Remember Father Moore at church? This man is like Father Moore. We're teaching her not to talk to strangers," the mother explained, meeting Tom's eyes. "But when I saw the clergy thing, I figured you must be the hospital chaplain or something."

Tom glanced down and saw his visitation stole was still visible, one purple edge peeking from his coat. *Or something.* That about summed it up.

"I'm just visiting someone from my church." Tom knelt slowly to be at eye level with the girl, his knees protesting the way they had since Vietnam.

The little girl studied him, then looked up at her mother for permission. Her mother nodded.

"My name is Charlotte." Her voice was small but clear, with a slight lisp.

"Charlotte." Tom extended his hand. "That's a beautiful name."

Charlotte's small fingers closed around three of his. A practiced handshake, surprisingly firm for someone so young.

"I love your ponytail," Tom said. "Did your mom do that for you?"

Charlotte's face lit up. "Mommy makes the best ponytails! Sometimes she even puts twists in them."

"Well, your mom is very talented." Tom pushed himself back to standing, gritting his teeth against the familiar ache. 'Battle-fatigued knees,' the VA doctor had called them. Another souvenir from Vietnam.

"But you know what? I think something's missing."

Charlotte's mother raised a curious eyebrow.

Tom reached into his pocket and pulled out one of the small plush toys. He held his closed fist out to Charlotte, then opened it slowly.

A purple unicorn. "Mommy..." Charlotte whispered. "It's purple!"

"Purple's her favorite color." The mother's voice caught. She pressed her fingertips to her lips. "How did you—"

"Lucky guess." Tom handed the toy to Charlotte, watching her face transform. This, at least, he could do. This small gesture that cost him nothing and meant everything to a scared little girl in a hospital. "I keep a few in my pocket. A unicorn for girls, an airplane for boys. Just in case."

Charlotte hugged the unicorn to her chest. For just a moment, the weight in Tom's chest eased.

"It's like you're..." The mother's eyes glistened. "It's like you're an answered prayer."

"An answered prayer?" The words came out rougher than he intended. Tom cleared his throat. "No ma'am. I'm just a guy with a toy in his pocket."

"You don't understand." She wiped at her eyes. "Charlotte left her stuffed animal at home. She's been beside herself all evening because..." Her voice cracked. "My husband is on this floor. But Charlotte's sister, Alysia, is down in pediatric ICU."

Tom looked down at Charlotte, who was running her small fingers over the unicorn's mane, oblivious to her mother's fear. Then he looked back up. The exhaustion and terror behind those tears were palpable.

"I'm so sorry." He brought his hands to his chest. It was a habitual gesture when he didn't know what else to do with them. "How are they doing?"

She pulled back her shoulders, taking in a breath that seemed to require effort. "The doctors say they'll both be okay. It's going to take longer for Alysia, but..." She managed a weak smile. "They should be home by the end of the month. That's what they tell us, anyway."

The end of the month. This month, between last month's Easter and next month's Pentecost. There's always so much to do. He should have been using this time to prepare. Instead, he'd been working around doctors' appointments and tests whose results he was still waiting to hear.

Easter was supposed to be about hope. About resurrection and new life. Had he given this woman any reason to hope? Or had he just handed her daughter a toy?

"Ma'am, I'm sorry. I never even asked your name."

"Maria." She extended her hand immediately. "My name is Maria."

Tom took her hand gently. "Tom. It's good to meet you both."

"Are you Reverend Tom? Father Tom?" Maria studied the purple edge of his stole. "I'm not sure how to address you properly."

The elevator dinged. The doors slid open with a grind.

"Just Tom." He moved toward the empty car, holding his arm across the door. The simple motion pulled at something in his chest. "I'm not much for formalities."

Maria guided Charlotte inside. Tom followed, letting the doors close behind them.

"I wasn't sure what kind of chaplains this hospital has," Maria said, pressing the button for the third floor.

"I'm the pastor at Great Witness Community Church. Spending time here with someone from the congregation."

The elevator hummed as it descended. Charlotte pressed her face against the unicorn, whispering something Tom couldn't quite hear.

"Tom." Something in Maria's voice made him look away from the floor numbers. Her eyes were direct. Determined. "Would you pray for them? For my husband Pete, and Alysia?"

The number of times Tom had been asked to pray for someone was incalculable. Hundreds of hospital rooms. Hundreds of bedsides. Thousands of promises that God was listening. Words that used to fill him with purpose.

He wanted so much to explain to Maria that it wouldn't be thoughts and prayers that would bring healing. It would be the skill and wisdom of the doctors. Medicine and time and the resilience of the human body. Things he could see and touch and trust.

But he also knew the power of hope. And if God was going to use him for anything anymore, maybe being an instrument of hope was enough. So, he did what had become a habit. "I'll keep them in my prayers," Tom said, forcing warmth into his voice. "In fact, I'm going to start right now by praying this elevator gets us down safely."

It was his standard deflection.

Maria's smile faded. Just for a second, but Tom caught it.

"Actually," she said, her voice smaller now. "I meant... would you pray now? Here? Before we get to Alysia's room?" She looked down at Charlotte. "I think it would help Charlotte to see someone pray for her sister."

The third floor was approaching.

Charlotte looked up at him, her small face serious, the purple unicorn clutched under her chin. "Will you make my sister better, Mr. Tom?"

The question hit him like a mortar landing in the next fox-hole.

Tom pulled his hands from his pockets and stared at them. These were the same hands that tore open that medical bag on that dark, thunderous battlefield. The same hands that tossed it to the medic when he screamed for morphine. The same hands that were so sure—

No. Not now.

He couldn't finish the thought. He wouldn't let himself remember. Just as his prayers had never changed anything, neither would recounting that night in some dense jungle while bombs exploded around him. A chaplain who'd failed at the one thing he was asked to do.

In the chaos and darkness, he'd grabbed what he thought was the morphine. And by the time they realized it, by the time dawn broke and they could see what had happened—

Tom's chest tightened. His breathing shortened. The elevator slowed.

"Mr. Tom?" Charlotte's voice pulled him back.

He looked at her. Really looked at her. She was maybe five years old, with her mother's dark eyes and a trust in her expression that he didn't deserve. Behind her, Maria's face was etched equally with exhaustion and hope.

He could deflect again. Promise to pray later. Add them to the church prayer list. Keep his doubts safely locked away.

Or he could pray. Right here, right now. Risk feeling like the hypocrite he thought he was. Risk speaking words that might fall on deaf ears. Risk failing them the way he'd failed so many others.

If he deflected now, what would that teach Charlotte? What message would that send to Maria, who was desperately trying to hold herself together?

The elevator dinged. The doors began to slide open.

Tom dropped to one knee. His joints protested, but he ignored them. The movement caused his coat to pull open, revealing a crisp powder blue shirt, complementing his blue-gray eyes, but a sharp contrast to the rough stubble shadowing his jaw. The morning was too hurried for shaving.

He reached out and took Charlotte's small hand in his left and Maria's trembling hand in his right. "Charlotte," he said, his voice rough, "I can't make your sister better. That's not something I can do. But I can pray. And I can ask God to be with her, and with your mommy and daddy, and with you." He looked up at Maria. "Is that okay?"

Maria's eyes filled with tears. She nodded.

Tom closed his eyes. For a moment, nothing came. The rehearsed words he usually relied on felt empty in his throat. The elevator doors began to close, then opened again.

Then quietly Tom began to speak.

"God..." His voice cracked. He cleared his throat and tried again. "God, I don't understand why this family is going through this. I don't understand why Alysia is sick, or why Pete is hurting, or why Charlotte has to be scared." He squeezed their hands. "But they need you. They need your presence. They need..." He paused, searching for honest words. "They need to know they aren't alone in this."

Charlotte's small fingers tightened around his.

"Please be with Alysia tonight. Be with the doctors and nurses taking care of her. Give Pete strength to heal. Give Maria courage to keep going." His voice dropped to barely above a whisper. "And help Charlotte know that her sister is in good hands. Better hands than mine."

The last four words came out before he could stop them. A confession hidden in a prayer.

Tom opened his eyes. "Amen," he said quietly.

Maria was crying openly now, but her expression had changed. Some of the tension had left her shoulders. "Thank you," she said, her voice filled with emotion. "Thank you for being honest."

Honest. That word stung because it was true. That was the most honest prayer he'd spoken in three years.

Tom stood slowly. "I'm glad I could help."

The elevator doors had stayed open, waiting. They stepped out onto the third floor together.

Charlotte held up the unicorn. "Thank you for the prayer, Mr. Tom. And for the unicorn. I'm going to let Alysia hold it when we go in."

"I bet she'll love that," Tom managed.

Maria guided Charlotte toward the pediatric ICU entrance, then turned back. "You're welcome to visit them, if you'd like. Pete would probably like to meet you."

"I'll keep that in mind," Tom said, though he wasn't sure he meant it.

They turned the corner and were gone.

Tom stood in the empty hallway for a long moment. Fluorescent lights hummed overhead. Somewhere down the hall, a monitor beeped. He turned back toward the elevator and pressed the button.

The descent to the lobby felt like an eternity. Tom leaned against the wall, exhausted. The prayer had taken something out of him he hadn't expected.

When the doors opened, he felt it immediately. The tightness. The shortness of breath. The dry cough. All worse than before. Tom made it three steps before his breathing became labored. He bent forward, hands on his knees, gasping for air that wouldn't come.

"Sir? Sir, are you alright?"

A nurse appeared at his side. Tom couldn't answer. The world had shrunk to the singular focus of trying to pull oxygen into lungs that refused to cooperate.

"Let's get you sitting down." The nurse guided him to one of the long benches along the lobby windows.

Tom collapsed onto the bench, still fighting for each breath. The nurse knelt beside him, checking his pulse, speaking in a steady stream of reassurance he couldn't quite process.

He watched her wave to someone at the reception desk. Watched other people glance his way with concern. Watched the world continue spinning while he drowned in air.

This is what happens when you stop hiding.

The prayer. The honest, vulnerable prayer. The admission that he didn't understand. The confession that his hands were inadequate. All of it had cracked something open inside him that he'd been holding closed for three years.

And now his body was paying the price.

Slowly—so slowly—his breathing began to ease. The desperate gasps became deep, shuddering breaths. The darkness at the edges of his vision receded. The muscles between his ribs screamed from the effort, but at least they were working again.

"There you go," the nurse said. "That's better. Can you tell me your name?"

"Tom," he managed. "Tom McGarvey."

"Okay, Tom. I think you should let me take you to the ER."

Tom shook his head. "I'm fine. This happens sometimes. I'm seeing my doctor next week."

The nurse frowned. "These episodes, how long have they been happening?"

"A few months." Tom straightened slowly, testing his breathing. Better. Not good, but better. "Really, I'm okay."

The nurse studied him, then sighed. "At least let me get your vitals."

While she checked his blood pressure and pulse, Tom stared out the window at the parking lot. The early evening was settling into dusk, streetlights beginning to flicker on. Somewhere upstairs, Charlotte was probably sharing her purple unicorn with Alysia. Maria was probably telling Pete about the kind pastor who prayed with them in the elevator.

And Gladys was probably sleeping peacefully, his earlier prayers already forgotten.

What do I even believe anymore?

The question had been haunting him for years. But tonight, kneeling in that elevator, something had shifted. He'd prayed honestly for the first time since Vietnam. It had terrified him. And exhausted him.

But he'd done it.

"Your blood pressure's elevated, and your pulse is still fast," the nurse said, writing something on her palm. "I really think you should be seen tonight."

"I will," Tom lied. He took a deeper breath, trying to prove he was okay. "This has happened before. I just need a little time."

The nurse gave him a long look, then handed him a small card with the hospital's number. "If this happens again tonight, call an ambulance. Understood?"

"Understood."

She stood, still skeptical, but nodded. "Take care of yourself, Reverend."

Tom nodded and watched her walk back toward the elevators.

He sat on that bench for another ten minutes, waiting for his body to fully return to normal. Waiting for the adrenaline to fade. Waiting for his thoughts to settle.

The symptoms were bad enough. The waiting for his appointment was worse. But this crisis of faith that had led him to pray honestly... that might be the worst of all. Because now he had to figure out what came next.

Tom pushed himself to his feet slowly, testing his balance. Steady enough. He pulled his coat tighter, tucking the visitation stole deeper into his pocket where it couldn't be seen.

Then he walked toward the exit, toward his car, toward home.

Toward whatever the future would bring.

CHAPTER
TWO

"Hello, I'm Kayla, Kayla Andersen. Here to meet Reverend Tom McGarvey."

The knock came just as Tom was reading the last line of Sheldon's letter for the third time.

Tom glanced up from his desk. The young woman in his doorway had the kind of smile that seemed to take up more space than her small frame. It was a bright, unguarded smile, and entirely too enthusiastic for a Thursday afternoon.

He folded the letter and motioned with a polite Midwestern two-finger gesture. "Come in, come in. Please call me Tom. Sheldon's told me all about you."

That wasn't entirely true. Sheldon's letter had been characteristically brief: *She needs a place to complete her externship. You need someone to remind you why we do this work. Consider us even.* Leave it to his old friend to frame a favor as if Tom were the one receiving it.

Kayla settled into the chair, her canvas bag hitting the floor with a thud as if she'd packed half the seminary library. Her eyes immediately went to the framed photograph on Tom's desk—a black-and-white picture of two younger men in combat fatigues, arms slung over each other's shoulders, grinning despite the dust and jungle behind them.

"Is that you and Rabbi Levine?"

"Seven years ago. Da Nang." Tom picked up the frame, studying his face for a moment before setting it back down—it was leaner, unlined. His hair was darker then, untouched by the gray that now threaded through it. And even in combat, his eyes looked clearer than the eyes that had been bearing the weight of pastoring a church since he got home. "A Christian minister named Tom and a Jewish rabbi named Sheldon in the same chaplain unit. Our commanding officer called it 'the Lord's idea of a joke.'"

"Rabbi Levine calls it 'providence.'" Kayla leaned forward, her hands clasped on her knees. "He says you two promised each other that if either of you ever needed anything, all you had to do was ask."

"And he's asking." Tom smiled. "So, tell me about yourself. Sheldon mentioned you studied English literature?"

"I did." The enthusiasm in her voice kicked up a notch. "I've always been a writer... or wanted to be. Novels, mostly. But senior year of college, I felt this... calling. Like I was supposed to do something more. Ministry seemed like the natural next step. I mean, it's all about crafting sermons, right? Writing that moves people?"

Tom let out a short laugh, the kind that came from recognition rather than humor. "I thought the same thing when I was your age. You're in for a surprise."

"That's what Rabbi Levine said you'd say." Kayla's grin turned playful. "He also said if anyone could bring you out of your funk, it's a feisty girl with a mission on her mind." She spread her hands. "So here I am."

Tom's smile faded. He set down the pen he'd been unconsciously tapping against his desk blotter. "He said that?"

She pointed to the folded paper on his desk. "Not in the letter. On the phone." Kayla's expression softened. "He's worried about you. Says you're carrying too much weight."

For a moment, Tom considered deflecting. He could offer some platitude about the challenges of ministry, about how every pastor goes through seasons of difficulty. Instead, he found himself exhaling slowly and leaning back in his chair.

"I don't know what Sheldon told you, but I'll be honest with you, Kayla. You're walking into a vocation that... well, it's not a sinking ship. Yet. But there are signs of decline."

He nodded toward the sanctuary beyond his office door. "Attendance is down a little from when I got here. Last board meeting, someone actually suggested cutting back on youth ministry."

He expected her face to fall, to see that bright enthusiasm dim. Instead, Kayla nodded as if he'd confirmed something she already knew.

"We talked about that in my Church and Society class," she said. "How the institution is losing its grip on American culture. How young people, especially, are walking away from organized religion." She paused. "But we also talked about why."

"People are losing faith." Tom heard the weariness in his own voice. "They're not praying enough. Not worshiping enough. Vietnam shook people's belief in everything, including God. If more people came back to Him, really came back, the church would be okay."

Kayla tilted her head, studying him. "How many prayer meetings does Great Witness have each week?"

"Two. Wednesday night and Sunday night after youth group."

"How many people attend?"

Tom shifted in his chair. "Ten, maybe twelve on a good week."

"And how many worship services?"

"Sunday morning, the eight o'clock and the nine-thirty services. We tried adding a Saturday night folk service last year. Guitars, contemporary hymns... thought it might bring in younger families."

"Did it work?"

"For about six months." Tom picked up his pen again, rolling it between his fingers. "Then they drifted away. Found other things to do on weekends, I suppose."

"Do you think it's because they weren't praying hard enough?" Kayla's tone was genuinely curious. "Or because they didn't see the point?"

Tom set the pen down with more force than he intended. "The point is connecting with God. Worship. Lifting up prayers for the community, for our boys still overseas, for the country. We have prayer chains, Kayla. We have weekly intercessory prayer meetings. I pray for this church every single day. Have since I arrived here. What more can we do?"

"You could feed someone."

The words hung in the air between them. Tom blinked.

"Excuse me?"

Kayla leaned forward, her voice taking on an intensity that seemed at odds with her youth. "Last spring, a church in my hometown closed its doors after eighty-five years. You know what their last deacon's meeting decided? To spend their remaining funds on a new pulpit Bible. Red leather, gilt edges... the works. It was beautiful. Meanwhile, three blocks away, families were lining up at the public assistance office because the factory laid off a hundred workers."

Tom opened his mouth, then closed it. He thought of the filing cabinet in the corner, stuffed with records from past outreach programs. "We've done mission work. Food pantries. Three years ago, we collected enough canned goods to fill half of Fellowship Hall."

"And last year?"

"About half that." The number tasted bitter. "But that's not because we stopped trying. It's because people stopped caring. About God. About church. About—"

"About what the church stands for," Kayla interrupted. "Tom, can I ask you something?"

Tom nodded.

"What do you think the first apostles spent more time doing: praying in the temple or feeding widows?"

Tom felt a flash of irritation. "That's not a fair comparison. They did both."

"Sure. But when the church in Acts had to choose between the two, what did they do?" Kayla counted on her fingers. "They appointed deacons to handle the food distribution so the apostles could focus on prayer and preaching. But notice, they didn't stop feeding people. That was nonnegotiable."

"Prayer is action," Tom countered, hearing the defensive edge in his voice. "It's intercession. It's—"

"It's important. I'm not saying it isn't." Kayla's voice softened. "But Rabbi Levine told me something you said to him once, back in Vietnam. You were talking about a village your unit helped rebuild after it was bombed. You told him, 'God doesn't have hands except ours.'" She paused. "Do you still believe that?"

Tom stared at her. The memory surfaced unwanted. Sitting with Sheldon in the mess tent, exhausted from a day spent helping villagers salvage what they could from the rubble. He'd been so certain then. So sure that faith meant getting your hands dirty.

When had that changed?

He looked away, his gaze drifting to the window. Outside, the church parking lot sat mostly empty in the afternoon sun, except for his '70 El Camino and just a handful of cars clustered near Fellowship Hall, where the women's prayer blanket group was meeting.

"You don't know what it's like," he said quietly. "To pour everything into something and watch it slowly die anyway. To try every program, every outreach, every new approach, and still see the empty pews gradually grow. At some point, you have to ask if maybe the problem isn't us. Maybe people just don't want God anymore. Not after everything that's happened."

"Or maybe," Kayla said, her voice gentle but unwavering, "they don't see Him in us."

Tom turned back to face her. She was watching him with an expression he couldn't quite read. Compassion mixed with challenge, understanding mixed with determination.

"So, what would you have me do?" He spread his hands. "What does your seminary education tell you is the answer?"

"I don't have all the answers. I'm just asking questions." Kayla looked out the window. "But here's one: What would this church look like if its members spent less time singing hymns and more time living them? If we did what Jesus actually did instead of just reading about it on Sunday mornings?"

Tom felt something stir in his chest. Not quite anger, not quite hope. Something uncomfortable and unsettling. He wanted to argue, to explain why it wasn't that simple, why she was naive, why the church had good reasons for being what it had become.

Instead, he found himself reading her face. The earnestness there. The fire. She reminded him of someone.

She reminded him of himself.

The realization hit him hard. When had he become the person who talked about why things couldn't change instead of how to change them?

Kayla must have seen something shift in his expression because she suddenly looked uncertain. "I'm sorry. I shouldn't have... It's my first day, and I'm already challenging everything. Rabbi Levine warned me I come on too strong."

"No." Tom's voice came out rougher than he intended. He cleared his throat. "No, you're... you're fine. It's good. I asked for your thoughts."

"Still." She offered a tentative smile. "I'm here to learn from you, not lecture you."

Tom looked at her for a long moment. He could feel the weight of a decision pressing on him, though he couldn't quite articulate what the decision was. He could thank her for coming, go over the externship paperwork, and set appropriate boundaries for a student-mentor relationship. Keep her at arm's length. Protect himself from whatever uncomfortable questions she might stir up.

Or...

"Kayla." He leaned forward, folding his hands on the desk. "I'm going to be honest with you. I don't know if I'm the right mentor for you. I don't know if I have much to teach you right now except how to manage decline." He paused, choosing his words carefully. "But maybe that's exactly why Sheldon sent you here. Not for what I can teach you, but for what you can teach me."

Her eyes widened slightly. "I'm not trying to—"

"I know. But you've already made me think more in the last twenty minutes than I have in the last year." He picked up the photo of him and Sheldon, the faces of two young men who'd been so certain they could make a difference. "So, here's what I'm proposing. You spend the semester here, completing your externship. I'll teach you what I know about ministry. The practical stuff, the hard stuff. But in return, you challenge me. Push back when I'm being cynical. Ask the hard questions. Make me prove my assumptions."

"Like... an accountability partner?"

"Like someone who remembers why we do this in the first place." Tom set the photo down and met her eyes. "Fair warning—I'm going to push back. I'm going to argue with you. I'm going to tell you all the reasons why your idealism won't survive contact with reality."

"And I'm going to prove you wrong." Kayla's grin was back, full force. "Deal?"

Tom felt the corner of his mouth twitch upward despite himself. He nodded with a smile. "Deal." He pulled out a folder from his desk drawer. "Now, let's go over the externship requirements. First thing you need to know about church administration..."

As they bent over the paperwork together, Tom caught himself glancing once more at the photograph. Sheldon's voice seemed to echo in his memory: *You need someone to remind you why we do this work.*

Maybe he'd been right about that.

Maybe providence had more to do with it than Tom wanted to admit.

AFTER KAYLA LEFT, TOM SAT ALONE IN HIS OFFICE AS THE afternoon shadows lengthened. He picked up the photograph again, really looking at it this time. Two young men who'd believed they could make a difference with their own hands—who'd believed God worked through action, not just intention.

When had he stopped believing that?

Tom set the photo down and pulled a yellow legal pad from his desk drawer. He uncapped his pen and stared at the blank page for a long moment. Then he wrote a single question at the top: "What would it look like to follow Jesus instead of just worshiping him?"

He stared at the words for a long moment. Then he tore off the page, folded it, and slipped it into his Bible, next to the bookmark he had placed weeks earlier in the Book of Acts.

It was just a question. Just words on paper.

But something had shifted. And Tom wasn't entirely sure how he felt about it.

CHAPTER
THREE

The red light on the Radio Shack answering machine blinked at him from across the den.

Tom stood in the doorway of his small ranch house, still wearing his clerical collar from the afternoon funeral service. Mrs. Henderson, at ninety-two, was the longest-serving member of the church. Her service was the second one this month.

He loosened his collar and pressed the play button.

Beep. "Tom McGarvey, this is Linda from Dr. Morrison's office. The doctor would like you to come in as soon as possible to discuss your test results. Please call us on Monday morning to schedule. Thank you."

Tom reached up and placed his open palm against his chest as he took in a deep breath. That didn't hurt nearly as much as what he'd gone through earlier in the week. Maybe the tests would come back fine. Maybe it was just stress. Maybe...

He stopped himself. He'd been playing the "maybe" game for months now.

The black and white photograph on the wall above his desk caught his eye. Him in Air Force chaplain fatigues, younger by a decade, standing with a medic named Paulson. The photo had been taken three days before the night that changed everything. Before the darkness. Before the screaming. Before he'd grabbed the wrong—

Tom looked away. No matter how many times he looked at that photo, it still affected him. Emotionally and physically. And yet, he wouldn't take it off the wall. Some might say he left it there as a reminder. To punish himself. He'd convinced himself he needed to see it, to never forget the life that was lost because of him.

He rubbed his ring finger, a finger that, until a year ago, used to wear a wedding band. Sarah had been patient. For years, she'd been patient with his silence, his nightmares, and his inability to let her in. But patience had its limits.

"I can't compete with your ghosts, Tom.

She had told him that over and over again. And was right.

The worn Bible on the counter had a bookmark sticking out of it, marking the Book of Acts, Chapter 17. Another reminder of disappointment in his life. He'd always wanted to preach on Acts 17:6, about the earliest Christians who were accused of "turning the world upside down." But he'd never pushed the elders hard enough to move away from the lectionary calendar, which didn't include that passage.

He opened the Bible to the passage, and there, next to the bookmark, was a handwritten note from Kayla. He'd hastily shoved it into the Bible after getting home the other day. With everything going on, he'd never gotten around to reading it.

He unfolded it and read what she wanted him to know.

Reverend McGarvey—

You might be right about the decline of the church. But that doesn't mean we should quit. I don't think ministry is a slow death if you care too much. Please don't give up on this until I'm fully ordained!

Also—Acts 17:6 is my FAVORITE passage. "These who have turned the world upside down have come here too." Why aren't you preaching on it?

— K

Tom let out a short laugh. "She's so idealistic," he said to the empty room. He recalled when he was young and full of energy and dreams. She was just as naive as he'd been, thinking he could change the world. She probably even thought she could be one of those accused of turning it upside down.

He folded the note and put it back next to the bookmark, then glanced at the clock. Nearly six. He should eat something. But the kitchen felt too empty, the silence too heavy.

The phone rang. Tom picked it up on the second ring. "Hello?"

"Tom, it's Howard." Howard Beckner, chairman of the church board. His voice had that careful quality it took on when he was about to deliver news Tom wouldn't like. "Got a minute?"

"Well, the finance committee met last night. We're looking at the numbers for the first quarter, and..." A pause. "Tom, we're down eight percent in giving compared to last year. If this continues, we'll have to make some decisions by summer."

Tom closed his eyes. "What kind of decisions?"

"The building fund is underwater. We might need to postpone the roof repair. And..." Another pause, longer this time. "Carolyn suggested we might want to consider combining the two Sunday services. Cut costs on utilities, organ rental, that sort of thing."

"Combining services would risk losing more members, Howard."

"I know. But we're running out of options." Howard's voice softened. "Look, I'm not saying we've given up. But we need to be realistic about where things are heading."

After Tom hung up, he stood in his kitchen and stared at nothing in particular. Eight percent down. Combining services. Postponing repairs.

Not a sinking ship yet. But taking on water.

"So, what exactly does a typical week look like for you?"

Kayla sat across from Tom in his office, notepad balanced on her knee. She'd arrived at nine sharp, eager and caffeinated, ready to shadow him through his daily routine.

Tom leaned back in his chair. "Monday mornings are for catching up. Usually. When there aren't urgent calls or hospital visits."

"And this week?"

"This week is typical. I need to start preparing the bulletin, follow up with a family from last week, and..." He glanced at the message slip on his desk. "I need to call Dr. Morrison's office."

"For you?"

The question was casual, but with concern behind it. "Routine follow-up. Nothing urgent."

Kayla made a note but didn't push. "What about the sermon for Sunday?"

"I'll start to prepare it today, if I have a chance. Then work on the specifics of it on Wednesday. And finish it up on Thursday if I need more time."

"What passage are you preaching on?"

Tom pulled out the lectionary calendar. "I'm going to change things up and preach on the Psalm reading — Psalm 150."

"A Psalm?" Kayla's eyebrows rose. "That's kind of taking the easy way out, isn't it?"

"People relate to the ancient texts."

"Do they?" She crossed her arms. "Or do they just tune them out because they've heard them so many times?"

Tom felt a flicker of irritation. "Do you remember Psalm 150? It's all about praising the Lord. And this being the time between Easter and Pentecost, it's an important reminder for the congregation to understand." He moved from behind his desk. "The lectionary is there for a reason, Kayla. It ensures we cover all of Scripture systematically."

"It also means you never preach on Acts 17:6."

Tom stared at her. "How did you—"

"Your note. In your Bible. I saw it when you were showing me your study resources last week." She met his gaze. "Why don't you just preach it anyway?"

"Because the elders prefer to follow the lectionary."

"Have you asked them about exceptions?"

"I..." Tom paused. When was the last time he'd actually pushed for something he wanted to preach? "It's complicated."

"Or maybe you're just tired of fighting." Her voice was gentle, but the observation stung because it was true.

Before Tom could respond, the phone rang. He picked it up, grateful for the interruption.

"Tom, it's Barbara Pritchard." Her voice was tight, controlled. "I'm at County Memorial with Dad. The doctors say... they say we should probably call family. I thought you should know."

George Pritchard. Eighty-six years old, a member of Great Witness since 1947. A man who'd taught Tom's Sunday school class when Tom was a boy visiting his grandparents in Stoneford.

"I'll be right there, Barbara."

Tom hung up and grabbed his coat. "We need to go to the hospital."

Kayla was already on her feet, notepad forgotten. "What happened?"

"George Pritchard... he's dying. That was his daughter." Tom checked his pocket for his visitation stole. "Welcome to a typical Monday in ministry."

County Memorial, Room 412

GEORGE PRITCHARD, DIMINISHED BY THE HOSPITAL BED and the web of tubes connecting him to various machines, looked nothing like the man who had helped raise funds for the new bell tower. Barbara sat beside him, holding his hand.

Her sister Linda stood by the window, arms crossed, staring out at nothing.

"Tom." Barbara's eyes were red. "Thank you for coming so quickly."

Tom moved to the bedside. George's eyes were closed, his breathing shallow and labored. "How is he?"

"They say it could be hours. Maybe less." Barbara's voice cracked. "He's not in pain. The morphine is helping with that."

Tom placed his hand on George's shoulder. Behind him, Kayla stood near the door, quiet and observant.

"Would you like me to pray with you?" Tom asked.

Barbara nodded. Linda turned from the window.

Tom bowed his head, and the familiar words came. Words about comfort and peace. About God's presence in the valley of the shadow. About the promise of resurrection and eternal life.

The words felt hollow, but he spoke them anyway because they were what the family needed to hear. When he finished, Barbara squeezed his hand.

"Thank you," she whispered. "That means so much."

They stayed for another twenty minutes. Tom sat with Barbara, listening as she shared memories of her father. George had been a farmer his whole life. Worked the land until arthritis finally forced him to sell. He'd never missed a Sunday service unless he was sick. Always sat in the third pew on the right side.

"Dad used to say the church was the backbone of this community," Barbara said. "He'd be heartbroken to see how things are headed. So many families gone. So many young people moved away." She paused, then looked at her dad. "Do you think the church will still be here… when it's my turn to—"

The question hung in the air. Tom felt Kayla's eyes on him, waiting for his answer.

"I hope so," he said finally. "I think so. But it will look different than it does now. It has to."

"How?"

"I'm still figuring that out."

On the drive back to the church, Kayla was quiet for several minutes before she finally spoke.

"That prayer. In the room. Did you mean it?"

Tom kept his eyes on the road. "What do you mean?"

"All that stuff about God's presence, about peace, about resurrection." She turned to look at him. "Do you actually believe it? Or are you just saying what you're supposed to say?"

The question was too direct, too honest. Tom felt his chest tighten, the familiar pressure that preceded an episode.

"It's what they needed to hear," he said carefully.

"That's not what I asked."

George died three hours later, with his daughters at his side. Tom and Kayla were back in his office when Barbara called to tell them.

After he hung up, the silence stretched between them. "You asked in the car if I meant what I said in that prayer," Tom said quietly. "The truth is, Kayla, in this line of work, sometimes you have to speak words that bring comfort even when you're not sure you believe them yourself. That's part of the job."

Kayla looked at him for a long moment, then nodded slowly. But her expression said what she wouldn't: Maybe that's part of the problem.

Thursday Afternoon

GEORGE PRITCHARD'S MEMORIAL SERVICE WENT SMOOTH-ly. It was a good turnout — nearly eighty people. Tom delivered a tribute that made people laugh and cry in equal measure. He spoke about his faithfulness, his kindness, and his decades of service to the church and community.

He did not mention that attendance at his funeral was nearly double the average Sunday service attendance.

After the reception in Fellowship Hall, after the last casserole dish had been claimed and the last guest had left, Tom returned to his office to finish Sunday's sermon. Kayla had spent the afternoon helping in the kitchen, insisting that part of ministry was serving wherever needed.

She appeared in his doorway now, drying her hands on a dish towel.

"That was beautiful," she said. "The service, I mean. You really honored him."

"He deserved it." Tom gestured to the chair. "Sit down. You've earned a break."

Kayla sat, still holding the dish towel. "Can I ask you something?"

"You're going to anyway," he said with a smile.

She returned the smile. "Why were there more people at the funeral than come to church on Sundays?"

Tom had been asking himself the same question. "People show up for the milestones. Births, deaths, weddings. But the week-to-week commitment? That's harder to maintain."

"Or maybe they don't see the point of showing up every week just to hear the same old sermons and sing the same old hymns." She leaned forward. "When's the last time this church did something that made people actually want to be here?"

"We do things. Food pantry, prayer meetings, Bible studies—"

"When's the last time the food pantry was open?"

Tom paused. "Last month. We distributed groceries to about fifteen families."

"Once a month. For two hours." Kayla's voice was more observant than accusatory. "What about the other twenty-nine days?"

"We don't have the volunteers to staff it more frequently."

"Have you asked for them?"

"Kayla—"

"I'm serious. When's the last time you stood up on Sunday and said, 'We need volunteers to feed hungry people in our community every week. Who's in?'"

Tom rubbed his eyes. The pressure in his chest was building again. "It's more complicated than that. There are liability issues, storage issues, coordination with the county assistance office—"

"So work through them." Her eyes were bright with that idealistic fire he'd seen on her first day. "Or is it easier to just keep doing the minimum and complain about decline?"

The words hit harder than she probably intended. Tom stood abruptly. "I think we're done for today. Go home, Kayla. Get some rest."

She stood slowly, reading his expression. "I'm sorry. I didn't mean—"

"It's fine. I'll see you Sunday."

After she left, Tom sat alone in his office as the afternoon shadows lengthened. The pressure in his chest had eased slightly, but not enough. He opened his desk drawer and pulled out the bottle of antacids he kept there, shaking two into his palm.

The phone sat on his desk. He still hadn't called Dr. Morrison's office.

He picked up the receiver, then set it back down. Monday. He'd call on Monday.

Thursday Evening

TOM SAT IN HIS DEN, THE TV PLAYING LOW IN THE BACKground. A documentary about archaeological discoveries in the Middle East. He'd turned it on for background noise but found himself actually watching it.

The narrator was discussing the Dead Sea. Ancient scrolls, preserved for centuries in clay jars, hidden in caves. Evidence of early Christian communities that practiced a radical form of communal living by sharing possessions, caring for widows and orphans, and taking in strangers.

"These communities," the narrator said, "represent Christianity in its most primitive and perhaps most pure form. Before institutionalization. Before hierarchies and doctrines and creeds. Just people trying to live out the teachings of Jesus in concrete, daily ways."

Tom leaned forward. On the screen, archaeologists carefully unrolled a fragment of ancient parchment, revealing faded script in Hebrew.

"The question historians continue to debate," the narrator continued, "is what happened to these radical communities. Why did this form of Christianity, focused on action and serving the poor, gradually give way to the institutional church we know today?"

The camera panned across a dig site in Israel. Tourists walked through ancient ruins, and a small village was visible in the distance.

Tom thought about Kayla's question. *What would this church look like if its members spent less time singing hymns and more time living them?*

The documentary cut to an interview with an elderly woman who lived near one of the dig sites. She spoke through a translator about how her family had lived in the region for generations, how they'd preserved old stories passed down through the centuries.

"My great-grandmother," the woman said, "used to tell us about an ancient ancestor who knew the apostles. She wrote down what she saw them do. Her writings were kept in our family for many, many years. Some say they were lost in a fire. Others believe they still exist today, hidden away, waiting to be found. But whether the writings survive or not, we remember the stories she told."

The camera moved on to another expert at another dig site. But Tom found himself thinking about that woman. About stories preserved for generations. About writings that documented what the apostles actually did.

Action. Not just belief, but action.

He turned off the TV and sat in the quiet. The Bible on his desk still had Kayla's note tucked into Acts 17. He opened it and read the passage again.

"These men who have turned the world upside down have come here too."

When was the last time anyone had accused him of turning the world upside down? When was the last time he'd even tried?

Tom pulled out a piece of paper and wrote at the top: *To Do.*

He wrote: *1. Visit the Holy Land. See where it all began.*

He stared at the single item for a long moment, then added: *2. Preach Acts 17:6 at least once.*

That was all he could think of. Two things. One big, one small. Both things he'd been putting off for years.

He folded the paper and put it in his wallet, then closed the Bible and turned off the lamp.

* * *

Sunday Morning

THE SANCTUARY WAS EXACTLY AS TOM EXPECTED. ABOUT seventy people were scattered across pews that could seat two hundred. Kayla sat in the back, observing.

Tom preached on Psalm 150. He'd prepared a practical sermon about praising the Lord and the rewards that come from it. People nodded at the right moments. A few even smiled at his illustration about instruments.

It was fine. Adequate. Forgettable.

After the service, Tom stood at the back door shaking hands as people filed out. The same compliments. "Lovely sermon, Reverend." "Very moving." "See you next week, Tom."

Kayla lingered after everyone else had left.

"You didn't preach what you wanted to preach," she said. It wasn't a question.

"I preached what the lectionary called for."

"You preached what was safe." She looked around the empty sanctuary. "And look how well that's working."

Tom felt something snap inside him. "What do you want me to say, Kayla? That you're right? That I'm playing it safe because I'm tired and burned out and don't have the energy to fight anymore?"

He looked at her, waiting for a response. Waiting for judgment, or worse, pity. But there was none. Her eyes weren't disappointed or triumphant. They were filled with compassion now, with an understanding that made his admission feel less like defeat and more like the first honest thing he'd said since his prayer with Charlotte in the elevator.

"Fine," Tom said, breaking the silence. "You're right. Is that what you wanted to hear?"

She didn't flinch. "No. I wanted to hear that you're going to do something about it."

"And what exactly am I supposed to do? Wave a magic wand and make people care again?"

"You could start by caring yourself." Her voice was gentle but firm. "You could preach what you actually believe instead of what you think people want to hear. You could stop going through the motions."

Tom looked at her. This young woman, with her idealism intact, her belief that passion and sincerity could change everything. Part of him wanted to protect that idealism. Part of him wanted to crush it before reality did it for him.

"It's not that simple," he said finally.

"It never is." She looked back toward the altar. "But that doesn't mean it's not worth trying."

After she left, Tom stood alone. Sunlight streamed through the stained glass windows, casting colored patterns across the worn pews. This building had stood for so long. Generations had worshiped here. Prayed here. Been married and buried here.

How much longer would it stand?

Tom walked to the front and sat in the first pew. He looked up at the simple wooden cross hanging above the altar. No corpus, just two pieces of wood nailed together. Plain. Protestant. Unadorned.

He thought about the documentary. About those early communities living radically, turning the world upside down. About that woman whose ancestor had written down what she'd seen.

He thought about Kayla's question. *What would this church look like if its members spent less time singing hymns and more time living them?*

He thought about the to-do list in his wallet. The Holy Land. Acts 17:6.

Things he'd been putting off because he was afraid. Of what the doctor might say. Of what change might require. And his biggest fear... of what failure might look like.

Tom pulled out his wallet and unfolded the paper. He stared at his two items, then added a third:

3. Stop playing it safe.

He didn't know what that would look like. He didn't know if he had the strength for it. But sitting in this empty sanctuary, with the colored light falling across his hands, he knew something had to change.

The question was whether that change would come in time, or whether he'd run out of time before he figured out what God was asking him to do.

He folded the paper and put it back in his wallet. Then he stood, turned off the lights, and locked the sanctuary door behind him.

Monday morning, he would call Dr. Morrison's office.

And maybe, just maybe, he'd find the courage to learn what it meant to turn the world upside down.

CHAPTER
FOUR

Tom sat in one of the vinyl chairs that lined the wall, his hands folded in his lap. The second hand on the clock above the receptionist's desk made its slow circuit in an office waiting room that smelled like industrial cleaner and old coffee.

Eleven forty-three.

His appointment had been at eleven-fifteen.

At County Memorial, other patients were also waiting. An elderly woman with a walker, a young mother holding a feverish toddler, a middle-aged man reading a tattered copy of *Reader's Digest*. They all seemed content to wait. But Tom felt his chest tightening with each passing minute.

More time passed before... "Thomas McGarvey?"

The nurse stood in the doorway, clipboard in hand. She wore a white pantsuit and had the kind of practiced smile that didn't quite reach her eyes. Tom had seen that smile before, on the faces of nurses who were about to deliver bad news.

He stood, his knees protesting slightly. "That's me."

"Dr. Morrison is ready for you now."

Tom followed her down a narrow hallway lined with examination rooms. Somewhere down the hall, a phone rang twice before someone picked up.

She stopped at a slightly rusted medical scale along the wall. "Here, let's get your weight."

The nurse slid the counterweights at the top of the scale. She read off his weight as she noted it in his chart. "One-forty-eight."

One-forty-eight. He'd lost nearly another ten pounds since his visit with Dr. Morrison last month, something the doctor had told Tom to keep an eye on.

The nurse showed him into a small office rather than an exam room. That was the first sign. Dr. Morrison's office had a desk cluttered with files, a diploma from Northwestern on the wall, and two chairs facing each other with nothing between them but worn carpet.

"The doctor will be right with you," the nurse said, then closed the door as she left.

Tom sat in the chair farthest from the desk. Through the small window, he could see the parking lot, his El Camino sitting in the third row. He'd parked under a tree, out of habit. Sarah used to tease him about that, about how he always looked for shade even on cloudy days.

He wondered if she knew. If anyone had told her. They'd been divorced for a year, but she still had friends at Great Witness. Word traveled fast in small towns.

The door opened. Dr. Morrison entered, carrying a large manila envelope and what looked like film negatives in a folder. He was in his late fifties, silver-haired, with reading glasses hanging from a chain around his neck.

"Tom." He shook Tom's hand, then settled into the opposite chair. Not behind the desk. Another sign. "Thanks for coming in."

"Your nurse said you have all my results."

"I do." Dr. Morrison set the envelope on his lap but didn't open it yet. "How have you been feeling since your last visit. I see here you've lost some more weight."

Tom's chest tightened again. "About the same. The breathing episodes come and go. Some days are better than others."

"Any pain?"

"In my chest, sometimes. Like someone's pressing down."

Dr. Morrison nodded, making a note on the file. "And the cough?"

"Worse at night. Dry, mostly. Sometimes there's..." Tom paused. "Sometimes there's blood."

The doctor's expression didn't change, but something flickered in his eyes. Recognition. Confirmation maybe.

"Tom, I'm going to show you something." Dr. Morrison pulled out the film negatives and held them up to the light from the window. "These are from the CAT scan we did. Do you know what that is?"

"Not really. Your nurse mentioned it was some kind of new X-ray machine."

"Essentially, yes. CT stands for 'computed tomography.' It's a new technology, only been available for a couple of years. It lets us see cross sections of the body in much more detail than regular X-rays." He pointed to one of the images. "This is a scan of your chest cavity."

Tom leaned forward, trying to make sense of the gray and white shapes. It looked nothing like the chest X-rays he'd seen before. This was more detailed, almost three-dimensional. "I'm not sure what I'm looking at," he said.

"These areas here and here—" Dr. Morrison pointed with his pen "—those are your lungs." He paused. "This here, this white area that shouldn't be there? That's a mass. It's in the main airway of your lung." Then, very matter-of-fact, "It's a tumor."

The word hovered in the air like a medivac helicopter waiting for the LZ to clear.

A tumor.

Tom stared at the image, trying to merge what he was seeing with what he was hearing. The mass looked strange on the film. How could something like that be causing so much trouble?

"How many?" Tom asked quietly.

"This one is the main one," Dr. Morrison pointed with his pen again. "We call this a primary tumor. Unfortunately, the CAT scan also shows that your lymph nodes are enlarged in that area. And…" He reached for a different film. "Do you see these small white areas below your lungs? Those are nodules on your liver. Those are called secondary tumors."

Tom had to remind himself to breathe.

Dr. Morrison set down the films and opened the manila envelope, pulling out pages of typed reports. "We also did blood work and a biopsy of the tissue from the procedure last month. The results came back last week."

Tom watched the doctor's face, reading what was coming before the words were spoken. "The tumors are malignant, Tom. There's no way to sugarcoat this… You have cancer."

There it was. The word everyone feared. The diagnosis that changed everything.

But Tom felt strangely calm. Almost detached, as if this were happening to someone else and he were merely an observer. "What kind?"

"Small cell lung cancer. It's aggressive, unfortunately. The blood work shows elevated markers, and, as you saw, it's already spread to the liver. We believe it's also in your lymph nodes based on what the CAT scan shows. 'Metastasis' is the medical term for all this."

Metastasis. Tom knew that word. He'd heard it from Herbert Williams two years ago. Herbert had lasted six months after his diagnosis.

"What are my options?" Tom asked, surprised by how steady his voice sounded.

Dr. Morrison set down the reports and leaned forward, his elbows on his knees. "I'm going to be honest with you, Tom. This type of cancer is particularly difficult to treat. Sometimes chemotherapy and radiation have an effect, but the response rates are not good. Especially once it's spread."

"Define 'not good.'"

"With aggressive treatment, a combination of chemotherapy and radiation to the primary tumor, you might gain some additional time. Maybe a year... a year and a half at best. But the treatment itself is brutal. You'd be very sick. The side effects are significant. In addition to losing your hair, you'd experience horrible nausea, fatigue, and your immune system would be weakened. Your quality of life would be severely impacted."

Tom thought about Margaret Henshaw, who'd undergone chemotherapy three years ago. He'd visited her during treatment, watched her waste away despite the poison they pumped into her veins. She'd lost fifty pounds and all her hair.

She couldn't keep food down. The cancer killed her anyway, four months after treatment began.

"And without treatment?" Tom asked.

Dr. Morrison leaned back. "Six months. Maybe less. The cancer would spread faster, but you'd maintain your quality of life longer. No nausea from chemo. No burns from radiation. Just management of symptoms. Pain medication and oxygen when needed. What's called 'palliative care' to keep you comfortable."

Six months.

Tom tried to process the timeline. Six months from now would be... October. Early autumn. The leaves would be turning. The harvest would be coming in.

He'd always loved October.

"What about experimental treatments? Clinical trials?"

"There are some trials happening at university hospitals. The closest would be Chicago, maybe St. Louis. But enrollment is limited, and honestly, Tom, the data so far isn't encouraging. We're talking about extending life by months, not years. And you'd spend most of that time traveling for treatments, feeling miserable."

Tom looked down at his hands. These hands that had baptized children and buried the dead. These hands that had failed Paulson on that dark night in Vietnam. These hands that would stop working in six months.

"I need some time to think about this," Tom said.

"Of course." Dr. Morrison stood and walked to his desk, pulling out a business card. "This is an oncologist in Springfield. Dr. Jane Chen. She's excellent. If you decide to pursue treatment, she's who I'd recommend." He handed Tom the card. "I'm also giving you prescriptions for pain medication and something to help with the cough. If the breathing gets worse, we can get you on oxygen."

Tom took the card and the prescriptions. The paper felt thin between his fingers, insubstantial. His entire future, reduced to a few pieces of paper.

"Tom." Dr. Morrison's voice was gentle. "I know this is a lot to take in. If you need to talk or if you have questions, call my office anytime. We'll get you through this."

Through this. Not *out of* this. The distinction wasn't lost on Tom.

"Thank you," Tom said, standing. His legs felt unsteady, but he kept his balance.

They shook hands again. Then Tom walked out of the office, down the hallway, past the waiting room with its vinyl chairs and industrial cleaner smell, out into the parking lot.

The spring air felt cool against his face. Clouds had moved in while he was inside, turning the afternoon gray. Tom stood in the parking lot, keys in hand, staring at nothing in particular.

Six months.

He got in his car and sat for a long moment, hands resting on the steering wheel. Through the windshield, he could see people coming and going from the hospital. A young couple walking out with a newborn, the mother cradling the baby against her chest. An elderly man being pushed in a wheelchair by an orderly. Life and death, all happening in the same building, separated by mere floors.

Tom thought about all the people he'd sat with in hospital rooms over the years. The prayers he'd prayed, the hands he'd held, the promises he'd made. *God is with you. You're not alone. Everything will be okay.*

Had any of it mattered?

He started the engine and drove home.

***

Back in His Den

TOM SAT AT HIS DESK, THE MANILA ENVELOPE SPREAD open in front of him. The CAT scan images lay on one side, the typed reports on the other. He'd been staring at them for twenty minutes, trying to make the words make sense.

Malignant neoplasm of the lung. Metastatic disease involving mediastinal lymph nodes as well as hepatic metastasis noted. Poor prognosis without intervention. Median survival 6–12 months.

Poor prognosis. A medical euphemism for *You're going to die.*

Tom picked up the CAT scan image and held it to the light from the window. There it was, that large mass and those smaller spots that were slowly killing him. How could a small picture of something be so deadly?

He set down the film and leaned back in his chair, closing his eyes.

Margaret Henshaw died weighing just ninety pounds.

Herbert Williams died gasping for air, his lungs too damaged to function.

Cathleen Foxhill just turned forty when she was diagnosed. She had chosen both chemo and radiation, hoping for a miracle... for her... and her young family. She lasted eighteen months. Tom had watched her transform from a vibrant woman into a hollow shell. There was no miracle. The treatments had stolen everything from her before the cancer finally did.

They were all dead now.

Every single person Tom had prayed with, every parishioner who'd undergone aggressive cancer treatment, was dead.

He opened his eyes and looked around his den. The walls were lined with books. Theology texts, commentaries, novels he'd never finished. On the shelf above his desk sat a row of bound sermons from his years at Great Witness. The file cabinet held records of baptisms, weddings, and funerals. A lifetime of ministry, documented and filed away.

What would he remember? What would he miss?

His eyes found another photo of him and Paulson from that night in Vietnam. The night he'd grabbed the wrong medication. The night a good man died because of his mistake.

He'd been living with that guilt for five years. Carrying it like a weight on his chest. A different kind of tumor, invisible but just as deadly.

Was this cancer God's way of evening the score? Payment for a life taken?

Tom shook his head. He didn't believe that. Couldn't believe that. If God worked that way, the world would be even more cruel than it already was.

He pulled open his desk drawer and found his sabbatical request. He'd submitted it in February, asking for two months starting June 1st. He'd planned to use May to transition his duties, then launch the veteran's program in early summer. It was a program for the men who came back from Vietnam, too hardened to find peace back home.

The board had approved it reluctantly, given the church's financial situation, but they'd approved it nonetheless. It was to be two months. Eight weeks of working to find ways to help those who came home changed versions of the people they once were. It was to be a way to honor the lives of the men who died there, but whose memories Tom held onto.

Now he had six months. Maybe less.

Tom set the sabbatical paperwork on top of the medical reports. The contrast was almost absurd. One document offering him time to create something good. The other, telling him his time was running out.

His eyes drifted across the desk, landing on the latest edition of *Sojourners* magazine. He'd been a subscriber since before they changed the name from *The Post-American* earlier this year. The magazine had moved from somewhere near Chicago to Washington, D.C., but Tom still felt connected to the contributors, to the editor Jim Wallis, to a vision of a Christianity that engaged with social justice rather than retreating from it.

The cover story this month was about the refugee crisis in Southeast Asia—Vietnamese families fleeing the fall of Saigon just a few weeks ago. Tom hadn't read it yet.

He flipped past the articles to the back pages, where the advertisements were: Christian bookstores, seminary programs, conference announcements.

And there, in the bottom corner of the third-to-last page, a small, boxed ad:

HOLY LAND TOUR
Limited Spaces Available
Contact: Pilgrimage Tours International

Tom stared at the ad. He'd seen dozens like it over the years, always in the back of religious magazines. He'd always told himself he'd go someday. When he had time. When he could afford it. When the church was stable enough for him to be away.

Someday.

He thought about his list, hastily written on a piece of paper and tucked in his wallet. *Visit the Holy Land. See where it all began.*

Tom looked at the medical reports again. *Six months. Maybe less.*

If he went on this trip, he'd use up two weeks of whatever time he had left. Two weeks that could be spent with the church, preparing them for his absence. Preparing them for his death.

But what would he be preparing them for, really? To carry on without him? They'd carry on regardless. The church had stood for decades before he arrived. It would stand after he was gone. Or it would close.

Either way, his presence or absence wouldn't change the outcome.

Tom found the phone number at the bottom of the ad and dialed before he could talk himself out of it.

"Pilgrimage Tours, Judith speaking."

"Hi, I'm calling about the Holy Land tour. The ad says limited availability. Is there space available for next month's tour?"

"Oh yes. Let me pull up that information." The sound of papers shuffling. "The tour runs from May 21st through the 30th. Ten days total. Our tours are small group tours, not the typical cattle call kind. Twelve people are assigned to each guide."

Tom barely held back a chuckle. A chance to be one of *The Twelve* was both absurd and intriguing. "Are there still spaces available?"

"We have... let me see... one space left for next month's tour."

One space out of twelve. Tom felt a strange urgency, as if the space might disappear while he was making up his mind. "What's the cost?"

"Twelve hundred dollars. That includes airfare from New York, all accommodations, most meals, and ground transportation. It doesn't include your flight to New York or personal expenses."

Twelve hundred dollars. Tom's breath caught slightly. He did the math quickly. He had about twenty-two hundred in savings. He'd been setting aside money for years, telling himself it was for an emergency.

If this wasn't an emergency, what was? "I'd like to take that last space," Tom heard himself say.

"Wonderful! Let me get some information from you..."

Ten minutes later, Tom hung up the phone. He'd given Judith his name and address and, because it was nearly last-minute, committed to sending the full amount by the end of the week.

He sat back in his chair, slightly stunned by what he'd just done.

He'd committed to spending most of his savings on a ten-day trip to Israel. He'd committed to doing something entirely for himself, something he'd been putting off for years because there was always a reason not to go.

Tom looked at the medical reports again, then at the magazine ad, then at his sabbatical paperwork.

Six months to live. Ten days in the Holy Land. A chance to see where it all began before everything ended.

He pulled out his wallet and unfolded the to-do list he'd written just days ago:

1.   *Visit the Holy Land; see where it all began.*
2.   *Preach Acts 17:6 at least once.*
3.   *Stop playing it safe.*

Tom picked up a pen and drew a check mark next to the first item. One down.

He didn't know what he expected to find in Israel. He didn't know if it would change anything about how he faced his death. He didn't even know if he believed God cared whether he went or not.

But for the first time in years, Tom had made a decision based on what *he* wanted rather than what was expected of him.

It felt terrifying. It felt right.

He folded the list and put it back in his wallet. Then he gathered up the medical reports and the CAT scan images and filed them in his desk drawer. He'd look at them again tomorrow. Make decisions about pain management and what Dr. Morrison described as palliative care.

And, of course, how to tell the congregation.

But tonight, he was going to sit with the knowledge that he'd done something for himself. That he'd chosen life, even if it was only for ten days in a different country.

Tom turned off the desk lamp and sat in the gathering darkness, listening to the house settle around him.

Six months. But first, the Holy Land.

First, he'd walk where Jesus walked.

Then he'd figure out how to die well.

CHAPTER
FIVE

Tom arrived at his office on Tuesday morning to find Kayla already there, sitting cross-legged on the floor in front of his bookshelf, surrounded by open volumes. She'd pulled out his entire collection on the Book of Acts, spreading them across the carpet like pieces of a puzzle she was trying to solve.

She looked up, her face bright with that enthusiasm he was beginning to recognize as her default setting. "Good morning! I hope you don't mind. I got here early to work on my research project. You have an amazing collection of commentaries on Acts. I've been comparing the different interpretations of Chapter 17, and—" She stopped mid-sentence, really looking at him for the first time. "Are you okay? You look..."

"Tired." Tom set his briefcase on the desk and lowered himself into his chair. "I didn't sleep well."

Kayla stood, brushing dust from her jeans. "Your appointment yesterday. With Dr. Morrison. How did it go?"

Tom had told her about the appointment on Sunday after the service. That he'd probably be late coming in on Monday, that he might need to reschedule their meeting depending on how long it took. She'd nodded and said she'd pray for good results.

He looked at her now, this young woman with her whole life ahead of her, her whole ministry just beginning. He felt the burden of what he was about to say.

"Sit down, Kayla."

Something in his voice made her move quickly. She pushed aside the books and sat in the chair across from his desk. "What is it?"

"The tests came back. The CAT scan, the biopsy, all of it." Tom pulled the manila envelope from his briefcase and set it on the desk between them. He didn't open it. "I have cancer. Lung cancer. It's already spread to other areas. The doctor says I have about six months. Maybe less."

She gripped the armrests of the chair. "No. No, that can't be. You don't smoke. You're young, you're only—"

"Thirty-nine."

"That's too young. How could... How can someone who's healthy get cancer?"

"I don't know," Tom answered, rubbing the back of his neck. "Some of the vets are talking about that crap they dumped from the air being bad for more than just the jungle. Agent Orange, they're calling it." He paused. "But it really doesn't matter how, does it?"

"But there has to be a way to treat it. What about chemotherapy or radiation? Aren't there clinical trials, experimental—"

"Kayla." Tom's voice was gentle but firm. "I've watched people undergo those treatments. Good people from this congregation. Every single one of them died anyway, and they spent their last months being poisoned, burned, and sick. I'm not doing that."

"But without treatment—"

"Without treatment, I maintain my quality of life. I'll be able to function, to do my work, to..." He paused. "To live, however much time I have left."

Kayla stared at him, her eyes filling with tears. "I don't understand. You're just going to give up?"

Tom smiled with a reassuring look. "I'm not giving up. I'm choosing how to spend my remaining time."

Kayla shook her head and closed her eyes. Her clenched fists caught Tom's eye.

He leaned forward. "Kayla, this is part of ministry," he said softly. "Sitting with people during these moments. Helping them process difficult news. Offering comfort when there are no easy answers. Usually, I'm the one offering that comfort. But right now..." He gestured between them. "Right now, you're the one ministering, and I'm the one who needs—"

Kayla stood abruptly, tears spilling down her cheeks. "I can't. I'm sorry, I can't be the minister right now. You're my mentor. You're supposed to teach me about ministry, not—" Her voice broke. "Not this. Not yet."

Tom moved around the desk sand stood in front of her. "This is exactly what ministry is. It's messy and painful and nothing like what they teach you in seminary. It's sitting with people in the worst moments of their lives and finding a way to be present even when you have no answers."

"I don't know how to do this." Kayla wiped at her eyes with the back of her hand. "I don't know what to say to you."

"Then don't say anything." Tom nodded warmly. "Just sit with me." He guided her back to the chair and then returned to his own seat. "That's what people need most of the time anyway. Not words. Not platitudes. Just presence... the ministry of presence."

They sat in silence for a long moment. Outside, the morning traffic moved along Main Street. The grandfather clock in the corner marked time with its steady tick.

Finally, Kayla spoke, her voice weak. "What happens now?"

"Now I figure out how to prepare the church. The board needs to know. The congregation needs to be told. There are practical things, like finding someone to cover my duties, arranging for guest preachers, making sure the administrative work doesn't fall apart." Tom pulled a legal pad from his open briefcase. "I've been making a list."

Kayla leaned forward, reading the items upside down. "You're already planning for when you're gone."

"I'm planning for when I can't work anymore. There's a difference."

"Not much of one," she said, barely above a whisper. She reached across the desk and turned the legal pad around to face her. Her eyes scanned the list: board meeting, pulpit supply, pastoral care coverage, financial review. Then her gaze caught on an item that made her pause. "What's this? 'Cancel sabbatical project'?"

"I'd planned to use my sabbatical to start a program. For Vietnam veterans. Men who came home from the war and couldn't find their way back to normal life. I thought... I thought I could help them. Use my experience as a chaplain to—" He stopped. "It doesn't matter now."

"Why not?"

"Because I don't have time to build something like that. It would take months just to get it off the ground, and I don't have that many months."

Kayla was quiet for a moment, still studying the list. Then her eyes moved to something else on his desk: a different notepad with the words "Pilgrimage Tours International" at the top. She picked it up. "What's this? 'Holy Land Tour, May 21–30,'" Kayla read aloud. "Tom, this is in three weeks."

"I know."

"Were you thinking about going?" She looked up at him, hope flickering in her eyes. "That might actually be good. Getting away for a while, seeing the places where it all began. Maybe it would help you—"

"I already booked it."

Kayla blinked. "What?"

"Yesterday. After the appointment. I called and reserved the last space." Tom took the notepad from her hands. "It's a ten-day tour. Small group; just twelve people. I leave in three weeks."

Kayla's expression shifted from surprise to something Tom couldn't quite read. "You just... decided? Just like that?"

"Just like that," he said.

"I know I just got here the other week, but that doesn't sound like you."

"No. It's not." Tom leaned back in his chair. "And I don't know how I feel about it. Part of me thinks I'm running away. That I should be here, preparing the church, making the most of whatever time I have left with the congregation."

He picked up the notepad, stared at the tour details. "But another part of me thinks... What if this is the only thing I've done in years that actually matters? What if dying in Jerusalem is more meaningful than dying in this office making lists?"

Kayla sat still, saying nothing. Practicing for the first time the ministry of just being present.

Tom could see her biting the inside of her cheek. Fighting the urge to speak, to fix, to offer solutions.

"Maybe that's the problem," Tom continued. "I've spent my whole life being careful and responsible, doing what was expected. And where did it get me? Divorced. Burned out. Dying at thirty-nine." He gestured to the notepad. "For once, I wanted to do something just because I wanted to. Not because it was smart or practical or approved by the board."

Kayla opened her mouth and closed it again. Then slowly, a smile spread across her face.

"Now I'm not sure what to think, Kayla."

Her first attempt at the ministry of presence didn't last long. "I think it's good," she burst out. She stood up, looked out the window, then turned back. "Do you know what I've seen since I got here? A man going through the motions. Preaching safe sermons. Avoiding conflict. Playing it safe because he's tired and doesn't want to fight anymore..."

"Go on."

She crossed her arms. "But this? This is the man Rabbi Levine told me about. The man who rebuilt villages in Vietnam. The man who believed God works through action, not just prayers. This is you actually living instead of just existing."

"Don't you think it's irresponsible?" Tom countered. "I'm the pastor of this church. I shouldn't just leave for ten days without—"

"Why not?" Kayla moved back to the chair and sat on the edge. "You're taking your sabbatical anyway, right? You said it starts June first. This tour is before that."

"By a week."

"So you leave a week early. The church will survive." She leaned forward, her eyes intense. "Tom, you just told me you have six months to live. Six months. And you're worried about leaving the church uncovered for ten days?"

"It's not that simple—"

"It is exactly that simple." Kayla pulled the legal pad toward her and picked up his pen. "You said the church needs to know. Fine, tell them. It doesn't need to be everything... not yet. Announce you're taking an early sabbatical for health reasons. Bring in guest preachers for the Sundays you're gone. I'll handle the day-to-day pastoral care. The board manages the administrative stuff they've been managing for years anyway."

"You can't handle pastoral care. You're not ordained yet."

"Then I'll shadow whoever you bring in. Or I'll call you if something urgent comes up. Or I'll figure it out." She looked into his eyes. "That's what you wanted, isn't it? Someone to challenge you? To push back? Well, I'm pushing back."

Be careful what you wish for, Tom. He felt something in his chest loosen slightly. "What if I get worse while I'm there? What if something happens and I'm halfway around the world?"

"Then you'll be halfway around the world, walking where Jesus walked, instead of sitting in this office making lists." Kayla set down the pen. "What's the worst that could happen? You die in Jerusalem instead of Stoneford? At least that's poetic."

Despite everything, Tom felt a laugh escape. "That's not comforting."

"Well, I'm not trying to comfort you. But I do want you to live. I want you to live your best days while you can." She stood and moved to his side of the desk, perched on the edge. "When I first got here, I asked you what this church would look like if its members spent less time worshiping and more time following Jesus. Remember?"

"I remember."

"You're getting the chance to actually do that. To follow Jesus. Literally. To walk the roads he walked, see the places he taught, stand where he stood." Her voice softened. "Don't waste this chance trying to be responsible."

Tom looked at her... this idealistic young woman who somehow saw past his cynicism to something he'd almost forgotten was there. Hope. Possibility. The belief that maybe, even now, something meaningful could happen.

"You need to go on this trip."

"The board meeting is Thursday night," he said slowly. "I'll tell them then. About the cancer, about the sabbatical, about needing pulpit coverage."

"What about you going on the trip?"

"I'll tell them I'm taking some time before the sabbatical officially starts. They don't need to know where I'm going."

"And the congregation?"

Tom thought about Sunday morning. The familiar faces, the empty pews, the routine of worship that had become so rote he could do it in his sleep. "I'll preach on Sunday. One more sermon. Then I'll announce the sabbatical. Tell them I need time for health reasons."

"You're not going to tell them about the cancer?"

"Not yet." Tom's voice was confident. "Once I tell them, everything changes. They'll start looking at me differently. Treating me like I'm already dead. I want..." He paused, searching for the words. "I want a few more weeks of normal before everything becomes about dying."

Kayla nodded slowly. "Okay. But Tom? You can't do this alone. You have to let people help."

"I know."

"No, I don't think you do." She slid off the desk and stood in front of him. "You've spent years taking care of everyone else. From Vietnam to here in Stoneford..." She looked around his office, "Where you've spent years visiting the sick, officiating funerals, and counseling the troubled. Now you're the one who needs care, and you have to let people give it to you. Starting with me."

Tom felt his throat tighten. "What do you mean?"

"I mean, instead of just your extern, I'd like to be... a friend. And I want to help you through this, whether you like it or not." She pulled the legal pad back toward her. "So, let's make a real plan. Not just for when you're gone, but for when you get back. Because you are coming back, and we need to make sure the church is ready for whatever comes next."

For the next two hours, they worked through the details. Kayla took notes while Tom talked through the pastoral care needs, the upcoming weddings and baptisms, and the families who might need extra support. She asked questions he hadn't thought of, pointing out gaps in his thinking, pushing him to be more specific about what he needed.

At some point, Tom wasn't sure when, she disappeared and returned with two cups of coffee from the little kitchenette down the hall, setting one down in front of him without breaking stride in her questioning.

She pulled out a calendar and started mapping out the next two months, including who would preach when, which board members could handle which responsibilities, and how they'd maintain continuity while Tom was away.

It struck Tom that she was better at this than he'd expected. More organized, more strategic, more confident. He'd thought of her as idealistic and inexperienced, but watching her work, he realized she was neither. She was prepared. And she was ready.

"What about the veteran's project?" Kayla asked, looking up from the calendar. "The one you were going to start during your sabbatical?"

Tom shook his head. "Eh, there's no point now. I don't have time to—"

"What if I did it?"

"Huh?"

"What if I took it on? As part of my externship. You could give me your notes, your contacts, whatever you've already planned. I could start laying the groundwork while you're gone. Then when you get back, we'd work on it together." She set down her pen. "It doesn't have to die just because you're... I'm sorry. I mean, just because you can't do it alone."

Tom stared at her. The project had been his way of making amends. His way of honoring Paulson and all the other men who'd died in Vietnam, and those who came back broken versions of themselves. The idea of handing it to someone else, of letting it become something he hadn't built himself...

"You'd do that?" he asked quietly.

"I'd be honored to." Kayla's voice was steady. "Let me help carry this, Tom. Let me help you leave something good behind. A part of your legacy."

Tom closed his eyes. He thought about the list he'd been making. All the things he'd planned to do, fix, to accomplish before he died. The veteran's project was at the top. A way to redeem something from his failure in Vietnam. To honor Paulson.

But maybe redemption didn't have to be something he did alone. Maybe it could be something he started and someone else finished. Maybe legacy wasn't about completing everything yourself but about planting seeds that others could tend.

"Okay," he said, opening his eyes. "I'll get you my notes. Everything I've collected. Names of veterans who might be interested, contacts at the VA, ideas for programming. It's all in the file cabinet."

Kayla's smile was radiant. "Thank you."

"No." Tom's voice was rough. "Thank you. For..." He gestured vaguely, unable to articulate what he meant. For caring. For not treating him like he was already dead. For pushing him to live. For offering to carry something he couldn't carry alone.

Kayla seemed to understand anyway. "That's what friends do."

They worked until noon, when Kayla finally stood and stretched. "I need to go. But I'll be back tomorrow morning, and we can keep planning."

"Okay."

She gathered her books and papers, stuffing them into her canvas bag. At the door, she paused and turned back. "Tom... I'm glad you booked that trip. I think it's exactly what you need to do."

"I hope you're right."

"I am right." She grinned. "I'm young and idealistic, remember? We're always right."

After she left, Tom sat in his office, looking at the work they'd done. The calendar was marked with names and dates. The legal pad filled with Kayla's neat handwriting, organizing his thoughts into actionable steps. The file on the veteran's project sat on the corner of his desk, ready to be handed off.

He'd come into the office this morning dreading the conversation, dreading Kayla's reaction, dreading the weight of telling someone else about his diagnosis.

Instead, he felt lighter.

He pulled out his wallet and unfolded the to-do list:

1. *Visit the Holy Land; see where it all began.* ✓
2. *Preach Acts 17:6 at least once.*
3. *Stop playing it safe.*

He stared at number three for a long moment. Then he picked up his pen and added a fourth item:

4. *Let people help.*

It would be the hardest item on the list. Harder than traveling to Israel. Harder than preaching a controversial sermon. Harder than taking risks.

But maybe it was the most important one.

Tom folded the list and put it back in his wallet. Then he turned to a clean notepad and began working on Sunday's sermon.

One more sermon. Then, three weeks to prepare. Then Israel.

Then whatever came next.

For the first time since meeting with Dr. Morrison yesterday, Tom felt something that wasn't quite hope but was close. Purpose. Direction. The sense that maybe, even with only six months left, there was still something meaningful ahead.

He just had to be willing to walk toward it. To walk into it. And then walk with it.

Even if it scared him. Especially if it scared him.

Tom took in a deep breath. Deeper than he'd been able to in weeks. And began to write.

CHAPTER
SIX

The eight members of the church board sat around the long table in the conference room, coffee cups and notepads in front of them. Howard Beckner had called the emergency meeting for seven o'clock, and they'd all shown up. Curious, concerned, and wondering what couldn't wait until the regular monthly meeting.

Tom stood at the head of the table. He'd rehearsed what he would say, practiced the words until they felt right. But now, looking at these faces—people who'd welcomed him three years ago and trusted him with their church—the rehearsed speech vanished.

"I'm dying," he said simply.

Silence followed. Eleanor Pritchard, George's widow, set down her coffee cup with a trembling hand. Bob Matthews, the treasurer, dropped his head. Carolyn Foster opened her mouth, but no sound came out.

Howard was the first to speak. "Tom, what are you—"

"Cancer." Tom sat down, unable to stand. "I don't understand most of it. The medical reports call it Small Cell Lung Cancer. And... it's already spread to my liver." He looked around the table, meeting each person's eyes. "I saw Dr. Morrison on Monday. He says I have about six months."

"Six months." Eleanor's voice was barely a whisper. "But you're so young."

"There must be treatment options," Bob said, leaning forward. "Chemo—"

"I'm not pursuing treatment." Tom's voice was steady. "I've watched too many people suffer through those treatments. I'm choosing quality of life over quantity."

Carolyn stood abruptly, her chair scraping against the floor. "Tom, there must be something... Howard, isn't your son-in-law a doctor? He's got to know someone—"

"Carolyn, it's okay. I've made peace with my decision."

"By giving up?" Her eyes were bright with tears.

"By choosing how I want to spend my remaining time."

"By abandoning your church?" Bob's voice cracked with emotion. "We need you. The church needs you."

Tom felt the words like a physical blow. He pressed his palm against his chest, trying to ease the tightness. "Bob, I'm not abandoning anyone. But the reality is..." He had to stop, catch his breath. "Every one of you has been here longer than I have. You know the church existed before I got here." Another pause. "And it'll exist after I'm gone. That's the reality... I'm not indispensable."

"But six months—" Eleanor wiped at her eyes. "That's not enough time."

"Which is why I'm telling you now. My sabbatical was approved to start June 1st. I'd like to move it up slightly. Take some time away before... before things get worse."

"How much time?" Howard asked carefully.

"I'm leaving next week. I'll be gone for about ten days."

"Ten days?" Howard started to stand. "Tom, you just told us you're dying, and now you're leaving for ten days? That's... a lot for us to process."

"I know it is. And I'm sorry for that." Tom looked around the table. "But I need this. I need time away from here, away from being a pastor, away from managing everyone's expectations about how I should die."

The board members exchanged glances. Finally, Howard cleared his throat. "What do you need from us, Tom? What can we do?"

Tom hadn't expected that question. He'd anticipated resistance, arguments, maybe even anger. But not... support. "Don't judge me?" The words slipped out as a question. "I'm sure that sounds strange, considering... But I can't tell you the guilt I'm feeling for making this decision. I feel like I'm abandoning you. What I need most... What I need most is your understanding."

"Tom?" Eleanor's soft voice cut through the tension. "May we offer you more than our understanding? Would you accept our love? And our prayers?"

Tom felt his eyes well up. When was the last time anyone had asked to pray *for him*? "I could sure use both, Eleanor."

"Tom, don't you worry about pastoral care concerns," Eleanor continued. "Our Stephen Ministers can step up. This is what we trained for."

The Stephen Ministers. In the whirlwind of the past week, Tom had forgotten about the newly trained Stephen Ministers in the congregation. "That's a wonderful idea, Eleanor. Kayla can handle what they're not comfortable with. She's more capable than any of you realize. And for anything she can't manage, I'm sure the neighboring churches will lend a hand."

"What about the pulpit?" Howard asked. "Who's going to preach while you're gone?"

"I'll make some calls. I know some retired ministers in the area who'll help. I'll arrange the guest preachers."

The meeting continued for another hour. Tom fielded questions about finances, pulpit supply, and what to tell the congregation. He answered what he could and deferred what he couldn't. By the time they adjourned at nine o'clock, a fragile plan was in place.

As the others filed out, Howard lingered. "Tom, I know you said you don't want people managing your death, but... are you okay?"

Tom thought about the question. Was he okay? No. Would he be okay? Probably not. But that wasn't what Howard was really asking.

"I'm scared," Tom admitted. "Terrified, actually. But I'm also... I don't know. Relieved, maybe? At least now I know. No more waiting for test results, no more wondering. Now I just have to figure out how to live with dying."

Howard nodded slowly. "If you need anything—"

"I know. Thank you."

After Howard left, Tom sat alone in the conference room for a long moment. One conversation down. One more to go.

THE SANCTUARY FELT DIFFERENT ON THIS SUNDAY MORNing. Tom stood in the pulpit, looking out at the seventy-some faces scattered across the pews, and wondered if they could sense it—a subtle shift in the air that comes before everything changes.

Kayla sat in the back row, as she always did during services. Their eyes met briefly, and she gave him a small nod of encouragement.

Tom had spent three days working on this sermon. Not the usual week of preparation. Just three full days of writing and rewriting, trying to find words that were honest. Honest and hopeful.

He'd chosen the 17th chapter of the Book of Acts as his text, focusing on the sixth verse.

"'These who have turned the world upside down have come here too,'" Tom read the verse slowly, letting it hang in the air. "That's what they said about the early Christians. Not that they prayed well. Not that they believed the right things. Not that they worshiped properly. They said these people turned the world upside down."

He closed his Bible and stepped out from behind the pulpit—something he rarely did. "I've been thinking a lot lately about what it means to follow Jesus. Not worship Jesus... we're already pretty good at that. We worship every Sunday morning. We sing hymns, say prayers, and listen to sermons. We're excellent at worship."

A few puzzled looks rippled through the congregation. This wasn't his usual style.

"But following Jesus? That's different. Following Jesus means doing what he did. Feeding the hungry. Visiting the prisoner. Welcoming the stranger. Taking care of widows and orphans... Loving so wastefully that people accuse you of turning the world upside down."

Tom walked to the edge of the platform. "When I first came to Great Witness three years ago, I had big plans. Programs to start, outreach to expand, ways to grow the church and make it vital again. And we've done some of that. We've had our food pantry once a month. We've collected clothes for outreach. We've prayed for the community."

He looked around the sanctuary at the empty pews, at the aging congregation, at the building that had stood for decades and might not stand much longer.

"But I wonder," he continued, "if we've been so focused on worshiping Jesus that we've forgotten to follow him. I wonder if the world looks at us and sees people who have turned anything upside down, or if they just see a nice building where nice people gather on Sunday mornings to sing nice hymns."

Tom returned to the pulpit, gripping its edges. "In today's reading from the Book of Acts, the apostle Paul went to a city and preached there for three weeks. Just three weeks to establish the church. And in that short of time, he and those with him made such an impact that the whole city was in an uproar."

Tom looked to the back at Kayla, who was smiling. "They dragged him and all the new converts before the city officials, saying, 'These men who have turned the world upside down have come here too.'"

He paused, letting the words sink in. "Their reputation in other towns preceded them. But three weeks. That's all it took to turn a city upside down. Not because of Paul's theology. Not because the apostle's prayers were more eloquent. But because he and the others lived out their faith in ways that disrupted the status quo. They challenged injustice. They welcomed outcasts... They lived as if the kingdom of God was already breaking into the world."

Eleanor Pritchard was crying quietly in the third row, George's pew. Tom felt his chest tighten but pushed on.

"I'm telling you this because I'm about to do something that might seem irresponsible or selfish or foolish. I'm taking my sabbatical early. Starting this week, I'll be away for about ten days. When I return, I'll preach as long as I'm able, and then we'll arrange for guest ministers."

He could see the question on their faces: Why? What's happening?

"The reason I'm taking this time is... personal. Health-related. Nothing I need you to worry about right now, but something that needs to be addressed." He swallowed hard. "And when I come back, I hope to come back with a better understanding of what it means to follow Jesus instead of just worshiping him."

Tom's voice gained strength. "While I'm gone, Kayla will be here. She'll be working with our new Stephen Ministers to handle pastoral care needs. She's more than capable, and I trust her completely.

"But I'm asking you... no, I'm challenging you... to use this time to think about that verse from Acts. To think about whether we're content being a church that worships, or whether we want to be a church that turns the world upside down. Even if it's just in our little corner of the world. Even if it starts with one act of radical love."

He pronounced the benediction, his voice steady and clear. As people filed out, shaking his hand at the door, Tom could see confusion and concern in their eyes. A few asked directly what was wrong. He deflected, saying he'd explain more when he returned and promised he was fine.

Only Eleanor lingered after everyone else had left. She stood in the narthex, small and frail in her Sunday best, looking at him with eyes that had seen too much death already.

"It's cancer, isn't it?"

Tom hesitated, then nodded.

"I thought so. You have that look George had. You've lost so much weight, haven't you?" She reached up and touched his cheek with her weathered hand. "Don't waste time, Tom. Don't waste whatever time you have trying to be strong for everyone else. Live. Really live. George waited too long to do the things he wanted to do, and then he ran out of time."

"I'm trying," Tom said, his voice not as convincing as he wanted it to be.

"Good." She patted his cheek once more and turned to leave. At the door, she paused. "Turning the world upside down. I like that. Maybe that's what this church needs. Maybe that's what we all need."

Kayla arrived at Tom's office with a three-ring binder, its tabs color-coded by category. "Good morning!" She set the binder on his desk with a thud. "I spent yesterday afternoon organizing everything. Blue tabs are pastoral care needs, organized by urgency. Green tabs are administrative stuff. Yellow tabs are—"

"Kayla." Tom held up a hand, overwhelmed. "Did you even sleep last night?"

"Some." She flipped open the binder to the first blue section. "Mrs. Henderson's daughter called again. She keeps wanting to talk about her mother, and goes through the same stories every time. I think she needs—"

"Someone to remember with her," Tom finished. "That's not about fixing anything. It's about presence."

"Ministry of presence," Kayla said, making a note. "Got it. Should I visit her?"

"Yes. And just listen. Don't try to make her feel better or move her along. She'll process her grief on her own time."

They worked through the binder together for the next two hours. Tom was impressed by how thoroughly she'd thought through the pastoral care needs, how she'd anticipated what the Stephen Ministers could handle, and which issues she should handle.

"What about the Carlsons?" she asked, flipping to another page. "Their son just got back from Vietnam last month. The mom called asking if we have resources for boys coming home."

"Tell her I'll get back to her when I return. That's actually going to be part of the veteran's project."

The veteran's project files filled an entire banker's box— his research, his contacts at the VA, his ideas for programming. Tom had brought the box in with him and set it on the floor in the back corner of the office.

"Everything's in there," Tom said, pointing to the box.

Before he could stop her, Kayla was on her knees, going through its contents. "This is ambitious," she said, flipping through a folder of program outlines. "Support groups, job training referrals, family counseling… Tom, this is a full-time ministry."

"I know. That's why I need you to start it."

"I don't know if I can—"

Tom bent down, rubbing his fingers along the top of the box, stopping at a specific folder labeled "Paulson Project." "This whole thing… it started with a man I knew in Vietnam. James Paulson. He was a medic in our unit."

Tom opened the folder, revealing a series of photos clipped to the inside cover. A group of men, arms slung over each other's shoulders. "That's Paulson at the end there," Tom said, pointing to the man in the far right of the photo. "He was one of the good ones. Always first to help, always checking on the guys who were struggling."

Tom stopped, letting his thoughts catch up to his mouth. *Why am I telling her this?* He had shared this story only once since having to answer questions from his C.O. about what had happened that night. That was to Sarah.

Kayla's warmth and genuine compassion were matured way past her age. This kid, so idealistic, so open and honest, made it easy to share even the most vulnerable parts of himself. But this one he wasn't sure of.

Kayla's voice interrupted his thoughts. "Penny for your thoughts."

It should have cost more than a single cent. And yet, he couldn't stop his words before his thoughts caught up. "Kayla, I'm not sure… I'm not sure I can… but I feel like I need to. I need to let this out. I need to let this go before I leave. Just in case I don't—"

"Tom," her voice soft, "in case you don't come back? Wherever it is that you take your final breath, you need to know you've touched countless lives. You've helped people not just from this congregation, but from all around town." She picked up the folder, looking at the photo. "You taught me about the ministry of presence. I'd like to think I'm also a safe person you can trust."

"I haven't trusted anyone since Sarah. I'm so confused right now."

"What if you showed yourself some grace? You know, the kind we're supposed to show others."

Grace. Every time Tom thought of that word, he recalled the passage from Paul's second letter to the church in Corinth. Paul had a thorn in his flesh and asked God three times to remove it. God's reply was blunt and comforting at the same time. "My grace is sufficient for you."

This felt more like a shard of glass than a thorn. But maybe Tom's grace to himself could also be sufficient.

"One night during a firefight, one of our men got hit bad. His pain was excruciating. He needed morphine." Tom took a breath. "Paulson got separated from his med bag. I found it and thought I could help." Sweat began to form on Tom's forehead.

"It was dark," he continued, shaking his head. "I wanted to help..."

Kayla set the folder on his desk and sat still.

He couldn't finish the story. Tom couldn't complete the thought, let alone the next sentence.

"Tom..."

He didn't respond. He kept his eyes focused on something only in his mind.

"Never mind." Kayla said, "You don't need—"

Tom picked up the folder, opening it to the photo. "Paulson never blamed me. He should have. But he didn't. He was killed three months later in another battle, and I never got the chance to make it right with him."

"Tom, I'm sorry."

"Don't be. It's my problem, not yours. I'm the one who's sorry." He dropped the folder in front of her. "This program is how I was supposed to make it right. Or it was supposed to be."

Kayla reached across the desk and grabbed his hand. "I got this, Tom. I promise you we'll make it happen. And it'll be everything you envisioned." She leaned back, looking at the contents of the box. "When you get back—"

"If I get back," Tom interrupted gently.

"*When* you get back," Kayla insisted. "We'll already have momentum."

***

TOM SAT IN DR. MORRISON'S OFFICE FOR WHAT HE EXpected would be his last appointment before leaving for Israel. This visit was to discuss pain management and travel precautions. The doctor prescribed stronger medication, explained warning signs to watch for, and gave him a letter to carry in case he needed medical attention abroad.

"You're sure about this trip?" Dr. Morrison asked as Tom was leaving.

"No," Tom admitted. "But I'm going anyway."

Dr. Morrison paused, then looked down at Tom's hands. "Let me see them," he said, pointing.

"My hands? Why do you want to see my hands?"

"Just put them out, like this." Dr. Morrison demonstrated with his own hands, palms down.

Tom did as instructed, confusion evident in his expression.

Dr. Morrison pressed down on each fingernail bed, one after the other. "I'm not liking what I'm seeing." He looked up at Tom. "Your fingernail beds should be refilling with color faster than they are." He squeezed down on Tom's thumb and let go again. "You see? Look how it stays pale. It should return to pink quickly."

"What's that mean?"

"It means you're developing hypoxia. Your blood oxygen levels are low. Your heart's not able to pump it through your body like it should." Dr. Morrison's expression shifted. "I think we should run more tests to see what's going on."

"No more tests." Tom's voice was emphatic. "What would be the use? No matter what they show, I'm not going to change my mind about my care."

Dr. Morrison nodded. "I understand, Tom. But I need to tell you that this could mean the cancer has progressed more than we first thought. Additional tests would give us a clearer picture of—"

"No more tests. No more scans. No more poking or sticking or... what was the last test called? Aspirating fluid?" Tom rubbed the side of his chest. "No more of it. I'm going to Israel. And I'm going without having to worry about more test results."

Dr. Morrison set down his reading glasses, rubbing the bridge of his nose. "I'm not trying to talk you out of going. I want to prepare you for what might happen while you're there. You need to understand the importance of resting if you get tired."

"I'll sit. I'll rest." Tom sat down slowly. "I'll take it easy. But I am going."

Dr. Morrison nodded and pulled out his prescription pad. "Stronger pain medication. Take them as directed on the bottle." He scribbled something, tore off the sheet, and pushed it across the desk. "Tom, if things get bad, get to a hospital. Promise me."

"I promise."

Dr. Morrison began writing on another sheet. After some time, he handed it to Tom. "This is a letter for you to carry. It explains your diagnosis and current treatment plan. If you need medical attention in Israel, show them this."

Before shaking hands and leaving, Tom took the letter, folded it carefully, and tucked it in his wallet next to his to-do list. Two pieces of paper, side by side. One documenting his death, the other his attempt to live.

THE NIGHT BEFORE TOM WAS TO LEAVE, THERE WAS A small gathering after the night's prayer meeting. Someone had made a cake.

Tom hung near the coffee urn, accepting well-wishes and hugs. Everyone was trying hard to be normal, to make this feel like a regular sabbatical send-off rather than what it actually was—possibly, goodbye.

Bob Matthews appeared as everyone began to make their way out. He quietly pressed an envelope into Tom's hand. "From the board. Two hundred in traveler's checks. For emergencies. Just in case."

Tom watched as people walked out the door, many of whom had become his church family. The magnitude of what he was leaving behind hit him. It wasn't forever. Not yet. But soon.

"Take care of yourself," Howard said, gripping his hand firmly.

"Take care of each other," Tom replied.

Kayla emerged from the kitchen, staying off to the side, not interfering with the moment. "That was nice. A nice touch from the prayer group."

"It felt like a funeral," Tom replied quietly. "They're all saying goodbye because they don't think I'm coming back."

"Are you?"

The question surprised him with its directness. "I don't know. I certainly hope so. I want to, that's for sure." His voice trailed off. "But if I get sick in Israel…"

Kayla was getting better at the ministry of presence.

Tom walked to the door. Turning to her, he said softly, "Take care of this place."

Kayla smiled. "I will. Now go home and get some sleep. You have a long day ahead of you."

Tom drove home through the quiet streets of Stoneford, past the houses where his parishioners lived, past the businesses that would open in the morning, and past the high school where members of the church's youth group attended. The town looked peaceful in the gathering darkness. Eternal and unchanging.

But Tom knew better. Everything changed. Everything ended. Even Stoneford would eventually fade, just like he would.

The thought should have depressed him. Instead, it gave him a strange sense of peace.

AT HOME, TOM'S PACKED SUITCASE SAT BY THE FRONT door, a battered brown Samsonite he'd borrowed from the church's lost-and-found. It had been sitting in the closet for two years, unclaimed. Tom had cleaned it out, finding a pack of gum and a yellowed boarding pass from a 1972 flight to Miami.

He'd folded his shirts and pants, rolled socks, and packed his toiletries. The travel itinerary sat on his nightstand. The prescriptions were in his carry-on.

Tom made himself a sandwich he didn't want and ate it standing at the kitchen sink, looking at his small backyard illuminated by two floodlights on either eave of the roof. The grass already needed to be cut. He wouldn't be here to do it. Maybe he'd never mow it again.

The phone rang at a quarter to ten. Tom answered, expecting Howard or maybe Eleanor.

"Hey," Kayla said. "Just wanted to make sure you're all packed."

"I am."

"Good. And Tom? Don't worry about anything here. I've got it covered. Just... be a pilgrim. Walk where Jesus walked. Let yourself be human for a while instead of a pastor."

Tom felt his throat tighten. "Thank you, Kayla. For everything."

"That's what friends do." A pause. "Come back, okay? I'm not ready to do this without you yet."

"I'll come back."

But after he hung up, Tom wondered if he was lying.

He wandered the house, touching things as if memorizing them. The worn couch where he'd spent his nights watching the evening news. The desk where he'd prepared and researched sermons. The photographs on the wall—his parents, now gone; his wedding photo, the marriage now over; a picture of him and Sheldon in Vietnam, both of them so young and certain they could make a difference.

At eleven-thirty, Tom sat on the edge of his bed and looked at the alarm clock set for 5:00 a.m. The car was filled with gas. The route to O'Hare was mapped out. Everything was arranged.

And yet...

Tom picked up the phone and dialed before he could second-guess himself.

"Hello?" Kayla's voice was dry with sleep.

"Kayla, it's me. Tom."

"Tom? Is everything okay?"

"I'm thinking about not going."

Silence. Then, more alert, "Why?"

"Because it's selfish." The words tumbled out. "Because the church needs me. Because I'm spending money I might need for medical bills. Because I—"

"Because you're scared."

Tom stopped. "Yes."

"Good." Her voice was clear now, more awake. "You should be scared. You should be terrified. You're about to do something brave and reckless and completely out of character." A pause. "That's exactly why you need to go."

"Kayla—"

"No. Listen to me." Her voice was as firm as a mother telling her child to get on the bus. "For years, you've played it safe.

You've managed decline, avoided conflict, and done what was expected. And where did that get you?"

There was a pause, but he dared not answer that question.

"Tom, this might be the most important thing you ever do. Not for the church. For you. Don't talk yourself out of it."

Tom closed his eyes, pressing the phone against his ear. "What if I die over there?"

"Then you die living instead of existing. And that's better than dying in that office making lists." Her voice softened. "Tom, remember what you preached on Sunday? About turning the world upside down? You can't turn anything upside down if you're too afraid to even turn yourself around."

After a long moment, Tom said quietly, "I'm going to hang up now and try to sleep."

"Good. And Tom? When you're standing in Jerusalem, walking where Jesus walked, remember this conversation. Remember that you chose to live."

Tom hung up. He double-checked the alarm. He turned off the light.

And he chose to go.

THE ALARM WENT OFF AT 5:00 A.M., PULLING TOM FROM A restless sleep. He'd dreamed of Vietnam again. The jungle, the firefight, Paulson's voice in the darkness. *When will these nightmares end?*

Tom dressed in comfortable clothes for the long journey. He chose khakis, a button-down shirt, and his most comfortable shoes. He cinched his belt tight to the last hole. His shirt hung loose on him. Signs of the weight he had lost. Even he couldn't ignore it now.

He made coffee and drank it while standing at the kitchen window, watching the first light of dawn break over Stoneford.

Before leaving, he walked through the house one more time. In his den, he opened the desk drawer and pulled out his wallet. The to-do list was there, folded next to Dr. Morrison's letter.

Tom unfolded the list and read it one more time:

1. *Visit the Holy Land; see where it all began.* ✓
2. *Preach Acts 17:6 at least once.* ✓
3. *Stop playing it safe. (In progress)*
4. *Let people help. (Learning)*

Two checked off. Two in progress. And now, driving away from everything familiar, about to board a plane while his body slowly betrayed him, Tom was living number three whether he felt ready or not.

He refolded the list carefully, as if it were something precious. Then he tucked it back in his wallet and carried his suitcase to the El Camino.

At 5:30, Tom backed out of his driveway. He turned back at his house one last time. This small ranch where he'd lived alone for a year, where he'd grieved his marriage, wrestled with his faith, and received his death sentence.

Would he see it again? Would he make it back from Israel, or would he die there, in some hotel room or on some tour bus, far from home?

Tom shook his head. He couldn't think like that. He had to believe he'd return. Had to believe there was still time.

He put the car in drive and headed north toward Chicago.

The drive took three and a half hours. Tom drove through the awakening Illinois countryside, passing small towns that looked like Stoneford, farms where early morning work was already beginning. The sunrise painted the sky in shades of pink and gold. *How many more sunrises would he witness?*

Six months. Maybe less. Maybe only a handful more.

Or maybe... if he was lucky... one perfect sunrise in Jerusalem.

As he approached the outskirts of Chicago, the traffic got heavier. Cars merged and divided, everyone rushing toward their own destinations, their own lives. *How many knew how precious this ordinary morning was? How many understood that every sunrise was a gift?*

He pulled into the long-term parking lot at O'Hare at 9:15. Two dollars per day for ten days. Twenty dollars total. Tom took his ticket from the attendant, then sat in his car for a moment, gripping the steering wheel.

This was it. The point of no return. Once he got on that plane, there was no turning back. He was committed.

Tom grabbed his suitcase and locked the doors. Then he stood in the parking lot, feeling the morning sun on his face, and looked up at a plane taking off overhead. Another plane would carry him away from everything he knew. Away from Stoneford, the church, Kayla, and the comfortable routines of life. Away from the familiar, toward the unknown.

Tom picked up his suitcase and walked to the terminal. Forward. That was the only direction now.

Six months to live. Ten days in the Holy Land. A chance to see where it all began before everything ended.

Tom McGarvey, thirty-nine years old and dying, walked through the automatic doors of O'Hare International Airport and stepped into Act Two of his life.

PART TWO
The Holy Land

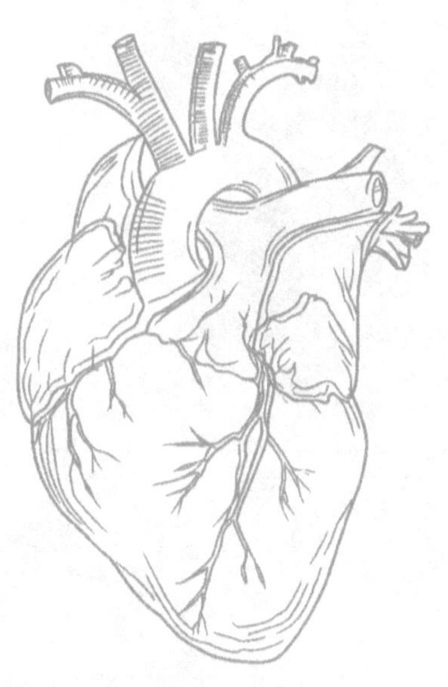

CHAPTER
SEVEN

O'Hare International Airport was chaotic. A swirling mass of travelers rushing in every direction, announcements crackling over loudspeakers, the smell of coffee and cigarettes filling the air, children crying, and businessmen shouting into payphones—all mixing into something uniquely airport-like.

Tom found the Eastern Airlines counter and joined the line.

"Next!"

Tom stepped up to the counter. The ticket agent, a young woman with her hair in a tight bun, barely looked at him. "Name?"

"Thomas McGarvey."

She flipped through papers and found his reservation. "Chicago to JFK, Flight 446. You're confirmed." She attached tags to his suitcase. "Gate B12. Boarding at 11:20."

Tom glanced at the clock on the wall behind her. 9:47. Almost two hours until boarding. "Is there somewhere I can... sit down?"

"Waiting area at the gate." She handed him his boarding pass. "Next!"

He found Gate B12 and claimed a seat facing the window. Outside, planes taxied and took off with mechanical precision. Tom watched them, trying to calm the flutter of anxiety in his stomach. He'd flown before—twice to conferences, once to visit Sarah's parents in Pennsylvania. But never alone. Never this far. Never while dying.

Through the glass, he could see the Eastern Airlines DC-9 being prepared. Fuel trucks, baggage carts, and ground crew moved with practiced efficiency.

"Attention passengers," the gate agent announced over the PA system. "We will begin boarding Flight 447 to New York's John F. Kennedy Airport in approximately ten minutes."

Tom pulled out his boarding pass. Row 8, Seat C. Aisle seat, specifically requested. Easier to get up if he needed to move around, less claustrophobic than the window or middle seat.

The pill he'd taken in the car was wearing off. He felt pressure returning to his chest, a slight wheeze in his breathing. He pulled out the pill bottle, shook one into his palm, and dry-swallowed it. The bitter taste made him wince.

Around him, other passengers were gathering their belongings, forming a loose line near the gate. A group of teenagers was loud and excited, laughing about something Tom couldn't quite hear. A mother with small children was trying to corral her kids, who seemed more interested in running in circles than staying near their gate.

Tom watched them all, these people living their normal lives, going about their business, unaware that the man sitting alone by the window was dying. Would die, probably, before any of them. Would be forgotten while they continued on, oblivious to the fact that they'd shared an airport waiting area with someone counting down his final months.

The thought should have been depressing. Somehow, it wasn't. It was oddly comforting. Life continued. The world kept turning. His death would be a small ripple in a vast ocean, barely noticed, quickly smoothed over.

"Now boarding all rows, Flight 447 to JFK."

Tom stood, grabbed his carry-on, and joined the line.

The DC-9 was as Tom had expected, with seats configured five across, two on one side of the aisle, three on the other. A businesswoman had already settled into the window seat at row 8 when Tom made his way there. She barely glanced at him, engrossed in a thick report on her lap.

The seat between them remained empty as other passengers filed past.

Tom watched them board. An elderly couple moving slowly down the aisle. A young man with a guitar case. And then a young mother with a small boy, maybe four years old, struggling with a carry-on bag. She stopped at row 8, directly across from Tom, trying to wrestle the carry-on bag into the overhead compartment while holding the squirming child. Tom stood and reached for the bag.

"Let me help."

She looked at him with exhausted, grateful eyes. "Thank you. I don't know why I thought flying alone with him was a good idea."

Tom lifted the bag into the overhead bin and closed it. "How old is he?"

"Four. And he barely slept last night." She settled into her seat with the boy on her lap, trying to fasten the seatbelt around both of them. The child, now crying in earnest, pushed against her, trying to escape.

"What's his name?"

"Marcus." She bounced him slightly, trying to soothe him. "We're going back home to Hoboken after visiting my parents. My husband couldn't get off work, so it's just us." She looked close to tears herself. "I know he's bothering everyone."

"He's not bothering me," Tom said, though he could see other passengers glancing over with expressions ranging from sympathy to annoyance.

The stewardess made her way down the aisle, checking seatbelts and closed overhead bins. "Ma'am, you'll need to secure your child in his own seat for takeoff."

"I'm trying," Marcus's mother said, but the boy was having none of it. He wailed louder, arching his back, refusing to be buckled.

Tom sat back down but kept watching. The mother finally got Marcus strapped in, but he continued to scream, kicking the seat in front of him. The businessman in that seat turned around and glared.

The plane taxied to the runway. Marcus's screaming intensified as the engines revved for takeoff. Tom could see the mother's shoulders shaking. She was crying now, too, overwhelmed and embarrassed.

The plane lifted off. The familiar pressure in his chest increased as they climbed, but he ignored it. All his attention was on the young mother and her distressed child across the aisle.

Once they reached cruising altitude and the seatbelt sign dinged off, Marcus unbuckled himself and tried to run down the aisle. His mother caught him, but he fought her, crying harder. She carried him back to their row, but he wouldn't sit still. He spilled his juice on the floor, threw his snack, kicked, screamed, and made everyone around them miserable.

The businessman turned around again. "Can't you control your child?"

The mother's face crumpled. "I'm trying. I'm sorry. I'm so sorry."

That's when Tom stood up.

He crossed the aisle and knelt in front of Marcus, meeting the boy at eye level. "Hey, buddy. My name is Tom. What's wrong?"

Marcus paused mid-scream, surprised by this stranger talking to him.

"Airplanes are scary, aren't they?" Tom said gently. "All the noise and the shaking, and you can't run around like you want to."

Marcus hiccupped, tears streaming down his face.

Tom looked up at the mother. "Is it okay if I tell him a story?"

She nodded, too exhausted to object.

Tom settled into the aisle, blocking it slightly, but he didn't care. "I know a little boy who went to church with his mom one Sunday. And he cried the whole time. He cried and cried and cried. And you know what happened?"

Marcus shook his head, transfixed.

"Some of the people in the church got upset. They said the little boy was being too loud. They said his mom should take him outside. But you know what the pastor said?"

Another head shake.

"The pastor said, 'This child has just as much right to be here as anyone else. His voice matters. His crying matters. He matters.'" Tom glanced at the businessman, who had the grace to look ashamed. "And that's true for you, too, Marcus. You matter. Your voice matters. Even when you're scared or upset. You matter."

The crying turned to barely a whimper. Marcus was listening now, really listening.

Tom looked at the mother. "Where did you say you were from? Hoboken?"

"Yes," she said, wiping at her own tears.

Kneeling next to Marcus, Tom began to sing. "This little light of mine, I'm gonna let it shine... All over Hoboken, I'm gonna let it shine. Let it shine, let it shine, let it shine."

Marcus's mother stared at him, then slowly began to smile.

Tom turned to the woman in the seat behind her. "Where are you from, ma'am?"

"Hainesville," she said quietly.

Tom sang again. "This little light of mine, I'm gonna let it shine. All over Hainesville, I'm gonna let it shine. Let it shine, let it shine, let it shine."

Tom stood and turned to face the passengers around them. His voice carried down the aisle. "I learned a song a long time ago. A song about letting your light shine. And I think Marcus here needs to hear where everyone is from."

A few nods. Most people just looked confused.

"Who's from Chicago?" Tom asked the passengers who were listening.

At least twenty hands went up. "Great!" Tom put his hands in the air like he was directing an orchestra. "Let's hear it for Chicago!"

He lifted his voice, louder than before, and most of the people with their hands raised joined in. "This little light of mine, I'm gonna let it shine. All over Chicago, I'm gonna let it shine. Let it shine, let it shine, let it shine."

About a third of the plane was now singing.

Someone yelled out, "Boston!" Tom started to sing, and most of the passengers joined in. "All over Boston..."

Tom moved down the aisle, asking where people were going, incorporating their hometowns into the song. Someone called out, "Old Bridge!" from the back.

Then "Springfield!"

Then "The Bronx!"

Soon, the entire plane was singing. Businessmen and families and teenagers and elderly couples, all calling out their hometowns, listening for the chorus of letting their light shine. Even the stewardesses joined in, their professional demeanors cracking into genuine smiles.

Marcus sat quietly in his mother's lap, watching with wide eyes as the plane full of strangers sang for him.

When the song finally ended, spontaneous applause broke out. Tom made his way back to his seat, slightly breathless from the exertion. His chest was tight again, and he'd need another pill soon, but it had been worth it.

The young mother leaned across the aisle. "Thank you. I don't... thank you."

"No need to thank me. Just remember, his voice matters. Don't let anyone tell you otherwise."

She nodded, still crying but now smiling too.

For the rest of the flight, Marcus was calm. He colored in a coloring book his mother pulled from her oversized purse. He ate his snack without throwing it. He even dozed off for the last thirty minutes.

As they descended into JFK, the businessman turned around. "I'm sorry," he said to Marcus's mother. "I shouldn't have been so impatient."

"It's okay," she said. "I understand."

Tom looked past the businesswoman, who'd never looked up from her report, out the window as the plane descended through the clouds. Below, he could see the sprawl of New York City, the Atlantic Ocean beyond. In a few hours, he'd be flying over that ocean, heading toward a land he'd only read about, only imagined.

He thought about what he'd just done—stood up in a plane full of strangers and led them in song for a frightened child. A month ago, he wouldn't have done that. A month ago, he would have sat quietly in his seat, uncomfortable but unwilling to make a scene.

But that was before the diagnosis. Before the list. Before he'd decided to stop playing it safe.

Tom pulled out the journal Kayla had given him yesterday and wrote:

Lesson 1: Sometimes ministry means making a spectacle of yourself. And that's okay.

JFK WAS EVEN MORE OVERWHELMING THAN O'HARE. Travelers from around the world filled the terminal. Families speaking languages Tom didn't recognize, businessmen shouting into payphones in German or French, women in saris, men in dashikis. The whole world seemed to be in motion, everyone going somewhere.

The layover was three hours, long enough to check in at the international terminal for the Tel Aviv flight and grab something to eat.

And take another pain pill.

Tom found a diner in the terminal and ordered a sandwich he barely tasted.

He called the church from a payphone, feeding dimes and quarters into the slot. Kayla answered on the second ring.

"Great Witness Community Church, this is Kayla."

"It's me. Just wanted to let you know I made it to New York."

"How was the flight?"

Tom smiled, thinking about Marcus and the singing. "Eventful. But good."

"Are you okay? You sound tired."

"I am tired. But I'm okay." Through the terminal windows, he could see planes taking off and landing, an endless stream of metal birds carrying people to destinations all over the world. "Kayla, thank you. For everything. For believing I should do this."

"You're going to have an amazing time," she said. "I can feel it."

After he hung up, Tom made his way to Gate 19. The gate area was already crowded with passengers for the Pan Am flight. Tourists with cameras, business travelers, and what looked like a few Orthodox Jewish families heading home.

And there, near the windows, he saw them. A small group of people wearing name tags that read "Pilgrimage Tours International" engaged in a friendly conversation.

His tour group.

Tom approached slowly, studying them. They were exactly what he'd expected. Middle-aged to elderly, mostly couples, dressed in practical travel clothes that screamed "American tourist." One woman was reading a book titled *The Land Where Jesus Walked*. A man was showing his wife brochures of the sites they'd visit.

They looked like nice people. Good people.

Tom just hoped they wouldn't ask too many questions about why he was there.

"Excuse me," a woman said, noticing his approach. "Are you part of the Pilgrimage Tours group?"

"I am. Tom McGarvey."

"Oh, wonderful! I'm Nancy Hudson, and this is my husband, Dale." She motioned to a tall man with gray hair. "We're from Oklahoma. Where are you from?"

"Illinois. Stoneford. Small town downstate."

"How lovely! Is this your first time to the Holy Land?"

"It is."

"Ours too! We've been planning this for three years. Saved up and everything. We're just so excited to see where our Lord walked and taught." She beamed at him. "What brought you on the trip?"

Tom hesitated, weighing his response. "I felt it was time to see it for myself."

"Time for a spiritual journey?" Dale asked, smiling.

"Something like that," Tom replied, feeling a warmth in their friendliness.

"Wonderful! While we're waiting, let me show you the brochures," Nancy said, waving him closer. Tom joined the group, even as a part of him remained guarded.

As they discussed the itinerary and shared their excitement, Tom realized he was no longer just a man with a terminal diagnosis. He was embarking on a pilgrimage. One that could lead him not just to historical places, but potentially to a new understanding of his life and purpose.

Tom felt his chest tighten. Why was he going on this trip? Cancer. The fear of dying without seeing the places that had shaped his faith. The desperate hope that maybe, somewhere in Jerusalem or Bethlehem or Nazareth, he'd find something he'd lost.

"So why now?" Nancy asked.

"Just felt like the right time," he said instead.

"Well, we're so glad you're here! This is going to be the trip of a lifetime."

I hope so, Tom thought. *Since it might be my last one.*

"Ladies and gentlemen, Pan Am Flight 201 to Tel Aviv will begin boarding in approximately thirty minutes."

Tom's heart rate picked up. This was it. The real journey. The threshold into Act Two.

The gate agent checked his ticket. "Mr. McGarvey, you're in 23C, nonsmoking. The aisle seat. Please wait until your row is called."

Tom stepped aside and watched the other passengers board. Families laughing together. Couples holding hands. A tour group from Brooklyn, all wearing matching blue T-shirts that read "Jerusalem or Bust!"

Tom was traveling alone. Would he die alone, too?

"Rows 20 through 30, please board at this time."

The Pan Am 707 was larger than the DC-9, with seats configured three on each side of the aisle. He made his way down the aisle, stowing his carry-on and settling in.

A woman in her late twenties occupied the window seat, her dark hair pulled back, wearing a simple dress. The middle seat between them remained empty as she stared out the window, her expression intense as if trying to commit every detail to memory.

Tom buckled his seatbelt and pulled out the Pilgrimage Tours itinerary he'd brought. Ten days. Jerusalem, Bethlehem, Nazareth, the Sea of Galilee, and Jericho. Places he'd only read about, only imagined. Soon he'd stand where Jesus had stood, walk where Jesus had walked.

If his body held out that long.

"Excuse me," the woman next to him said suddenly, her voice tight. "Is this your first time flying?"

After the eventful flight he'd just gotten off, Tom was looking forward to a restful flight. He held the tour itinerary in his hand, hoping she'd see it and leave him alone. But when he looked over at her, her strained knuckles gripping the armrest caught his attention. "No, ma'am. I've flown before. Why?"

"Because it's mine." She turned to face him, tears glistening in her eyes. "And I'm terrified."

Tom set down the itinerary. "Flying is actually very safe. Statistically, it's safer than driving."

"I know. Everyone keeps telling me that. But knowing something in your head and feeling it in your body are two different things." She tried to smile, but it came out as more of a frown. "I'm sorry. I'm sure you don't want to spend ten hours sitting next to someone having a panic attack."

Just because he was 900 miles from his church didn't mean he was free of his responsibilities to anyone needing comfort. So much for a restful flight. "It's okay," Tom said with a warm smile. "I'm a minister. I'm used to people having panic attacks around me." He extended his hand. "Tom McGarvey."

She shook it, her hand trembling. "Rachel Stein."

"Where are you flying to, Rachel?"

"Tel Aviv. Then to Jerusalem. My father lives there. He's..." She paused, swallowing hard. "He's dying. I got the call two days ago. They said I should come quickly if I want to say goodbye."

The word... *Dying*. It hit Tom hard. He'd been trying not to think about his own death, losing himself in the logistics of travel and the distraction of other people's lives. But here it was again, reflected back at him through this stranger's grief.

"I'm so sorry," Tom said quietly.

"He went back to Israel after my mother died four years ago. Said he wanted to spend his final years there." Rachel wiped at her eyes. "I thought I had more time. I was going to visit next year, when work wasn't so busy. But then the call came, and..." She gestured helplessly.

Tom understood that gesture. He'd seen it a hundred times in hospital rooms and church offices. That helpless, empty-handed gesture that said, *I don't know what to do with this grief. I don't know how to hold this pain.*

"Tell me about him," Tom encouraged.

As the plane prepared for takeoff, Rachel described her father. Tom gently asked questions while the plane sped down the runway and climbed into the air. Rachel was so focused on sharing the details about her father that she didn't even notice the sensation of acceleration.

Tom looked at her hands. They were no longer gripping the armrests. Instead, they rested on her lap or motioned in the air.

For the next hour, Rachel talked. She told him about a tailor who'd survived the camps, rebuilt his life in America, and never lost his faith despite everything he endured. She told him about her mother, who'd been the light of her father's life, and how something had broken in him when she died. She spoke of her own life—already divorced, no children, and a career in accounting that paid the bills but didn't fulfill her soul.

Tom listened. He didn't offer cliches or empty comfort. He just listened and let Rachel fill the space between them with her words.

Finally, she paused and looked at him with red-rimmed eyes. "I'm sorry. You didn't sign up for a therapy session."

"I don't mind. Really." Tom paused, weighing how much to share. "My wife left me a year ago. Divorced me. Said she couldn't compete with my ghosts. And she was right. I've been haunted by things I can't fix, can't change, can't make right. I understand what it's like to carry something heavy and not know how to put it down."

Rachel studied him. "You said you're a minister. What denomination?"

"Does it matter?"

"I suppose not. My father always said God didn't care about denominations, only about whether you did justice, loved mercy, and walked humbly."

Tom smiled. "Your father sounds like a wise man."

"He is. Was. Is." She shook her head. "I don't know what tense to use anymore. He's still alive, but I keep thinking about him in the past tense, like he's already gone."

"I understand that too," Tom said quietly.

Something in his tone made her look at him more closely. "Are you okay?"

The question was so direct, so unexpected, that Tom almost laughed. "Why do you ask?"

"You have that look. Like you're carrying something. And you keep rubbing your chest when you think no one's watching."

Tom glanced down at his hand, which had indeed been pressed against his sternum. He lowered it. "You're very perceptive, Rachel."

She smiled but didn't respond. Her eyes told Tom she was waiting for his reply.

"You're not the first... but you'll be the first person other than my friends who I've told." He took in a breath, holding it for a moment. "Lung cancer. I was diagnosed a few weeks ago. They say six months, maybe less."

Rachel's eyes widened. "Oh my God. I'm so sorry. Here I am going on about my father, and you—"

"It's okay. Honestly, it helps to focus on someone else's problems for a while." Tom settled back into his seat. "That's why I'm going to Israel. I wanted to see it before... before I can't anymore."

"Are you scared?"

"Terrified. Rachel. But I'm more scared of wasting whatever time I have left being safe and careful and responsible." He looked out the window at the darkness beyond. They were over the Atlantic now, thirty-some-thousand feet above the ocean, suspended between continents. "So here I am. Flying to the Holy Land because if I'm going to die anyway, I might as well die having done something that mattered to me."

Rachel reached over and squeezed his hand. "Thank you."

"For what?"

"For listening to me. For being honest with me. For reminding me that I'm not the only one carrying something heavy." She smiled, and this time it was a genuine smile. "Maybe we can help each other carry it for a while."

The stewardess came by with drinks and snacks. Rachel accepted ginger ale and pretzels, her fear of flying apparently forgotten in the wake of their conversation.

They talked for another hour. About faith and doubt, about regret and hope, about what it meant to live well in the face of death. Rachel told him about the Jewish concept of *tikkun olam*—repairing the world—and how her father had lived that principle every day of his life.

"He used to say that the purpose of life wasn't to be happy or successful or even good," Rachel said. "The purpose of life was to leave the world a little better than you found it. Even if it was just by one small act of kindness."

Tom thought about the veteran's project. About Kayla carrying it forward. About the possibility that maybe his life had meant something after all, even if he hadn't finished everything he'd planned.

Eventually, the cabin lights dimmed for the overnight portion of the flight. Rachel pulled out a book and tried to read, but Tom could see her eyelids drooping.

"You should try to sleep," he said. "You'll need your strength when you see your father."

"I don't think I can sleep. Too nervous."

"Try anyway."

Rachel nodded and closed her eyes. Within ten minutes, her breathing had deepened and evened out.

Tom pulled out his journal and wrote in the dim reading light:

Lesson 2: Sometimes the people you're trying to help end up helping you instead.

He should try to sleep too. His body was exhausted, the medication making him drowsy. But he was afraid of the dreams. The nightmares that had been getting worse since the diagnosis. Always variations on the same theme. Vietnam. The darkness. Paulson's face. The wrong medication. The screaming.

Tom closed his eyes anyway. He'd learned long ago that you couldn't outrun your nightmares. Eventually, they always caught up.

SLEEP DIDN'T COME QUICKLY, BUT THE NIGHTMARE CAME fast.

He was back in Vietnam—not the base, the mess tent, or any of the safe places. He was in the jungle, the dense darkness pressing in on all sides. Explosions lit up the night sky. Screaming. So much screaming. Someone was calling his name.

"Chaplain! We need a chaplain!"

Tom ran toward the voice. A strange medical bag banged against his hip. He pushed through the undergrowth, branches tearing at his clothes and face. The screaming got louder.

He found an injured soldier on the ground next to Paulson, blood everywhere. Too much blood. Paulson's eyes were wide, looking at Tom with the kind of trust that comes from believing someone can save you.

"Help me," the injured soldier gasped. "Please, Chaplain."

Tom opened the medical bag. His hands shook as he searched for morphine. Found it. But in the darkness, he couldn't see the label. Couldn't read what he was holding. He threw it to Paulson anyway because Paulson was screaming the soldier needed help, and he had to do something, had to help. Had to—

"No," Paulson said after he injected it into the soldier. His voice changed. Flattened. "Wrong one."

Tom looked down at his hands. The syringe was wrong. The medication was wrong. Everything was wrong.

"I'm sorry," Tom said. "I'm so sorry. I didn't mean—"

But the soldier was already fading, his eyes going distant, his breathing slowing. And then he was gone.

Paulson stood up and looked down at Tom with shame. "No!"

Then the sound of a single bullet whizzing through the air. It hit Paulson in the chest and exploded out of his back. Paulson's eyes fixated on Tom as they lost focus. "Why…"

Paulson fell to the ground next to the dead soldier.

"Your fault," a voice said in the darkness. "Your fault they died."

Tom looked at his hand. He was now holding a pistol instead of a syringe.

Another voice. A voice filled with evil. "Use it. Put it to your head and pull the damn trigger!"

Tom jerked awake with a gasp, his heart hammering, his shirt soaked with sweat. He was trembling uncontrollably, his hands squeezed into tight balls.

"Tom?" Rachel's voice, soft and concerned. "Tom, are you okay?"

He couldn't answer. Couldn't catch his breath. Couldn't stop shaking.

He heard Rachel unbuckle her seatbelt. She flipped up the armrest and slid over into the empty middle seat. Then her arms were around him, holding him steady, grounding him in the present.

"Breathe," she said quietly. "Just breathe. You're safe. You're on a plane. You're okay."

Tom tried to breathe. In through the nose, out through the mouth. But his lungs wouldn't cooperate. The pressure in his chest was crushing, and he couldn't get enough air.

"I'm going to get a stewardess," Rachel said.

"No." Tom managed to grab her wrist. "Please. Just... stay. It'll pass. It always passes."

So she stayed. She held him while he shook, whispered reassurances while he fought to breathe, kept him anchored to reality while the nightmare slowly released its grip.

Gradually. So gradually, the shaking subsided. His breathing evened out. The pressure in his chest eased enough that he could think again.

"I'm sorry," Tom said, his voice hoarse. "I didn't mean to—"

"Don't apologize." Rachel squeezed his hand. "What do you need? Water?"

"Medicine. My medicine... in my bag. Blue bottle."

She retrieved the pill bottle from his carry-on and shook one into his palm. She watched as he swallowed the pill and took several slow sips of water.

"Thank you," Tom said. "I'm okay now. You can go back to your seat."

"I don't think so." Rachel settled more comfortably in the middle seat, still holding his hand.

"You sat with me when I was panicking before we took off. Now I'm sitting with you. Fair is fair."

"You don't have to."

"I know. I want to." She looked at him in the dim cabin light. "Want to talk about it?"

"Not really."

"Okay. Then we'll just sit."

And they did. For the next hour, Rachel sat in the middle seat, holding Tom's hand, not asking questions, not demanding explanations. Just being present.

Finally, Tom's breathing returned to normal. The medication kicked in. The nightmare receded into whatever dark corner of his mind it had crawled out of.

"Vietnam?" Rachel asked quietly.

Tom nodded. "It's always the same... The same dream. The same nightmare." He looked down at his hands. "And I always wake up just before I pu—" His tongue short-circuited inside his mouth.

"It's okay," Rachel said softly. "You don't have to—"

"I grabbed the wrong medication in the dark," Tom interjected. "Threw it to a medic working on an injured soldier... My fault."

Rachel listened.

"A medic... Paulson. That's who I threw the wrong medication to. He never held it against me—the mistake I made that night. But I feel like I killed him, too. I killed a part of him that night. I doubt he ever recovered from it. It was my fault.

Two men. One died an earthly death, and the other died a spiritual death. Both my fault."

"I'm sorry."

"Everyone says that. But it doesn't change what happened." Tom looked out the window at the darkness beyond. "I've been carrying that for five years. Can't put it down. Can't make it right. Can't bring him back."

"My father would say you're doing tikkun olam wrong."

Tom looked at her. "What do you mean?"

"Tikkun olam isn't about fixing the past. It's about repairing the present and building the future. You can't bring back the man you lost. But you can honor his memory by helping others. By being present. By showing up even when it's hard." She squeezed his hand. "Like you're doing right now. Flying to Israel while you're dying. Helping a stranger on a plane. Sitting with someone else's fear even when you're carrying your own."

Tom felt tears prick at his eyes. "I don't feel like I'm doing much."

"That's because you're in the middle of it. But I see what you're doing. And I'm grateful for it."

They sat together in comfortable silence as the plane droned on through the night. Around them, other passengers slept or read or watched the in-flight movie. Normal people living normal lives, unaware that in row 23, two strangers were sharing their grief and fear and hope.

Eventually, Rachel returned to her window seat, and Tom leaned back and closed his eyes. But this time, sleep came without the nightmares. And when he woke a few hours later, as the captain announced their descent into Tel Aviv, he felt something he hadn't felt in weeks.

Peace.

However temporary, however fragile, however unlikely. Peace.

The plane touched down at Ben Gurion Airport at 6:47 a.m. local time. Tom had lost track of the time zones, didn't know what day it was anymore, and couldn't remember the last time he'd slept in an actual bed.

But he was here. In Israel. In the Holy Land.

He followed the other passengers through customs and immigration, collected his suitcase from baggage claim, and made his way to the arrivals area, where a sign read "PILGRIMAGE TOURS INTERNATIONAL."

The tour guide, a middle-aged Israeli man with black hair that had turned silver at the temples, introduced himself. "Welcome, welcome! I am Dr. Rami Bar-El, your guide for the next ten days. We have a bus waiting to take you to Jerusalem. Please gather your luggage and follow me."

Rachel appeared beside Tom, pulling a small suitcase. "This is it," she said. "I'm taking a taxi to the hospital. My father's there."

"I'll pray for you," Tom said. "And for your father."

"Thank you." She hugged him quickly, fiercely. "Take care of yourself, Tom McGarvey. And try to let people help you carry what you're carrying. You don't have to do it alone."

Then she was gone, disappearing into the crowd of travelers.

Tom followed Dr. Bar-El and the other pilgrims to the waiting bus. The drive to Jerusalem took an hour through landscapes that were simultaneously familiar and alien. Hills dotted with olive trees, ancient stone buildings, and modern highways cutting through ancient land.

Tom pressed his face to the window, trying to take it all in. Somewhere in this land, Jesus had walked. Had taught. Had lived and died, and if you believed the stories, risen again.

And now Tom was here. Dying, exhausted, haunted by nightmares and grief and regret. But here.

The bus pulled up in front of the Eden Hotel on Giladi Street, near the tourist area. Dr. Bar-El stood at the front of the bus. "Please check in and rest for the day. Tonight, at seven o'clock, we'll have a meet-and-greet reception in the lobby. I look forward to getting to know you all. Shalom."

Tom checked into his room. It was small but clean, with a window overlooking the street. He set his suitcase on the floor, splashed water on his face, and looked at himself in the mirror.

He looked terrible. Dark circles under his eyes. Face gaunt from weight loss. The weariness of the journey was etched into every line of his face.

But he was here.

Tom pulled out his journal and wrote:

Day 1 continued: Made it to Jerusalem. Exhausted. Scared. But here. Whatever comes next, at least I made it this far.

He set down the pen and lay on the bed, fully clothed, just for a moment. Just to close his eyes and rest.

He woke six hours later to the sound of traffic outside his window and the realization that he'd slept through most of the day. The clock read 6:15 p.m.

The meet-and-greet started in forty-five minutes.

Tom showered, changed into clean clothes, and made his way down to the lobby. The other members of the tour group were already gathering. Nancy and Dale Hudson from Oklahoma, an elderly couple from Texas, a middle-aged woman traveling alone, and several others whose names Tom hadn't caught.

Eleven of them. Tom made it an even twelve. He again laughed at the irony of that number. Would this group of tourists become known as the *New Twelve?*

Dr. Bar-El welcomed them all.

Rami Bar-El, retired professor of archaeology at the Hebrew University of Jerusalem. One of the most respected academics in the area, Dr. Bar-El was known for more than just his scholarship. He was also known for his ability to make the ancient world breathe.

Dr. Bar-El's tours blended scripture, archaeology, and personal reflection. Tom had been in search of all three.

After formally introducing himself, Dr. Bar-El offered wine and cheese and invited each person to introduce themselves and share why they'd come on the pilgrimage.

"I'm Nancy Hudson, and this is my husband, Dale. We're from Tulsa. We've been saving for this trip for three years because we wanted to walk where Jesus walked and deepen our faith."

"I'm Harold Jensen. My wife, Peg and I are celebrating our fortieth anniversary. She always wanted to see the Holy Land."

One by one, they introduced themselves. Faithful Christians. Devout believers. People who talked about Jesus with the easy familiarity of a personal relationship.

Next, Edward Hartwell spoke up. *The Reverend* Edward Hartwell. He was nearing sixty, perhaps, with white hair and the confidence of someone used to being in charge. "My name is Edward Hartwell, senior pastor of First Baptist Church in Atlanta. This is my wife, Margaret. I have led several Holy Land tours over the years, and we never get tired of walking where our Savior walked."

His voice carried the kind of practiced cadence of a career preacher. "For me, this trip is about connecting with the roots of our faith, understanding the historical and geographic context of scripture, and of course, sharing that knowledge with my congregation when I return."

Several in the group nodded appreciatively. Tom felt a flicker of unease. Reverend Hartwell seemed nice enough, but there was something about him that reminded Tom of the ministers at those pastor conferences he'd attended. Men so certain of their theology, so confident in their interpretations, that there was no room for questions.

Then it was Tom's turn.

"I'm Tom McGarvey. I'm a pastor from Illinois. I came here because..." He paused, searching for words. "Because I needed to see this place for myself. To understand what it means to follow Jesus, not just worship him."

Nancy beamed. "Oh, how wonderful! Another minister in the group! What denomination are you?"

"Does it matter?"

Her smile faltered slightly. "Well, I suppose not. We're all Christians here. We know the Bible as the Word of God. The inerrant Word of God. At least we can all agree on that."

Tom felt a familiar tightness in his chest. "I believe the Bible is inspired and sacred. But I also believe it's a human document written in specific historical contexts, and we need to interpret it with wisdom and humility."

The room went quiet. Nancy's smile disappeared entirely.

"So, you don't believe the Bible is true?" a man asked from the back.

"I believe the Bible contains truth. That's not the same as saying every word is literally, historically accurate. While I don't read the Bible literally, I do take it seriously."

"But it is still the Word of God," Nancy's husband, Dale, retorted. "Every word in the Bible is true."

"I agree. Every word in the Bible is true. It's when we put them together to form sentences that we end up misunderstanding most of them."

"I see." Nancy exchanged glances with her husband. "Well, I suppose we'll just have to agree to disagree on that."

But her tone suggested they wouldn't be agreeing on anything.

Tom tried to explain, to clarify, to bridge the growing divide. But the more he talked about historical context, metaphorical interpretation, and the importance of social justice, the more alienated he became from the group.

By the time the reception ended, most of the group was avoiding him. Nancy and Dale were pointedly talking to others. Harold and Peg had moved to the far corner of the room. The woman traveling alone gave him a sympathetic look but didn't approach.

Tom had ostracized himself from the tour group before the first day of official touring had even begun. *Had he just become Judas among the other eleven disciples?*

He returned to his room and stood at the window, looking out at the darkened streets of Jerusalem. Tomorrow, the tour would begin in earnest. Tomorrow he'd visit the sites he'd dreamed of seeing. Tomorrow, he'd walk where Jesus had walked.

But he'd be walking alone, isolated from his group. A stranger in a strange land.

Tom pulled out his journal and wrote:

Lesson 3: Sometimes being honest about what you believe means being alone. And maybe that's okay. Maybe the journey was never meant to be taken in a crowd.

He closed the journal and climbed into bed. Outside, Jerusalem hummed with life. Ancient and modern, sacred and secular, a city that had seen countless pilgrims come and go over thousands of years.

Tom was just one more pilgrim. One more dying man searching for something he couldn't quite name.

But at least he was searching. At least he was here.

At least he'd stopped playing it safe.

And tomorrow. Tomorrow, the real journey would begin.

CHAPTER
EIGHT

Stoneford, Illinois
May 21, 1975
7:49 a.m.

Kayla sat at Tom's desk in the church office, surrounded by books she'd pulled from his shelves. *Women in Early Christianity* lay open to a chapter on female disciples. "The Forgotten Apostles" was bookmarked at a section about Mary Magdalene. A thick commentary on the Gospel of Luke sat beneath a yellow legal pad covered in her notes.

She'd been here since 5:30, preparing for Sunday's sermon. Her first real sermon. Tom had convinced her to preach for the next two weeks, and she was terrified.

The coffee maker filled the office with the smell of cheap grounds. Kayla took a sip from her mug—her third cup already—and returned to her notes.

The liturgical reading for this Sunday was from the tenth chapter of the Gospel of John, verses 22–30. But she had chosen to preach on a passage from Luke's gospel.

She wrote the passage from Luke 8, verses 1–3, as it was found in the Revised Standard Version Bible:

Soon afterward, he went on through cities and villages, preaching and bringing the good news of the kingdom of God. And the twelve were with him, and also some women who had been healed of evil spirits and infirmities: Mary called Mag'dalene, from whom seven demons had gone out, and Jo-an'na, the wife of Chu'za, Herod's steward, and Susanna, and many others, who provided for them out of their means.

Three women named Mary Magdalene, Joanna, and Susanna. And the phrase that haunted her: "... *and many others*".

How many others? Ten? Twenty? Fifty?

And who were they? What were their names? What did they see? What did they do?

Kayla flipped through the commentary, looking for more information. But the scholar spent three paragraphs analyzing the phrase "provided for them out of their means" (discussing ancient patronage systems and the economic structure of itinerant ministry) and barely mentioned the women themselves.

As if they were footnotes. As if their names didn't matter. As if their witness didn't count.

She reached for another book, *Silenced Voices: Women in the Jesus Movement,* and found a chapter that made her sit up straighter.

The early Christian movement included numerous women who were witnesses, teachers, and leaders. Yet by the second century, their voices were being systematically erased. Letters were edited. Names were removed. Stories were rewritten with male protagonists. The women who funded Jesus' ministry, who witnessed his death, who were first to see the resurrection—they became "the women," "some women," or simply disappeared from the record entirely.

Kayla set down her coffee cup and stared at the passage. Erased. Systematically erased.

She thought about Sunday school lessons she'd learned as a child. The twelve disciples—all men. Paul and his missionary journeys—all men. The early church leaders—all men.

But Luke said women traveled with Jesus, funded his ministry, and were part of his inner circle. So where were their stories?

Kayla pulled her legal pad closer and began writing.

Sermon notes:

- Jesus included women in his ministry (scandalous for the 1st century)
- They traveled with him, funded him, learned from him
- Luke names three: Mary Magdalene, Joanna, Susanna
- But there were "many others"—unnamed, unremembered
- Question: What did they see that we don't know about?
- What did they witness that no one wrote down?
- What voices were silenced?

She paused, chewing on her pen. This was the message taking shape. Jesus elevated women, included them, and taught them. But the church that came after him slowly pushed them back into the shadows.

The phone on Tom's desk rang, startling her. Kayla checked her watch—almost seven o'clock. Who would call the church this early?

"Great Witness Community Church, this is Kayla."

"Oh, thank goodness someone's there." It was Barbara Pritchard, sounding worried. "I know Tom's away, but my mother fell this morning. She's okay, just shaken up. I'm taking her to the hospital to get checked out, but I thought someone from the church should know."

Kayla grabbed a pen. "Of course. I'll meet you there. Which emergency room?"

"County Memorial, the main entrance. But you don't have to—"

"I'll be there in fifteen minutes."

Kayla hung up and looked at her sermon notes, at the stack of books, and at the coffee growing cold in her mug. The work would have to wait. Ministry was calling.

She grabbed her canvas bag and headed for the door, already mentally shifting gears from scholar to pastor.

As she locked the office behind her, Kayla thought about those unnamed women in Luke 8. They'd probably done the same thing by dropping everything when someone needed them. Fed the hungry. Comforted the suffering. Did the actual work of ministry while the men got their names in the book.

As difficult as it was for a woman, especially a young woman in 1975, maybe she would continue their tradition.

The Galilee Region
30 AD
Late Afternoon

SHE CROUCHED AT THE EDGE OF THE CROWD, CLOSE enough to hear but not so close as to draw attention. A woman in her position learned to make herself small. She was unmarried, past the age when most were given to husbands, and living on the charity of distant cousins.

The Teacher sat on a flat rock. The twelve who followed him gathered around him in a loose circle. Behind them, crowds of people had gathered to listen. Farmers and fishermen, mostly. A few merchants. Women with children. The poor and desperate and curious who always followed when word spread that the Nazarene was teaching.

She had been following for nearly a year now, staying at the edges, listening. There was something about his words that had lodged in her chest like a stone. She couldn't explain it. Couldn't articulate why she kept coming back to him, why she continued to follow him. But she did.

Today, he was teaching about the kingdom of God. Again. He talked about it constantly. This kingdom that was somehow already here but not yet fully arrived. It confused most people. But she thought she understood. He was talking about the world as it should be, as God intended it. A world where the hungry were fed and the oppressed were freed and the last became first. A world where the marginalized were made to feel like they belonged.

A world that didn't exist yet. But might.

"Teacher," one of the twelve asked, "what will it be like when the Son of Man comes in his glory?"

The Teacher was quiet for a moment, his eyes distant. Then he began to speak, his voice carrying across the hillside.

"When the Son of Man comes in his glory, and all the angels with him, then he will sit on his glorious throne. Before him will be gathered all the nations, and he will separate people one from another as a shepherd separates the sheep from the goats."

She leaned forward. This was something new. A parable, perhaps. The Teacher loved to speak in parables.

"He will place the sheep on his right, but the goats on the left." The Teacher's voice was steady, and his eyes went to everyone listening. "The King will say to those on his right, 'Come, you who are blessed by my Father, inherit the kingdom prepared for you.'"

The crowd was silent, listening intently.

"For I was hungry..." He moved his open palm at those nearest him. "And *you gave me food*."

Making the gesture again, he said, "I was thirsty and *you gave me drink*."

He stood up so everyone could see him. "I was a stranger and *you welcomed me*."

Looking down at his tattered cloak. "I was naked and *you clothed me*."

The Teacher spotted a small child in the crowd and smiled. "I was sick and *you visited me*."

He lifted his hands to those at the edges of the crowd. "I was in prison and *you came to me*."

She moved a little closer. This wasn't about belief or ritual or keeping the law. This was about *action*. About doing.

The Teacher continued. "Then the righteous will answer him, saying, 'Lord, when did we see you hungry and feed you, or thirsty and give you drink? And when did we see you a stranger and welcome you, or naked and clothe you? And when did we see you sick or in prison and visit you?'"

He paused, allowing the question to hang in the air. Then his voice grew stronger, more insistent.

"And the King will answer them, 'Truly, I say to you, as you did it to one of the least of these my brothers, you did it to me.'"

The words hit her. *As you did it to one of the least of these, you did it to me.*

The judgment wasn't based on knowledge or faith or prayers. It was based on what you did—how you treated the hungry, the thirsty, the stranger, the naked, the sick, the imprisoned. The least. The forgotten. The ones no one else saw.

People like her.

The Teacher went on to describe the goats—those who failed to help, who turned away from those in need, and their condemnation. But she barely heard it. Her mind was still caught on that phrase "the least of these."

She looked around. Most were nodding along, as if they were absorbing the teaching. But she wondered, *Would they remember this?*

The twelve were there, listening. Surely one of them would write it. Surely this teaching, so radical, so clear, would be preserved.

But what if it wasn't?

What if, like so many other things, it faded into memory and then into nothing?

The teaching session ended as the sun began to sink toward the horizon. The crowd dispersed slowly, people discussing what they'd heard, debating interpretations. The twelve gathered closer around the Teacher, asking questions in voices too low for her to hear.

She should leave. Should head back to her cousin's house before dark. But her feet wouldn't move.

Finally, when most of the crowd had gone, she stood. Her legs were stiff from sitting so long. She took a breath, gathering courage, and walked toward the group.

One of the twelve noticed her first. His expression shifted from welcoming to wary. "It is late. The Teacher needs to rest."

"I just want to ask him something," she said, keeping her voice respectful. "Please."

He looked like he was going to refuse, but the Teacher raised a hand. "Let her come."

She approached, her heart pounding. Up close, the Teacher looked tired. His cloak was dusty from the road, his face weathered by sun and wind. But his eyes were kind.

"What is your name?" he asked gently.

"Sheerah."

"Sheerah, wife of..."

"I am just Sheerah. Never married. I have no one."

Just Sheerah. A woman with no husband to protect her, no father to take care of her.

"Your father, Sheerah. Where is he from?"

"He died two years ago." Sheerah's eyes blinked with tears. "And my mother died before him. I live now with my cousin's family. I am... I am not anyone important."

Her mother's death was the truth. But her father... that was different. Although he was probably still alive, she was sure she was dead to him. He was wealthy. Wealthy enough to hire a private teacher for her when she was a young child. Smart enough to make sure no one knew of it.

"God does not measure importance the way people do," the Teacher said. His voice was soft, but there was iron beneath it. "What did you want to ask?"

Sheerah looked at the twelve men clustered around him, whose names she didn't know. All men. All listening.

"Your teaching today," she began hesitantly. "About the sheep and the goats. About helping the hungry and the stranger and the imprisoned. Will... will it be forgotten?"

The Teacher was watching her face. "You are afraid it will be lost," he said. It wasn't a question.

"Yes, Teacher." Sheerah's voice was barely above a whisper. "So much is lost. So many people, so many voices. Especially..." She trailed off, unsure how to continue.

"Especially the voices of women," the Teacher finished quietly.

Sheerah's eyes widened. He understood.

"I see you," the Teacher said, and the words seemed to mean more than just physical sight. "I see all of you. The women who follow and listen and serve. The Father sees you. I see you."

Tears spilled down Sheerah's cheeks before she could stop them.

"But the world..." She couldn't finish the sentence. The world didn't see. The world didn't remember. The world wrote its stories about important men doing important things, and women like her disappeared.

The Teacher reached out and gently touched her shoulder. It was a move that made several of the twelve shift uncomfortably. It wasn't proper for a rabbi to touch a woman he wasn't related to. But he didn't seem to care.

"If you believe this teaching matters," he said, his voice low and intense, "then you make sure it is remembered. The kingdom of God is near. Repent and preserve what you believe is important."

Sheerah stared at him. "But I am... I'm just a woman. No one will—"

"I am telling you to do it." The Teacher's voice was firm now. "Repent and preserve it. Your witness matters, Sheerah. Do not let anyone convince you it does not."

He released her shoulder and stepped back. The moment broke, and the fleeting intimacy dissolved. The disciples were murmuring to each other, some looking disapproving.

But Sheerah barely noticed them. Her mind was racing. *Preserve what is important.*

She bowed quickly. "Thank you, Teacher."

Then she turned and hurried away before the tears could overwhelm her completely.

Sheerah's Cousin's House
Three months after the crucifixion

THE HOUSE WAS SMALL—ONE MAIN ROOM WITH A COOKing area and sleeping mats rolled against the wall. Sheerah's cousin Deborah and her husband Levi had three children, and space was tight. Sheerah slept in the corner, behind a curtain that gave the illusion of privacy.

After the evening meal, made of lentil stew, bread, and olives, and after the children were settled and the adults were preparing for sleep, Sheerah waited. She listened. When she was sure everyone else was asleep, she carefully retrieved the small clay lamp from the shelf and lit it with an ember from the dying fire.

Then she pulled out her most precious possession: a scroll of parchment her father had given her before she left. "For your wedding contract," he'd said. "So you will have something of value to bring to your husband."

But there had been no husband. No wedding. Just Sheerah, growing older and becoming a burden on Deborah's household.

The parchment had sat unused for years. Until now.

Sheerah also retrieved the small writing kit her father had bought for her. Reed pens and a tiny jar of ink made from soot and gum arabic. He'd given her this new kit after she worked the last one dry. Her father had no idea of her whereabouts after she left the safety and wealth of her family, and was now living among the people of the land.

As a peasant in this land, she had become a follower of this man. This teacher spoke differently about life. He gave people like her hope.

And, like so many others, she was drawn to his presence immediately. Her father, who paid for her to have an education that no other girl had, could not understand why she had left everything he wanted to provide for her.

Her father could provide many things for her, but she yearned for more. And this man, whom she had been following for months now, provided nourishment for her soul. He provided hope for the future. He provided a promise that was unheard of in that part of the empire.

Sheerah was strong. Just like her namesake. But unlike the woman her father named her after from ancient scripture, she had no desire to build cities. Instead, this man she was now following helped her find a calling to build a different way of doing things.

In the dark corner of the room, Sheerah unrolled a portion of the parchment and weighed it down with stones. Her hands trembled as she dipped the reed pen into the ink.

Your witness matters, the Teacher said.

She closed her eyes and recalled his words from that afternoon. The parable about the sheep and the goats. About feeding the hungry, welcoming the stranger, and visiting the imprisoned. About how what you did to the least of these, you did to him.

His words, Sheerah imagined, would be recorded. But the teachings of what others felt and what they feared would be lost. Unless she acted.

Sheerah began to write.

Her letters were uneven at first, the ink blotching in places. But she persisted, forming words carefully, spelling out what those who heard him felt about the real message he was sharing.

She wrote slowly, pausing frequently to think, to get the words right. The lamp flickered, and she adjusted the wick. Outside, a dog barked in the distance.

I was hungry and you gave me food; I was thirsty and you gave me drink...

As she wrote, something shifted inside her. This wasn't just copying words. This was an act of resistance. Of preservation. Of faith.

The world would try to forget. It would try to erase the voices of women like her. It would try to turn the teacher's radical message into something safe and comfortable and acceptable to the powerful.

But not if she could help it.

As you did it to one of the least of these my brothers, you did it to me.

She thought about the Teacher's insistence on action over words. About how the judgment in the parable wasn't based on what people believed or said, but on what they *did*.

An idea began to form. Sheerah dipped her pen again and began to write more.

Sheerah set down her pen and read what she'd written. It was bold.

But then again, the Teacher had told her to preserve it. Had told her that her witness mattered. He'd given her permission to write down what might otherwise be lost.

Sheerah carefully rolled up the parchment and sealed it with a bit of wax from the lamp. Then she hid it beneath her sleeping mat, her heart pounding.

Tomorrow, she would find a better hiding place. Tomorrow, she would begin the work of preservation.

But tonight, in the flickering lamplight, Sheerah—unmarried, unimportant, easily forgotten—had done something the world might one day discover:

She had shared her fears. She had kept the truth alive.

Stoneford, Illinois
May 21, 1975
11:30 a.m.

"WHAT IS THIS?" MR. WESCOTT DEMANDED, AS HE BARGED into the room holding Sunday's bulletin, the smell of the mimeograph ink still wet on the pages. "Why is this week's gospel reading from Luke and not what the liturgical calendar calls for?"

Randolph Wescott, board member and head of the worship committee. A close friend of the board's chairman, Howard Beckner. A "force to be reckoned with" is how Tom described him.

Kayla had just returned to the church office after three hours at the hospital. Eleanor Pritchard had suffered a mild concussion from her fall but would be fine. Her daughter, Barbara, had thanked Kayla repeatedly, squeezing her hand and saying how glad she was that someone from the church was there.

That was ministry. Real ministry. Not theological theories or sermon preparation. But showing up when people needed you. She felt good about it—until...

"Answer me," his voice as firm as his words. "Tom might be able to get away with it, but you? A young... *woman*... I mean, a seminarian who isn't even ordained yet. You don't get the same latitude as *Reverend* Tom McGarvey."

Kayla sank into Tom's desk chair and looked at her scattered notes, her open books, her cold coffee. The sermon on Luke's commentary on the importance of women still needed work.

"I'm sorry," she said firmly, but with enough respect that she wouldn't be accused of insubordination. "Before he left, Tom told me to preach on what I was most comfortable with. He said it wouldn't be a problem for the couple of weeks he was gone."

"Reverend McGarvey needs to remember there's a worship committee for a reason. Just because I've been away doesn't mean he can decide what readings are more important than others. Especially when he's off on a sabbatical somewhere."

"Like I said, he told me it wouldn't be..." Kayla caught herself. *If he's been away, does he even know about Tom's diagnosis?* "Mr. Wescott, you said you've been away. May I ask when you got back?"

"I got in this morning. I came right here to check on things—where I learned that our pastor has up and left us, and the board doesn't even know where he is."

"So, you don't know. You haven't heard the news?"

"What news?"

"About Tom... about his diagnosis."

"What diagnosis?"

Kayla took the next few minutes to fill Mr. Wescott in on Tom's diagnosis. She reminded him that Tom had asked the board to keep his diagnosis confidential until he returned. He wanted to be the one to tell the congregation.

Mr. Wescott's jaw softened. So did his brow. "I... I wasn't made aware." It wasn't an apology, but at least his tone had changed. "Well, Miss... for this week," he held up the bulletin, "it's okay. But going forward, you make sure to run any changes to the calendar through me."

"I will."

"I appreciate that. Good day."

"Well, that was fun," Kayla let out as soon as he left.

Is this a part of ministry, too? It was a question that would have to wait for later. Everyone at Great Witness had been so kind to her up until this point. She wasn't about to let one bad apple spoil the whole bunch.

She got back to the work at hand—her upcoming sermon. Her first sermon in a *real* church.

She had the main idea down. Her research showed that women were central to Jesus' ministry and had been slowly erased from the story. But she wasn't sure how to land it. How to make it matter to the congregation.

She picked up *Silenced Voices* for the second time and flipped to a chapter titled "The Lost Gospels." It discussed documents that hadn't made it into the official Bible—some discovered recently, others known only from references in ancient texts.

We can only guess at how many writings were lost, the author wrote. *How many accounts of Jesus' life and teachings, how many letters, how many testimonies from eyewitnesses. Some were deliberately suppressed. Others were simply... forgotten. Lost to time and neglect.*

Kayla thought about Tom, halfway around the world in Jerusalem. Walking where Jesus walked. Seeing the places where these lost stories had once been told.

What if there were still writings out there? Still hidden? Still waiting to be found?

It was a hopeful thought. Wishful thinking, probably.

But then again, the Dead Sea Scrolls had been discovered just thirty years ago. Who knew what else might be hidden in caves or sealed in jars or tucked away in family collections?

Kayla pulled her legal pad closer and added to her sermon notes:

What voices have been silenced? What stories have been lost? What witnesses have been erased?

And how can we... today... make sure we don't repeat that pattern? How can we honor ALL the voices, not just the ones that fit comfortably into our expectations?

She thought about Eleanor at the hospital, grateful that someone had shown up. About Barbara, relieved to have support in a scary moment. About the unnamed women in Luke's Gospel who had followed Jesus and funded his ministry. And who witnessed his death and resurrection.

Many others, the author of Luke had written. *But who were they? What were their names?*

And why hadn't anyone thought their stories were worth preserving?

Kayla set down her pen and closed her eyes, offering a prayer that surprised her with its intensity.

God, if there are still voices waiting to be heard, help us hear them. If there are still stories waiting to be told, help us tell them. Don't let us forget. Don't let us erase. Don't let us silence those who need to be heard.

She opened her eyes and looked at her notes again. The sermon was taking shape. It would challenge people. It might make some uncomfortable. And that was a good thing, according to one of her professors, who told her, "A good sermon is one that makes those who are comfortable feel uncomfortable and gives comfort to those who are uncomfortable."

Tom didn't preach on comfort before he left. He had preached on turning the world upside down. Maybe it was time for someone to actually try it, regardless of how uncomfortable it made others feel.

Kayla picked up her pen and began to write in earnest, her words flowing faster now, the message crystallizing.

Jesus included women. Taught them. Empowered them. Sent them as the first witnesses to the resurrection.

But somewhere along the way, we forgot that. We erased them from the story. We made them footnotes.

It's time to remember. It's time to honor their witness. It's time to stop silencing the voices that need to be heard.

Outside, the late-morning sun poured through the church office windows.

In Jerusalem, Tom was probably sleeping off jet lag in his hotel room.

And somewhere in the ancient past, a peasant woman's words were written on parchment. Never meant to be found as much as they were destined to be given.

God has always had a way of bringing hidden things to light.

CHAPTER NINE

Wednesday, May 21, 1975
Eden Hotel, Jerusalem
6:45 a.m.

The sound of the morning Muslim call to prayer drifted through Tom's open window. *Allahu Akbar.* God is great. The melodic chant echoed across the city—ancient and insistent—reminding everyone that this was holy ground, whether they wanted to remember it or not.

He'd slept poorly. The bed was hard, the room too warm, and jet lag had his body convinced it was the middle of the night. Tom lay still for a moment, listening to Jerusalem wake up around him. Car horns, voices shouting in Arabic, the rattle of metal shutters being opened on storefronts. All distinctly different from the morning sounds back home.

He was here. Actually here. In the city where Jesus had walked, taught, died, and risen.

So why did he feel so... empty?

Tom pushed himself out of bed, immediately feeling tightness in his chest. The dry air and the stress of travel conspired to make breathing harder. He reached for his pill bottle on the nightstand and dry-swallowed one of Dr. Morrison's pain medications.

The bathroom mirror showed a man who looked older than thirty-nine. His face was drawn, his eyes shadowed. He'd lost more weight. The loose-hanging T-shirt on his frame was an outward sign of the cancer that was eating him from the inside out.

"Six months," Dr. Morrison had said. But looking at himself now, Tom wondered if even that was optimistic.

He showered in the cramped bathroom, dressed in khaki pants and a short-sleeved button-down shirt, and packed his small canvas bag for the day. Inside went his Bible, thermos, sunglasses, the journal, and his prescriptions. Then he made his way downstairs for breakfast.

The hotel's small dining room was already full. The Pilgrimage Tours group sat around two long tables pushed together, plates heaped with pita bread, hard-boiled eggs, sliced cucumbers and tomatoes, white cheese, and jam. Coffee flowed freely, and the conversation was animated.

"Good morning, Brother McGarvey!" Reverend Hartwell called, gesturing to an empty chair. "We were just discussing today's itinerary. Dr. Bar-El says we'll start at the Garden Tomb, then move into the Old City. Should be a magnificent day."

Tom took the offered seat between Patricia, the woman traveling alone, and one of the Millers from Texas. "Morning, everyone."

"You look tired," Patricia said quietly, pouring him coffee. "Did you sleep?"

"Not much. Jet lag."

"Me neither." She offered a sympathetic smile. "I kept thinking about where we are. It feels surreal."

Dr. Bar-El stood at the head of the table, checking his clipboard. "Alright, everyone, here's the plan. We leave at eight o'clock sharp. Dress modestly. Covered shoulders, no shorts. We'll be at the Garden Tomb for about an hour, then walk through the Christian Quarter of the Old City. I'll show you the Via Dolorosa, and we'll end at the Church of the Holy Sepulchre. We should be back at the hotel by three o'clock. Questions?"

"Will we have time for shopping?" Mrs. Miller asked. "I promised my daughter I'd bring back some olive wood nativity sets."

"Plenty of time tomorrow," Dr. Bar-El assured her. "Today is about experiencing the holy sites."

Tom spread jam on a piece of pita and tried to eat, but his stomach rebelled. Everything tasted like cardboard. He forced down a few bites and drank the coffee, hoping the caffeine would help.

Reverend Hartwell was holding court at his end of the table, explaining the theological significance of the Garden Tomb. "Most scholars agree that this is likely the authentic site of Jesus' burial, not that Catholic shrine over at the Church of the Holy Sepulchre. The geography matches the biblical descriptions perfectly. It's outside the city walls, near Golgotha—a tomb cut from rock..."

Tom tuned him out. He'd heard this debate before. Protestant evangelicals preferred the Garden Tomb because it was quieter, prettier, more "spiritual." Catholics and Orthodox Christians insisted the Church of the Holy Sepulchre was the real site, backed by centuries of tradition and archaeology.

He didn't particularly care which was authentic. What mattered was the meaning, the message of the resurrection—not the location.

Patricia leaned over. "He's already exhausting me, and it's only seven-fifteen."

Tom suppressed a smile. "Long week ahead."

"At least we can suffer together." She raised her coffee cup in a mock toast.

At eight o'clock, the group gathered outside the hotel where a van awaited them. It was smaller than a bus, with fewer amenities, including no air-conditioning. The morning sun was already hot, the sky a brilliant blue without a single cloud. Tom climbed aboard and claimed a window seat near the middle. Patricia sat beside him.

The van wound through Jerusalem's streets, navigating traffic that seemed to have no rules. Cars honked constantly, motorcycles weaved between lanes, and pedestrians crossed wherever they pleased. Dr. Bar-El stood at the front, narrating as they drove.

"We're heading north now toward the Damascus Gate. Jerusalem has been continuously inhabited for over 3,000 years. David captured it around 1000 BCE and made it his capital. Solomon built the First Temple here. The city has been destroyed and rebuilt multiple times. By the Babylonians, the Romans, the Crusaders..."

Tom watched the city pass by his window. Modern apartment buildings stood next to ancient stone walls. Orthodox Jews in black coats and fur hats walked past Arab women in colorful hijabs. Israeli flags hung from balconies. The Dome of the Rock glinted gold in the distance.

This was nothing like he'd imagined. It was grittier, more complicated, more *real* than the sanitized Holy Land of his imagination.

The van pulled into a parking area near a limestone cliff face. Everyone filed off, squinting in the bright sunlight. Dr. Bar-El led them through a gate into a beautifully maintained garden filled with flowers and shaded pathways.

"This is the Garden Tomb," Dr. Bar-El announced. "Discovered in 1867, many believe this to be the authentic site of Jesus' burial and resurrection. You'll see why in a moment."

They walked along a path that led to a rock-cut tomb. The entrance was low, requiring visitors to duck slightly to enter. A stone bench ran along the inside wall, and there was a channel cut in the floor where a rolling stone might have sat.

The group gathered around the entrance, and Reverend Hartwell stepped forward. "I'd like to lead us in a communion service, if that's alright. I brought elements from home... bread and juice. And I can't think of a more appropriate place to remember our Lord's sacrifice."

Murmurs of approval rippled through the group. Everyone formed a loose circle around the tomb entrance. Hartwell unpacked a small plastic container of broken crackers and a thermos of grape juice.

"Let us pray," he began, his voice taking on the practiced cadence of public worship. "Lord Jesus, we gather at this tomb, this place of death that became a place of life. We remember your broken body, your shed blood, your victory over death..."

Tom bowed his head and tried to focus on the prayer, but his attention kept drifting. This was supposed to be meaningful. This was supposed to be profound. He was standing where Jesus might have been buried, where the stone might have been rolled away, where Mary Magdalene might have encountered the risen Christ.

But all he felt was tired, hot, and vaguely nauseated.

Hartwell passed around the crackers, then the cups of juice. Everyone partook solemnly, murmuring "Amen" at appropriate moments. Tom took the elements mechanically, the words "This is my body, broken for you" echoing hollowly in his mind.

Broken for you.

Tom's chest tightened. Not now. Not here. He tried to breathe deeply, but the air felt thin.

"Let us sing," Hartwell announced, "'Amazing Grace.' All together now."

The group began to sing, their voices rising in the garden. Tom opened his mouth but couldn't manage more than a whisper. His throat felt tight, his lungs struggling.

And then, through the gap in the garden wall, Tom saw him.

A man. Maybe in his early thirties, with dark sun-weathered skin and a patched tunic hanging loosely on his thin frame. He stood just outside the gate, watching the group with an expression Tom couldn't quite read—neither hostile nor begging. Just... watching.

The man's eyes met Tom's, but Tom looked away. The group was singing the third verse now. He should focus. He should be present in this moment.

But when he glanced back at the gate, the man was still there.

The impromptu service ended, and Dr. Bar-El gave everyone fifteen minutes to explore the garden and take photographs. Most of the group dispersed toward a viewpoint overlooking the Old City. Tom remained near the tomb, trying to process what he was supposed to feel.

Nothing. He felt nothing.

"Brother McGarvey." Reverend Hartwell approached, his face beaming. "Wasn't that powerful? To take communion at the very site of the resurrection?"

"It was nice," Tom managed.

Hartwell's smile faded. "Nice? My dear brother, it was transformative! Surely you felt the presence of the Holy Spirit in this place?"

Tom didn't know how to respond. Before he could formulate an answer, he noticed the man from the gate had entered the garden. He was walking along the path, moving slowly, as if trying not to draw attention.

Up close, Tom could see more details. The man's cotton tunic was patched everywhere, but clean. His baggy trousers were tattered at the hem, and his sandals were worn through at the heels. His hands were calloused, the fingernails rimmed with dirt. But his eyes were intelligent and alert, taking everything in.

The man paused near the tomb entrance, studying the ancient rock face. Then his eyes found Tom again.

"Excuse me," the man said in accented English. "I am thirsty."

Not now. Not when I'm trying to feel something. Tom's thoughts became even more personal... *Why is he asking me?*

Even when he avoided direct eye contact, the man persisted. "I am thirsty."

Christ, it's only water. Right? Maybe if he gave this man what he wanted—what he needed—he'd go away. Tom looked down at the metal thermos in his canvas bag. He'd filled it at the hotel before getting in the van.

"I, uh..." Tom hesitated.

"Brother McGarvey," Hartwell said sharply, his voice low. "We're trying to have a spiritual experience here. These beggars are everywhere in Jerusalem. If you give to one, ten more will appear."

The man heard this. His expression didn't change, but something in his eyes shifted. Not anger. Something sadder. Resignation, maybe.

Tom looked at the thermos in his hand. Then at the man. Then at Hartwell's disapproving face.

Standing here, in this place of sacred history, Tom closed his eyes and saw the title of one of his favorite books in his office: *In His Steps: What Would Jesus Do?* prominently displayed behind his desk. The eighty-year-old book was as timeless as it was moving.

He'd forgotten how many times he recommended it. And when he did, he tweaked the subtitle just enough to suggest that we are called to act. Instead of asking, "What would Jesus do?" Tom asked his parishioners, "What would Jesus want you to do?"

Tom squeezed his eyes shut even tighter. *I was thirsty and you gave me drink.*

Then he opened them and held out the thermos. "Here."

"Tom—" Hartwell started.

"It's just water," Tom said, more sharply than he intended.

The man took the thermos carefully, as if it might be snatched away. "Thank you," he said. Then he drank deeply.

When he finished, he screwed the cap back on and handed the empty thermos back to Tom.

"God bless you," the man said quietly before turning and walking back toward the gate.

Tom stood there holding the empty thermos, aware of Hartwell's disapproval radiating beside him.

"Well," Hartwell said after a moment. "I hope you're satisfied. You just encouraged him to beg from every tourist who comes through here. They need our prayers, not handouts."

"He asked for water," Tom replied. "Not money."

"It's the same thing. These people—" Hartwell stopped himself and sighed. "Never mind. I know you mean well. But this isn't why we came to Jerusalem."

Hartwell walked away to rejoin his wife, leaving Tom standing alone with his empty thermos.

What if this is exactly why we came? Tom thought.

But he didn't have an answer to that question.

THE GROUP REUNITED AT THE GATE AND FOLLOWED DR. Bar-El into the Old City. They entered through the Damascus Gate, immediately plunging into a maze of narrow stone streets crowded with people. Merchants called out from tiny shops selling everything from spices to carpets to religious icons. The smell was overwhelming. Incense, roasting meat, unwashed bodies, donkey dung, fresh bread.

Tom's senses were on overload. Every direction he looked, something was happening. Children ran past, chasing a soccer ball. Old men sat on stools playing backgammon. Women haggled over vegetables in Arabic. Tour groups in matching T-shirts clogged the walkways.

Dr. Bar-El led them along the Via Dolorosa, the Way of Suffering. It was the route tradition said Jesus walked carrying his cross. This would be a quick pass on the route to get to where they needed to be. A more thorough walk, filled with explanations of each station, would come another day.

Tom tried to engage, to imagine it: Jesus stumbling through these streets, bleeding and beaten, carrying the instrument of his execution. But this moment was too loud, too immediate, too chaotic to allow room for the past.

"Are you okay?" Patricia nudged his elbow. "You look pale."

"Just hot," Tom said, though it was more than that. His chest felt tight again, and he was having trouble catching his breath.

"Maybe you should sit down for a minute."

"I'm fine."

But he wasn't fine. The heat, the crowds, the stress. It was all compounding. Tom's vision blurred slightly.

And then, impossibly, he saw the man again. The same man from the Garden Tomb. He was standing in a doorway about twenty feet ahead, watching Tom.

Tom blinked. Was he hallucinating?

The man lifted a hand in a small wave. Then stepped out of the doorway and began walking away down a side street.

"Tom?" Patricia's voice sounded far away. "Tom, are you sure you're—"

"I'll be right back," Tom heard himself say. Then, before he could think better of it, he left the group and followed the man down the narrow alley.

The alley was quieter than the main street, shaded by buildings on either side. The man walked slowly, glancing back occasionally to make sure Tom was still following.

Finally, the man stopped and turned around. Up close, in better light, Tom could see that his face was weathered but kind. His eyes were brown and intelligent, with laugh lines at the corners.

"You followed me," the man said. It wasn't a question.

"I... I don't know why," Tom admitted.

"I do." The man smiled slightly. "You have a good face. A troubled face, but a good one."

Tom didn't know what to say to that.

"I think you need to sit down before you fall down," the man said.

Tom realized he was swaying slightly. The world had taken on a strange, tilted quality.

The man stepped forward and took Tom's arm, guiding him to a stone step. "Sit. Put your head down."

Tom did as instructed, dropping his head between his knees. The pressure in his chest was building, familiar and terrifying. *Not now. Not here.* Not in front of a stranger in a Jerusalem alley.

"Breathe," the man said calmly. "Slowly."

Tom tried. The air wouldn't come at first—his lungs refusing to cooperate. But gradually, painfully, the episode began to pass. His vision cleared. The pressure eased slightly.

When he could finally lift his head, he found the man sitting beside him on the step, patient and unconcerned.

"Better?" the man asked.

"Yes. Thank you."

"You are sick."

It wasn't a question, but Tom answered anyway. "Cancer."

The man nodded as if this explained everything. "And you come to Jerusalem to die among the holy stones?"

"Something like that."

"A waste," the man said matter-of-factly.

Tom looked at him sharply. "Excuse me?"

"The stones do not care if you die here. They have seen too many deaths already." The man motioned around them. "Thousands of years of death: Crusaders, Romans, zealots, martyrs. One more American tourist will not make the stones holier."

Tom felt a flash of irritation. "I didn't come here to die. I came to see where Jesus lived. To walk where he walked."

"Ah." The man's smile was knowing, almost teasing. "A religious tourist. You want to see the holy places and feel spiritual without the inconvenience of being holy."

"That's not—" Tom stopped. Was it true? "That's not fair."

"No?" The man stood, brushing dust from his tunic. "Tell me, when you see me—a poor man in his worn clothes asking for water—what do you see?"

Tom hesitated. "I see... a man who needs help."

"Do you? Or do you see an interruption to your pilgrimage?" His voice wasn't cruel, just honest. "You gave me water because your Jesus taught you to. But you did it with annoyance in your heart. I saw it in your eyes."

The words stung because they were true. Tom had given the water, but he'd resented it. He'd seen the man as an inconvenience, a distraction from the "real" pilgrimage.

"I'm sorry," Tom said quietly.

"Do not be sorry. Be better." The man extended a hand to help Tom up. "Your tour group is probably missing you. Your reverend friend will be very angry that you wandered off."

Tom accepted the hand and stood, his legs still shaky. "How did you know—"

"I know many things." The man's eyes flickered. "I know you will see me again. And you will have to choose: the holy stones or the holy person."

Before Tom could respond, the man turned and walked away down the alley, his tunic fluttering behind him.

Tom stood there for a long moment, processing what had just happened. Then he made his way back to the Via Dolorosa, where he found the group waiting at the twelfth station.

Dr. Bar-El looked relieved. "There you are! We were about to send out a search party."

"I'm sorry. I just needed a moment."

Reverend Hartwell's expression was less forgiving. "Brother McGarvey, we can't have people wandering off. This is a busy city, and it's easy to get lost."

"Yeah, I know. It won't happen again."

But even as Tom said it, he suspected it wasn't true.

<hr>

That Evening

THE GROUP DINNER AT A RESTAURANT NEAR THE HOTEL was loud and cheerful. Everyone shared their favorite moments, exuberating over the sites they'd seen.

Tom sat at the end of the table, picking at his chicken and rice, only half-listening to the conversation.

Mrs. Thompson was the loudest. "The Garden Tomb was just as beautiful as the pictures! And that communion service... I'll remember that for the rest of my life. I have chills just thinking about it!"

"I took at least fifty pictures," Mr. Miller added. "Can't wait to get them developed when we get home."

Reverend Hartwell was holding court at the other end of the table, explaining the historical accuracy of the route to anyone who would listen. His wife, Margaret, sat beside him, nodding along, occasionally touching his arm to moderate his enthusiasm.

Patricia slid into the empty seat next to Tom. "You've been quiet."

"Just tired."

"That man you followed today. Who was he?"

Tom looked at her in surprise. "You noticed that?"

"I notice things." Patricia sipped her wine. "You looked like you'd seen a ghost."

"He's... I don't know what he is. Homeless, I think. He asked for water this morning at the Garden Tomb."

"Ah, yes. The one Reverend Hartwell was so disapproving about?"

"That's the one."

Patricia was quiet for a moment. "My husband David used to say that God has a way of putting people in our path when we're not looking. People who need us, or people we need. He said the trick is recognizing which is which."

Tom thought about that. "Did you? Recognize?"

"Not always. Sometimes not until much later." Her eyes were distant. "There was a homeless woman who used to sit outside our church. Every Sunday. David wanted to start a feeding program for her and other homeless people. But the church board said it would bring 'the wrong element' into the neighborhood. David was furious. Said Jesus spent most of his time with the wrong element." She smiled sadly. "We were still arguing with them about it when he died."

"I'm sorry."

"Don't be. He was right." Patricia set down her wine glass. "I came here hoping to find... I don't know. Meaning. Purpose. Something to help me understand why David was taken and I was left alone." She looked at Tom. "But maybe the meaning isn't in what's here. Maybe it's who's here."

Tom thought about the homeless man's words. The stones don't care if you die here.

"Maybe," he said.

After dinner, Tom excused himself and returned to his room. He pulled out his journal and began to write.

Day 1 – Wednesday

We visited the Garden Tomb today. Took communion at the place where Jesus might have been buried. Everyone else seemed deeply moved. Hartwell said it was "transformative." I felt nothing.

Then I met a homeless man. He asked for water, and I gave it to him... but only after hesitating. Only after Hartwell told me not to.

Later, the same man found me in the old city. He said I came to Jerusalem to see holy places without the inconvenience of being holy. That stung. Because it's true.

I gave him water, but I resented it. Saw him as an interruption to my pilgrimage. As if the

pilgrimage is about seeing sites rather than...
what? I don't know anymore.

The homeless man said I'd see him again. And
I'd have to choose: the holy stones or the holy
person.

Tom closed the journal and lay back on the narrow bed. Through the window, he could hear Jerusalem settling into night. The distant sounds of traffic, voices in the street below, and the final call to prayer echoing across the city drowned out his own thoughts. And he was okay with that.

Tomorrow, they would visit Bethlehem. The birthplace of Jesus. Another holy site. Another opportunity to feel spiritual without being holy.

Tom finally closed his eyes, falling into an uneasy sleep, dreaming of thermoses, communion cups, and a man in a patched tunic who seemed to see right through him.

Thursday, May 22
7:30 a.m.

THE VAN TO BETHLEHEM DEPARTED PROMPTLY AT EIGHT. Tom had slept slightly better, waking only twice with breathing difficulties. He'd taken his morning medication, forced down some breakfast, and tried to prepare himself for another day of heat, crowds, and forced spirituality.

Dr. Bar-El stood at the front of the van. "Today we're traveling about six miles south to Bethlehem. It should take about thirty minutes, depending on traffic and checkpoints. Bethlehem is technically in the West Bank, so we'll need to show our passports."

"Is it safe?" Mrs. Miller asked nervously.

"Perfectly safe," Dr. Bar-El assured her. "We make this trip all the time. Just stay with the group, and everything will be fine."

The van wound through Jerusalem's southern neighborhoods, eventually reaching a military checkpoint. Israeli soldiers boarded, checked passports, and waved them through. Tom watched the landscape change. It was more rural now, with olive groves and stone terraces carved into the hillsides.

"Bethlehem means 'House of Bread,'" Dr. Bar-El narrated. "It's one of the oldest cities in the world, mentioned in the Bible as the birthplace of both King David and, of course, Jesus Christ. Today it's a predominantly Christian city, though the population has been declining due to emigration."

The van pulled into a parking area near the Church of the Nativity. The group filed off into bright morning sunlight. The church was ancient and imposing, its entrance famously low, requiring visitors to stoop to enter.

"The Door of Humility," Dr. Bar-El explained. "It was reduced in height during the Ottoman period to prevent people from riding horses or camels directly into the church. Now it serves as a reminder to bow before entering the birthplace of the King of Kings."

One by one, they stooped and entered. Inside, the church was dark after the brilliant sunshine outside, lit by oil lamps hanging from the ceiling. The air smelled of incense and centuries of candle smoke. Orthodox priests in black robes moved through the shadows, tending to various chapels.

Dr. Bar-El led them down ancient stone steps to a grotto beneath the main sanctuary. A fourteen-point silver star marked the traditional spot where Jesus was born.

"Here," Dr. Bar-El said softly, "according to tradition, is where Mary gave birth to Jesus. Where God entered the world as a helpless infant."

The group gathered around, taking turns kneeling by the star, praying, and taking photographs. Tom waited his turn, feeling the weight of expectation. He should feel something here. This was the birthplace of his faith, literally.

But when his turn came and he knelt beside the silver star, all he felt was the cold stone beneath his knees and the pressure of people waiting behind him.

He stood quickly and moved aside.

Outside, they had ninety minutes of free time before lunch. Most scattered toward nearby shops selling olive wood carvings and mother-of-pearl jewelry. Tom found a shaded bench near the church entrance and sat down, suddenly exhausted.

"You okay?"

Tom looked up to find Patricia standing beside him.

"Still tired, I think," he said, not sure if she'd buy his white lie.

She sat down beside him. "Or still not feeling the spiritual awakening?"

"Is it that obvious?"

"Only to someone who's also not feeling it." She smiled. "I keep waiting for that moment. The one where everything makes sense, where I feel God's presence, where I understand why David died. But so far, nothing."

"Maybe we're doing it wrong," Tom suggested.

"Or maybe—" Patricia stopped mid-sentence, her attention caught by something across the plaza.

Tom followed her gaze and saw him. The homeless man. Standing near a stone wall, watching them.

"That's him, isn't it?" Patricia asked. "Your homeless friend."

"That's him, but he's not my friend," Tom said automatically. Then, realizing how that sounded, he added, "I mean, I barely know him."

"Well, he seems to know you. He's walking this way."

Sure enough, the man approached, his patched tunic making him stand out among the better-dressed tourists.

"Hello, American tourist," the man said, stopping in front of them. "You came to see where Jesus was born. A baby in a stable. Very humble."

"Hello," Tom said, resigned. "What are you doing in Bethlehem?"

"I go where I am needed." The man's eyes moved to Patricia. "And who is this?"

"Patricia," she said, extending her hand. He shook it formally. "I'm traveling with Tom's group."

"I see. Another religious tourist seeking the holy places." But his tone was gentler with Patricia than it had been with Tom. "Have you found what you're looking for?"

"Not yet," Patricia admitted. "But I'm still looking."

"That is good. It is the looking that matters, not the finding." The man turned back to Tom. "I am hungry."

Tom felt the familiar surge of resistance. He'd packed a sandwich from the hotel breakfast. Pita bread with cheese and vegetables wrapped in a napkin. It was supposed to be his lunch.

"I have a sandwich," Tom said slowly. "But—"

"Then I will take half, and you will keep half." The man smiled. "This is fair, yes? We share."

Tom wanted to say no. Wanted to explain that he was sick, that he needed to keep his strength up, that this sandwich was for him. His stomach was empty, and he was hungry himself. But under Patricia's watchful gaze and his own memory of yesterday's shame, he pulled out the sandwich and tore it in two.

"Here," he said, handing over the larger half.

The man accepted it with a slight bow. "Thank you. This is better than yesterday. Yesterday you gave with annoyance. Today you give with resignation. In the future, perhaps, you will give with joy."

"Don't hold your breath," Tom muttered.

The man laughed. It was a warm, genuine sound. He looked at Patricia. "Your friend has humor. This is good. God likes humor." He bit into the sandwich, chewing thoughtfully. "This cheese is good. Not as good as my grandmother makes, but good."

"You have family?" Tom asked, surprised.

"Of course. Did you think I was born homeless?" His eyes danced. "I have a grandmother, two uncles, four cousins, and many friends. I am rich in family, even if poor in money."

"Then why—" Tom stopped, realizing the question was rude.

"Why do I live as I do?" the man in tattered clothes finished the thought. "That is a long story. Perhaps one day I will tell you. But not today. Today, you have a tour to catch up with and holy places to photograph." He finished the last bite of the sandwich and wiped his hands on his tunic.

"Thank you for the food. It is good to eat with friends."

"We're not—" Tom started, but the man was already walking away.

Patricia watched him go. "He's interesting."

"He's infuriating," Tom corrected.

"Maybe that too." Patricia stood, brushing dust from her pants. "But I think he's right. You did give with less annoyance today. Progress?"

"Toward what?"

Patricia just smiled. "Come on. We should probably find the others before Reverend Hartwell sends out another search party."

THE AFTERNOON TOUR INCLUDED THE SHEPHERD'S Fields, where tradition said the angels appeared to announce Jesus' birth. The group stood in a sunbaked field dotted with scrubby bushes while Dr. Bar-El read from Luke 2.

"And there were shepherds living out in the fields nearby, keeping watch over their flocks at night. An angel of the Lord appeared to them, and the glory of the Lord shone around them, and they were terrified..."

Tom tried to imagine it. Tried to picture shepherds in this very spot 2,000 years ago, seeing the sky filled with angelic hosts. Even if it was just a story, he wanted to visualize it. But all he could see was the field as it was now. A hot, dusty, unremarkable pasture.

On the ride back to Jerusalem, Reverend Hartwell sat in the empty seat across from Tom.

"Brother McGarvey, may I speak frankly?"

Tom's stomach sank. "Of course."

"I'm concerned about you. Yesterday, you wandered off from the group. Today, I saw you giving food to that beggar in Bethlehem. The same man who accosted you at the Garden Tomb, I believe."

"He didn't accost me. He asked for help."

"Semantics." Hartwell waved a dismissive hand. "My point is, you seem distracted from the purpose of this pilgrimage. We came here to walk in Jesus's footsteps, to experience the holy sites, to deepen our faith. Yet you seem more interested in these... street people."

Tom felt his jaw tighten. "Jesus spent most of his time with street people."

"Yes, but he was Jesus. We're just tourists with limited time in the Holy Land. Shouldn't we prioritize the spiritual over the physical? We're human, and we can't be held to the same standards as Jesus."

"Of course not," Tom replied. "But we can ask ourselves, 'What would Jesus want us to do?'"

Hartwell shook his head, and his expression shifted. "I heard you were having some health troubles. Is that why you're here? Some kind of last pilgrimage before..."

He trailed off, but the implication was clear.

"Something like that," Tom said tightly.

"Then all the more reason not to waste your time." Hartwell leaned forward, voice earnest now. "If you're dying, you should be soaking in these holy places, storing up spiritual nourishment for the journey ahead. Instead, you're frittering away your precious time on people who will forget you the moment you leave."

Tom looked out the window at the passing landscape. Was Hartwell right? Was he wasting his time?

But then he remembered the homeless man's words: *The stones don't care if you die here.*

"Thank you for your concern," Tom said finally. "I'll take it under advisement."

Hartwell studied him for a moment longer, then sighed and leaned back in his seat.

Patricia, who'd been pretending to sleep but had clearly heard everything, opened one eye. "He means well," she whispered.

"I know."

"But he's also wrong," she said softly.

Tom looked at her in surprise.

"David used to say that the church's biggest sin was prioritizing the building over the people. Caring more about maintaining the institution than actually following Jesus." Patricia sat up and looked directly at Tom. "I think that homeless man has given you the chance to explore what following Jesus actually looks like." She pointed to Reverend Hartwell. "And it's making him uncomfortable because it challenges everything he's built his ministry on."

"You're giving a homeless man a lot of credit for someone who might just be looking for handouts."

"Maybe." Patricia settled back in her seat. "Or maybe God placed him in your path for a reason. Stranger things have happened."

Tom didn't have a response to that. He closed his eyes and tried to rest, but his mind kept circling back to the same questions.

Why had he come to Jerusalem? To see holy places or to be holy? To take spiritual pictures or to actually live his faith? To worship Jesus or to follow him?

The words from his sermon on the Book of Acts gnawed at him: *These who have turned the world upside down have come here too.*

Was his world being turned upside down? And if so, was he resisting it or embracing it?

Tom didn't know.

Friday, May 23
Mount of Olives
9:30 a.m.

THE MORNING BEGAN WITH A PANORAMIC VIEW OF JERUsalem from the Mount of Olives. The group stood on a viewpoint overlooking the Kidron Valley, with the Old City spread out below like a postcard. The Dome of the Rock gleamed gold. The walls of the Old City traced their ancient path. Church bells competed with the Muslim call to prayer.

"This is the view Jesus would have seen," Dr. Bar-El explained, "when he wept over Jerusalem, predicting its destruction. From this vantage point, you can understand why this city has been so contested throughout history. It's strategically positioned, easily defensible, and sacred to three major religions."

Cameras clicked as everyone took photographs. Tom stood slightly apart from the group, trying to see it through Jesus's eyes. A city he loved. A city he knew would reject him. A city worth dying for.

O Jerusalem, Jerusalem, killing the prophets and stoning those sent to you...

The words from Matthew's gospel rose in his mind. Jesus had loved this city enough to weep over it. Loved it enough to die for it.

What did Tom love enough to die for?

Before he could pursue that thought, the group moved on. They walked down the slope toward the Garden of Gethsemane, passing through ancient olive groves. Dr. Bar-El explained that some of these trees were over 2,000 years old, possibly witnesses to Jesus' prayer the night before his crucifixion.

The Garden of Gethsemane was smaller than Tom expected. It covered just a few acres, filled with carefully tended olive trees behind an ornate iron fence. A church built in the 1920s dominated one side, all dark stone and dramatic architecture.

"This church is called the Church of All Nations," Dr. Bar-El said, "because it was funded by donations from multiple countries after World War I. Inside, you'll find the Rock of Agony—the traditional location where Jesus prayed, 'Father, if thou art willing, remove this cup from me; nevertheless not my will, but thine, be done.'"

They entered the church, which was cool and dark after the bright morning sunlight. The ceiling was painted with a night sky, and alabaster windows filtered light into purple and blue hues. In the center, protected by a metal fence, was a large rock.

The group gathered around it, silent and reverent. Reverend Hartwell read from Luke 22.

"And being in agony, he prayed more earnestly, and his sweat became like great drops of blood falling down upon the ground."

Tom stared at the rock. Jesus had been here. Had knelt here. Had asked to be spared from what was coming. Had begged the Father to find another way.

And the Father had said no.

Not my will, but yours.

Tom felt his chest tighten. Not the cancer this time. Something else. Something deeper. The recognition of shared suffering. Jesus had asked to be spared; Tom had asked to be spared. And they'd both gotten the same answer: No.

The tightness increased. Tom's breathing became labored. Not here. Not in front of everyone.

He pushed past the group and stumbled outside into the garden. The bright sunlight was disorienting. He made it to a stone bench beneath an olive tree before his knees gave out.

The breathing episode hit hard and fast. His lungs refused to expand. The pressure in his chest was crushing. Tom leaned forward, his head between his knees, fighting for air that wouldn't come.

Is this what dying is like? He thought with strange clarity. *Right here in the Garden of Gethsemane... where Jesus prayed before his death. Is this what dying feels like?*

Tom remembered the homeless man's calm voice that cut through his panic the other day. *Breathe, my friend. Slowly.*

Even though he wasn't standing with him, Tom sensed his presence. It soothed him. With enough focus, Tom was able to find his pills and take one with a gulp of water from his thermos.

Air eventually began to flow again.

Six months, Tom thought. *Maybe less.*

He thought about the past three days. The Garden Tomb, the Via Dolorosa, Bethlehem, the Shepherd's Fields. All sacred sites. All empty of the meaning he was seeking. With air filling his lungs, Tom looked around the garden at the ancient olive trees, at the church built over a rock where Jesus had prayed. He came here to find meaning before he died.

Now, he didn't know. Was he looking in the wrong places? Everything he'd seen so far was beautiful. Sacred. But these places aren't where God lives. He tapped himself on the chest, partly to loosen the mucus and partly to remind himself where God really lives.

What if the holiest place in Jerusalem is not a church or a tomb? What if it's wherever love is practiced? Wherever mercy is shown? Wherever the hungry are fed and the thirsty are given drink?

Tom sat there for a long time, processing what had just happened. His breathing was back to normal now, but his mind was reeling.

What you do to the least of these... you do to me.

The Jesuits had it right. Seeing Jesus in the faces of those he served should be more sacred than the stones of ancient churches.

Patricia found him eventually, concern written across her face. "Tom? Are you alright? Everyone's worried."

Tom answered with his now all-too-familiar reply. "I'm fine." Then he stood, testing his legs. Steady enough. "Just needed some air."

"What's going on? You know, besides your health?"

Tom thought about how to answer that. "I think... I think I'm supposed to be learning something. Something I've been missing."

"And have you figured out what it is?"

"Maybe." Tom looked back at the Church of All Nations, at the rock where Jesus had prayed for deliverance. "Jesus asked to be spared from his suffering. But he went through it anyway because it was the only way to save people. Maybe..." Tom paused, trying to articulate the thought forming in his mind.

"Maybe what I'm supposed to learn isn't in avoiding suffering or finding some grand spiritual experience. Maybe it's in choosing how I suffer. Choosing what I do with the time I have left. Choosing to see Jesus in the faces of people like a homeless man instead of just looking at holy rocks."

Patricia was quiet for a moment. Then she said, "I think David would have liked that answer."

They walked back to the group together. Reverend Hartwell looked relieved to see Tom upright and walking, though his expression suggested a lecture was coming later.

But for the first time since arriving in Jerusalem, Tom didn't care what Hartwell thought. Something was shifting inside him. Something he didn't fully understand yet, but that felt strangely like hope.

As they boarded the van back to the hotel, Tom could have sworn that he caught a glimpse of the homeless man in the distance, watching from beneath an olive tree. Their eyes met across the garden, and the man raised a hand in a small wave.

Tom waved back.

⸻

That Evening

BACK IN HIS HOTEL ROOM, TOM PULLED OUT HIS JOURNAL.

Day 3 – Friday

Had a breathing episode in the Garden of Gethsemane. I might have had an epiphany. I'm looking for God in the wrong places. God lives in people, not stones.

I learned that the holiest place in Jerusalem is wherever love is practiced, mercy is shown, the hungry are fed, and the thirsty are given drink.

I gave a homeless man water and food, but I didn't want to. I did it out of obligation, not love. Out of guilt, not compassion. And the man knew it. He said I first gave with annoyance, then with resignation. He's waiting for me to give with joy.

I don't know if I can. I'm too tired, too sick, too focused on my own dying to have much joy left for anyone else.

But maybe that's exactly the point. Maybe the way to find meaning in death is to stop being so focused on dying and start actually living. Even if only for a few more months. Even if only for a few more days.

I'm afraid I've been so focused on finding Jesus in ancient churches that I missed him standing right in front of me, asking for a sandwich.

Tomorrow we're walking the Via Dolorosa again and visiting the Church of the Holy Sepulchre. More holy places. More stones.

I wonder if the homeless man will show up.

Part of me hopes he won't. Because he's inconvenient and demanding and forces me to confront uncomfortable truths about myself.

But a bigger part of me hopes he will. Because even though he frustrates me, even though I give to him begrudgingly, I think he might be the only real thing I've encountered in this city full of sacred stones.

Kayla was right when she said I needed to come here. I just don't think she knew, or I knew, what "here" would actually mean.

What if it's not about the places? What if it's about the people? What if it's about learning to see Jesus in the least of these?

God help me actually learn that lesson before my time runs out.

Tom closed the journal and lay back on the bed. Through the window, Jerusalem settled into evening. Somewhere out there, the homeless were finding places to sleep. Probably in a doorway or a tent or wherever they found shelter in this ancient city.

If Tom were to see him again, would he choose annoyance, resignation, or joy?

He wasn't sure he was capable of joy yet. But maybe, just maybe, he was moving in that direction.

One reluctant sandwich at a time.

CHAPTER TEN

Saturday, May 24, 1975
Eden Hotel, Jerusalem
6:15 a.m.

Tom woke before his alarm, which rarely happened anymore. For a moment, he lay still in the predawn darkness, trying to understand what felt different. Then he realized he was thinking about the homeless man. Wondering where he'd slept last night. Whether he'd found food, and whether he was safe.

He was confused by what had happened. How could a homeless man stop being an irritation and become... what? A concern? A responsibility? Something more?

Tom got out of bed and went through his morning routine, taking his medications with water from the bathroom faucet. His reflection in the mirror showed a man who looked marginally better than three days ago. Maybe because he'd been walking so much or because something had shifted internally, making the external seem less important.

Or maybe he was just fooling himself, and the cancer was eating him alive regardless of his mental state.

Downstairs at breakfast, the group was in high spirits. Today, they would complete the Via Dolorosa and visit the Church of the Holy Sepulchre, one of the most significant sites in Christianity.

"This is the day I've been waiting for," Reverend Hartwell announced to the table at large. "The actual site of Jesus's crucifixion and resurrection. Everything else has been preparation for this moment."

Mrs. Thompson clapped her hands together. "Oh, I can hardly wait! I've dreamed about this since I was a little girl."

Tom spread jam on a piece of pita and said nothing. Three days ago, he might have shared their enthusiasm. Now he found himself wondering if he'd see that homeless man again. And if he did, what would Tom choose: the Church of the Holy Sepulchre or the man in the patched tunic?

Why was that even a question?

Patricia slid into the seat beside him. "You're quiet this morning."

"Just thinking."

"About your friend?"

Tom shook his head and couldn't control the roll of his eyes. "My friend? I wouldn't—" He stopped mid-thought. "I don't know what I'd call him... or any of this. I just don't know."

"Maybe that's the point. Maybe you're not supposed to know yet. Maybe you're just supposed to pay attention." She poured herself coffee. "David used to say that God speaks in whispers, not shouts. You have to be still enough to hear it."

"I've never been good at being still."

"Neither was I. Still aren't, really." Patricia stirred sugar into her coffee. "But maybe that's what this whole trip is about. Learning to be still enough to hear what God is trying to tell us."

———

THE VAN DROPPED THEM AT THE DAMASCUS GATE AT eight-thirty. Dr. Bar-El led the group through the warren of the Old City toward the beginning of the Via Dolorosa. The morning sun was already heating the ancient stones, and the streets were filling with people.

Tom found himself scanning faces in the crowd. Looking for a patched tunic. A weathered face. Brown eyes that saw too much.

"Alright, everyone," Dr. Bar-El called, gathering them near a small chapel. "This is the First Station of the Cross, where Pilate condemned Jesus to death. We'll walk the route Jesus took, stopping at each station, and end at the Church of the Holy Sepulchre, where we'll see both Golgotha and the tomb."

Reverend Hartwell had brought a small prayer book and began reading: "Lord Jesus, unjustly condemned, help us to stand up for what is right even when it costs us..."

Tom half-listened, his attention divided between Hartwell's prayer and his continued surveillance of the crowd. That man across the street... was that him? No, a different man. That one by the vegetable stand? No, too young.

Why was he looking for him?

They moved to the second station, then the third. At each stop, Hartwell or another member of the group would read a meditation. Other tour groups were doing the same thing, creating a steady stream of pilgrims retracing Jesus's final walk.

At the fifth station, where Simon of Cyrene helped carry the cross, Tom noticed a commotion ahead. Two Israeli police officers were questioning a group of men clustered near a doorway. The conversation was heated, conducted in rapid Arabic or Hebrew that Tom couldn't understand.

And there, at the edge of the group, was the homeless man.

Tom's heart rate picked up. The man looked different today. He was more disheveled than usual. His tunic, which had been patched but relatively clean earlier in the week, was torn along the shoulder seam. A long rip exposed a gray shirt beneath.

As Tom watched, one of the police officers gestured sharply at the man, clearly ordering him to move along. The man responded with something that made the officer's face harden. The situation was escalating.

"Brother McGarvey?" Hartwell's voice cut through Tom's focus. "We're moving to the next station."

One of the officers grabbed the man's arm, then threw him face-first to the ground. Another officer kneeled on his back. One of his knees pressed the man's neck against the filthy pavement. The man—his friend—made eye contact with Tom.

"I'll catch up," Tom said, already moving toward the homeless man pinned to the street under the weight of now two police officers.

"Tom, we need to stay together—"

But Tom was no longer listening. He pushed through the crowd until he reached the group of men. The police officers turned toward him, immediately suspicious.

"Can I help you?" one officer asked in heavily accented English.

"I'm with him," Tom said, gesturing to the man. It wasn't exactly true, but it was true enough.

The homeless man's eyebrows rose slightly, but he said nothing.

"This man was loitering," the officer said, pulling handcuffs from his belt. "We have laws about beggars harassing tourists."

"He's not a beggar. He's my guide." The lie came easily, surprising Tom with its smoothness.

The officer looked skeptical. "Your guide?"

"Yes. He's been showing me parts of Jerusalem that most of us tourists don't see." Tom pulled out his passport, bent down, and showed it to the officer. "I'm an American. A minister. This man has been helping me understand the culture here."

The two officers looked at each other. One of them nodded. The handcuffs went back into the belt.

"If he's with you, that's different. But keep him out of trouble." The officers stood up, then looked at the homeless man. "You understand?"

The man nodded, his expression carefully neutral.

The two officers moved on to another cluster of men down the street. Tom and the man were left standing in the narrow street, watching each other.

"Thank you," the man said finally. "That was... unexpected."

"What was that about?"

"What it is always about. They do not like us standing in groups. They think we are planning something." The man's smile was bitter. "As if a dozen men without jobs or money could threaten the Israeli state."

Tom noticed the torn tunic again, the exposed shoulder. "What happened to your clothes?"

The homeless man glanced down as if seeing the tear for the first time. "Ah. This. This is the price of living where I live. It's nothing."

"It's not nothing. You need that repaired."

"And I will repair it. When I have time. When I have thread." He shrugged. "For now, it serves its purpose."

Tom looked around the Via Dolorosa. His tour group had moved on without him. He could see them gathered at the next station, about fifty yards ahead. Dr. Bar-El would be annoyed. Hartwell would be disappointed. They'd probably have to wait for him again.

Or he could go another direction entirely.

"Come with me," Tom said.

"Where?"

"Wherever you are going to take me to get you a new shirt."

The man's expression shifted to something like amusement. "American pastor wants to buy me clothes? This is new."

"Do you want it or not?"

"I want it." Youssef gestured down a side street. "The souk is this way. We can find cheap clothing there."

Tom followed him through increasingly narrow streets until they reached a covered marketplace—the souk. It didn't seem possible that any place could be more chaotic than JFK, but this was. Vendors shouting, spices perfuming the air, bright fabrics hanging from stalls, and the press of bodies in the confined space.

The man led Tom to a stall selling men's clothing, mostly traditional Arab garments but also some Western-style shirts. The vendor, a heavyset man with a magnificent mustache, greeted the homeless man warmly in Arabic. They had a rapid conversation that Tom couldn't follow.

"He says twenty shekels for a good shirt," the man translated. "But I can get him to fifteen."

Tom pulled out his wallet. He had about sixty shekels left from the money he'd exchanged at the hotel. "Tell him we'll take a shirt."

"That is very kind of you, American—"

"What are those?" Tom asked, pointing to a row of robe-like garments hanging behind the counter. They were of a better quality than the patched tunic the homeless man wore and looked like something a more modern man would wear.

"They are too expensive. Too much."

"I didn't ask what they cost. I asked what they were."

"That is a thobe," the man answered. "But only men who can afford such clothing wear it."

"Tell him we'll take one of them as well. You choose the color."

The homeless man looked at Tom sharply. "That's too much."

"It's not enough. Tell him."

Another rapid conversation in Arabic. The vendor's eyes lit up. He pulled out a neatly folded thobe in dark blue, along with a simple white button-down shirt.

"Fifty shekels," he said. "For both."

Tom handed over the money. The vendor wrapped the clothes in brown paper and tied the package with string.

Outside the stall, the man stood holding the package, his expression unreadable. "Why did you do this?"

"Because you needed it."

"That's not an answer. The other day, you gave me food with resignation. Today you buy me clothes with... what? Obligation? Guilt?"

Tom thought about it. Why *had* he done it? Not out of obligation. Not really out of guilt. He'd seen the man's torn tunic and thought: *I can fix that. I should fix that.*

"I did it because I wanted to," Tom said finally. "Is that acceptable?"

The man's face broke into a wide smile. It was the first truly unguarded expression Tom had seen from him. "Yes, American pastor. That is very acceptable." He tucked the package under his arm. "But now you have missed your tour. Your reverend friend will be very angry."

"Probably."

"And you do not care?"

Tom realized with surprise that he didn't. Three days ago, missing the Via Dolorosa walk would have seemed like a tragedy. Now it seemed... less important than making sure this man had clothes that weren't torn.

"No," Tom said. "I don't care."

"Good." He clapped Tom on the shoulder. "Then you are learning. Come, I will show you the real Via Dolorosa. Not the tourist version with the pretty stations and the prayers. The real one, where people actually live."

FOR THE NEXT TWO HOURS, THE MAN LED TOM THROUGH the Christian Quarter, but not the parts tourists saw. They walked through residential streets where laundry hung from balconies and children played in doorways. They visited a small shop where an elderly man repaired watches with a jeweler's loupe screwed into his eye. They stopped at a bakery where the owner, a friend of the man's, gave them fresh ka'ak bread still warm from the oven.

"This is Father Mikhail's church," he said, gesturing to a small stone building sandwiched between two larger structures. "Greek Orthodox. Very old. When the tourists go to the big churches, Father Mikhail stays here and serves his neighborhood. Twenty families. Not impressive to your tour guides, but very important to those twenty families."

They entered the church, which was tiny and dark, smelling of incense and old stone. A priest in a black robe was lighting candles in front of an icon of the Virgin Mary.

"Youssef!" the priest exclaimed in accented English, turning with a broad smile. "My friend! It has been too long!"

They embraced, and the priest kissed Youssef on both cheeks.

Tom dropped his head. He had interacted with this man for three days now. Patricia even called him Tom's friend. And yet, Tom hadn't even asked the man his name. He just saw him as *the homeless man*. Tom felt the shame that reddened his face.

Then the priest turned to Tom with interest. "And who is this?"

"An American pastor," Youssef said. "He's learning that there is more to Jerusalem than holy stones."

Father Mikhail laughed, a deep belly laugh that echoed in the small space. "Ah, yes. The pilgrims. They come, they see, they take pictures, they leave. But they never stay long enough to see the real miracle."

"What's the real miracle?" Tom asked.

"That we survive." Father Mikhail gestured around the church. "Look at this place. Tiny. Poor. Hidden away where the tourists never come. But we survive. For centuries, through wars and occupations and disasters, we survive. Because we do not wait for miracles from heaven. We create miracles for each other. Food, shelter, community, love." He smiled at Tom. "That is the real Via Dolorosa. The way of suffering that ends in resurrection. Not once, two thousand years ago, but every day."

Tom thought about his church in Stoneford. The declining membership. The financial struggles. The slow death that everyone could see but no one knew how to stop.

"What if you're losing?" Tom asked. "What if the church is dying, and nothing you do seems to make a difference?"

Father Mikhail considered this. After a brief moment, he said, "Then perhaps you are measuring the wrong things. We count bodies in pews, yes? Money in the offering plate? But God counts something different. God counts how many hungry people were fed. How many lonely people were visited. How many suffering people were comforted." He looked at Youssef. "My friend here is not a member of my church. He is Muslim. But he is part of my ministry because when I have extra food, I share it with him. And when he meets someone who needs help, he brings them to me. We are the body of Christ together, even though we do not agree on theology."

"Your church would be scandalized," Tom said.

"Probably." Father Mikhail grinned. "But Jesus was not very concerned with scandal, was he? He ate with tax collectors, he touched lepers, he let prostitutes wash his feet. I think if Jesus came to Jerusalem today, he would spend more time in this little church, helping twenty families, than in any of the big holy places with their crowds, tourists, and gift shops."

They stayed for another thirty minutes, drinking strong coffee that Father Mikhail brewed in a tiny pot over a camping stove. He told stories about the neighborhood, about families he'd served for decades, and about children he'd baptized who were now adults with children of their own.

At the door, Father Mikhail thanked them for stopping by. Tom then had his second revelation at this church—not only had he not asked Youssef his name, but he had also never introduced himself to Youssef.

"Youssef, thanks to Father Mikhail, I now know your name. I'm sorry I never asked you what it was. There's no excuse. Please let me introduce myself to you." He reached out his hand. "My name is Tom, Tom McGarvey."

Youssef looked at Tom's hand and pushed it aside. He then embraced Tom the same way he was embraced by Father Mikhail, including a kiss on both cheeks.

As they left, Tom felt something he hadn't felt in years. Envy.

Father Mikhail had so little. A tiny church, a small congregation, no resources or prestige. But he had something Tom had lost: a sense of purpose. A connection to real people doing real things.

It was nearly noon when Tom finally made it back to the meeting point near the Church of the Holy Sepulchre. The group was just emerging from a long tour of the church, looking overwhelmed and spiritually saturated.

Dr. Bar-El spotted Tom and hurried over, his clipboard clutched to his chest. "Mr. McGarvey! Where have you been? We've been worried sick!"

"I'm sorry. I got... sidetracked."

"Sidetracked?" Reverend Hartwell appeared, his face flushed with anger. "You missed the entire Church of the Holy Sepulchre! Do you have any idea what you—" He stopped mid-sentence, his eyes narrowing. "Is that the beggar's package?"

Tom looked down. He was still carrying the brown paper bundle of Youssef's old tunic. Youssef had insisted that Tom take it. "For remembering," he'd said cryptically.

"His name is Youssef," Tom said quietly. "And he's not a beggar. He's a man."

"A man who has been deliberately interfering with your pilgrimage since we arrived!" Hartwell's voice was rising. "You've missed major sites at every stop. You've wandered off from the group multiple times. And today... today! You missed the Church of the Holy Sepulchre, arguably the most important site in all of human history, to spend time with a beggar."

"I was helping someone who needed help."

"There will always be people who need help!" Hartwell's face was red now. "That's not the point! You came here for a specific purpose. To see the holy sites, to deepen your faith, to prepare yourself spiritually for what's ahead. Instead, you're wasting your time and money on people who will forget you the moment you leave!"

"I'm not concerned about being forgotten here. I'm concerned about helping someone who is poor."

"My brother, perhaps it would do you good to recall what our savior said about the poor: 'For you will always have the poor with you, but you will not always have me.'"

Tom felt something inside him snap, and he didn't hesitate. "Perhaps it would do you good to recall what Jesus said one chapter earlier, Reverend Hartwell." The entire group, including Dr. Bar-El, was watching.

"I was hungry and you gave me food. I was thirsty and you gave me drink. I was a stranger and you welcomed me. I was naked and you clothed me." Tom held up the brown paper package. "I just clothed someone. Does that count? Or does it only count if I do it after I've properly toured all the sacred sites and taken all the right photographs?"

"That's not fair—"

"You're right. It's not fair." Tom's voice was steady now, certain. "It's not fair that I have money for tours, hotels, and restaurants while Youssef sleeps in doorways. It's not fair that I have the luxury of flying to Jerusalem as a tourist while he can't even walk these streets without being harassed by police. It's not fair that I have six months to live while some people don't even know if they'll survive today."

Tom then looked past Hartwell to the group. "But you know what? Jesus didn't call us to be fair. He called us to be faithful. And I'm starting to think faithfulness looks less like visiting churches and more like helping people."

Hartwell opened his mouth, closed it, and opened it again. "I'm trying to help you, Tom. You're dying. This is your last chance to experience these holy places, and you're throwing it away."

"Maybe," Tom said. "Or maybe I'm finally experiencing what's actually holy."

He walked away before Hartwell could respond, leaving the older minister standing in the plaza with his mouth still open.

Patricia caught up with Tom near the van. "That was brave."

"That was stupid," Tom corrected. "I just alienated the senior minister on the tour."

"No. You just told the truth." Patricia smiled. "David would have been proud."

THE RIDE BACK TO THE HOTEL WAS TENSE. TOM SAT alone near the back, and no one attempted to sit with him except Patricia. Hartwell held court at the front, describing the wonders of the Church of the Holy Sepulchre to anyone who would listen, with occasional pointed glances back at Tom.

Tom stared out the window and tried not to care. But he did care. He'd been trained his whole ministry to care about what other clergy thought, to maintain good relationships, to avoid conflict.

Yet he didn't regret what he'd said. Every word had been true.

Back at the hotel, Tom skipped the group lunch and went straight to his room. He pulled out his journal and began to write.

Day 4 - Saturday

I bought Youssef clothes today: a shirt and a thobe. Fifty shekels, almost all the money I had left.

And I missed the Church of the Holy Sepulchre—the tomb of Christ, the place every Christian dreams of seeing.

Hartwell was furious. He said I'm wasting my pilgrimage. Maybe he's right. Maybe I'm being foolish.

But Youssef showed me something today. He took me through the real Christian Quarter, not the tourist version. We met Father Mikhail, a Greek Orthodox priest serving twenty families in a tiny church. He said God doesn't count bodies in pews or money in offering plates. God counts hungry people fed, lonely people visited, and suffering people comforted.

I think Father Mikhail understands something I've forgotten: that the church isn't a building full of programs and activities. It's people serving people. It's love in action.

I gave Youssef clothes today, and I wanted to. Not out of obligation or guilt. I saw his torn tunic and thought, I can fix that. And I did.

Hartwell thinks I'm throwing away my last chance to see holy places. But I think I'm finally seeing what's actually holy.

Tomorrow is a free day. No scheduled tours. Everyone's planning to sleep in or go to church and then explore on their own.

I'm going to find Youssef. Not because he needs me, but because I think I need him. He keeps pointing me toward something I can't quite see yet—something about the way Jesus actually lived versus the way we worship him.

"What you did for the least of these, you did for me," keeps echoing in my head.

If that's true—if feeding Youssef is feeding Jesus, if clothing Youssef is clothing Jesus—then maybe I haven't been missing the pilgrimage at all.

Maybe I've been living it.

Tom closed the journal and lay back on the bed. Through the window, he could hear the sounds of Saturday afternoon in Jerusalem. Children playing, merchants calling... the distant sound of church bells.

Tomorrow, he and Youssef would meet again. And this time, he wouldn't wait for Youssef to find him.

* * *

Sunday, May 25
7:30 a.m.

TOM WOKE EARLY, RESTLESS WITH PURPOSE. HE DRESSED quickly, took his medications, and skipped breakfast at the hotel. Instead, he bought bread and cheese from a corner shop near the Damascus Gate and set off into the Old City.

He had no idea where Youssef lived, or even if "lived" was the right word. But Tom had noticed that Youssef seemed to frequent the Christian Quarter, particularly the area near the Via Dolorosa. So that's where Tom headed.

The Old City on Sunday morning was quieter than weekdays. Many shops were closed, and the usual crush of tour groups hadn't yet materialized. Tom walked through nearly empty streets, scanning doorways and alleyways.

He found Youssef near the fifth station, sitting on a stone step with his eyes closed, face tilted toward the morning sun.

"Good morning, American pastor Tom," Youssef said without opening his eyes.

"How did you know it was me?"

"Your footsteps. Americans walk differently than Palestinians. Heavier. Like you own the ground beneath you." Youssef opened his eyes and smiled. "You are wearing a new shirt."

Tom looked down at the blue cotton shirt he'd bought on the way to find Youssef. It was different from the one he'd bought for Youssef, but from the same stall. "I needed something besides my tour clothes."

"Ah. You are becoming less of a tourist." Youssef stood, brushing dust from the new thobe Tom had bought him. In the morning light, the dark blue fabric looked almost regal. "What brings you here today? No holy places to visit?"

"I wanted to find you."

"And now you have found me. What will you do with me?"

Tom held up the bag of bread and cheese. "Share a late breakfast?"

Youssef's smile widened. "That is acceptable. Come, I will show you where I live. It's not far."

They walked through winding streets, moving away from the tourist areas into residential neighborhoods. The buildings here were older, more weathered. Laundry hung from windows. TV antennas sprouted from rooftops like metal fingers.

Finally, Youssef stopped at what looked like an abandoned building: a two-story stone structure with boarded windows and a heavy wooden door that hung askew on its hinges.

"This is it?" Tom asked.

"This is it." Youssef pushed through the door into a dim interior.

Tom followed. His eyes took a minute to adjust to the darkness. The building had once been a shop of some kind. He could still see remnants of shelving on the walls. But now, it was clearly being used as shelter. Blankets and cardboard mats covered the floor. A few belongings—plastic bags, water jugs, and a camping stove—were scattered around.

And there were people. At least a dozen men, women, and children throughout the space. Some were sleeping. Others were sitting in small groups, talking quietly.

"Welcome to the palace," Youssef said with mock grandeur. He called out something in Arabic, and heads turned toward them.

A young woman approached. She was maybe twenty-five, with intelligent eyes and a blue hijab. She looked at Tom with curiosity but not hostility.

"This is Nadia," Youssef said. "She speaks better English than I do. Nadia, this is Tom. The American pastor I told you about has a name."

"The one who buys nice clothing for Youssef," Nadia said, amusement in her voice. She extended her hand, and Tom shook it. "Youssef has been talking about you."

"Has he?"

"He said you were learning to see." Nadia gestured around the space. "Now you can see where we live. It is not much, but it is dry and relatively safe."

Tom looked around more carefully now. Despite the obvious poverty, there was organization here. The space was cleaner than he'd expected. People's belongings were neatly arranged. Children's drawings decorated one wall.

"How many people live here?" Tom asked.

"It changes," Youssef said. "Right now, fourteen. Sometimes more, sometimes less. When the police find us, we scatter for a few days, then come back."

"Why don't you go to a shelter?"

Youssef and Nadia exchanged glances. "The shelters require things," Nadia explained. "Identification papers, proof of residency, permission from authorities. Many of us do not have those things or cannot get them. Or have reasons for staying invisible."

Tom thought about the police encounter yesterday. The tension. The suspicion. "Because you're Palestinian."

"Because we are *poor Palestinians*," Youssef corrected. "That is two strikes against us."

An older woman called out from the corner. Youssef responded in Arabic, then turned to Tom. "That is Mama Farah. She wants to know if you brought food."

Tom held up the bag. "Bread and cheese. Not much."

"It is enough." Youssef took the bag and began distributing the food, tearing the bread into pieces, dividing the cheese. Every person got a portion, though none were large. When he was done, there was nothing left.

"You didn't keep any for yourself," Tom observed.

"I ate yesterday. Some of these have not eaten in two days." Youssef shrugged. "Besides, you brought it for all of us, not just me. In this place, we share everything."

Tom watched the group eat, the careful way they made the small portions last, the gratitude in their eyes. He thought about the breakfast spread at the Eden Hotel—more food than twelve people could eat, most of it thrown away.

"Come," Youssef said. "Let me introduce you properly."

For the next hour, Youssef took Tom around the space, introducing him to each person. There was Mama Farah, who'd lost her home in 1967 during the Six-Day War. There was Hassan, a teenager who'd run away from an abusive stepfather.

There was a young couple, Rami and Leila, with a baby who never cried because crying required too much energy.

Each person had a story. Each story was a tragedy. And yet there was something here that Tom hadn't expected: community. Real community. Not the polite fellowship of church potlucks and committee meetings, but the raw, necessary community of survival.

"They take care of each other," Tom said, watching Nadia help Mama Farah stand up.

"Of course," Youssef said. "What choice do we have? No one else will take care of us. The government does not see us. The charities have too many rules. The tourists take our pictures but then walk away." He looked at Tom. "You are the first tourist who has stayed."

"I'm not a tourist anymore," Tom said.

"No?" Youssef smiled. "Then what are you?"

Tom didn't have an answer to that.

AROUND THREE, SOMEONE BROUGHT FOOD. ACTUAL food, not just bread and cheese. A member of the group worked at a restaurant and had managed to smuggle out a large pot of lentil stew and a stack of pita bread.

They sat in a circle on the floor, passing around the pot, each person taking a portion. Tom ended up sitting between Youssef and Nadia, with the baby Leila asleep in her mother's arms across from him.

"This is the Eucharist," Tom said suddenly.

Everyone looked at him.

"Sorry," Tom said. "I just... this reminds me of communion. Breaking bread together, sharing a meal, being a community."

"We do this every day," Nadia said. "When we have food. Is that so different from your churches?"

Tom thought about the communion services at Great Witness on the first Sundays of the month. The small cubes of bread. The cleanly polished chalices containing wine. Everyone lining up, taking their portion, and going back to their pews. Neat. Orderly. Sanitary.

"Very different," Tom admitted. "This is more like what Jesus probably did. A real meal with real people, not a symbolic ritual."

"Jesus was one of us," Mama Farah said through Nadia's translation. "Poor. No home. Dependent on charity... The church forgot that."

"Yes," Tom said quietly. "We did forget that."

After the meal, Tom helped clean up, carrying the empty pot to a water spigot outside where Nadia washed it. When he came back inside, he found Youssef sitting alone near the boarded window, staring at nothing.

Tom sat down beside him. For a long moment, neither spoke.

"You want to know my story," Youssef said finally.

"Only if you want to tell it."

"My family had a house in East Jerusalem. A good house, with a garden. My father was a teacher. My mother made the best baklava in the city." Youssef's voice was distant, remembering. "I had two brothers and a sister. We were happy."

"What happened?"

"1967. The Six-Day War. The Israelis took East Jerusalem. Some families were allowed to stay. Some were not. We were not." Youssef's hands clenched into fists. "They gave us three days to leave. Three days to pack up a lifetime. My father tried to fight it, went to the authorities, filed papers. But in the end, we left. We had no choice."

"Where did you go?"

"A refugee camp in Jordan. We lived there for five years. My father never recovered. He died in 1972. My mother followed him six months later." Youssef's voice was flat now, emotionless. "My brothers left for America. My sister married and moved to Lebanon. I came back here."

"Why?"

"Because this is my home. This is my city." Youssef looked at Tom, and his eyes were fierce. "They can take my house. They can take my family. But they cannot take Jerusalem from my heart. I will die here. And until I die, I will live here as best I can."

Tom thought about his own losses. His marriage, his health, his faith. They seemed small compared to what Youssef had lost. "I'm sorry."

"Do not be sorry. Be better." Youssef's voice softened. "You lost family, yes? You are losing your health. But you still have choices. You still have the power to do good. Use it."

"I'm trying."

"I know. That is why I keep finding you." Youssef smiled slightly. "My grandmother says there is an old story in our family about a person who would come someday. A person who would see the least of these and help them without being asked. Without expecting anything in return. Just because it was right."

Tom's heart rate picked up. "What else did your grandmother say?"

"That when this person came, we would know them by their actions. By the way they feed the hungry and give drink to the thirsty and welcome the stranger." Youssef looked at Tom meaningfully. "You have done all those things this week."

"I've barely done anything."

"You have done more than you know." Youssef stood and extended his hand to help Tom up. "Come. My grandmother is waiting to meet you."

"Now?"

"Now." Youssef's eyes sparkled with something Tom couldn't quite read. Anticipation? Excitement? "She lives nearby. We can walk there."

Tom felt a flutter of something in his chest. Not the cancer, but something else. Nervousness? Expectation?

"Alright," he said. "Let's go."

But before they could leave, Tom felt it. The familiar tightening in his chest, the warning sign.

"Youssef," he managed, "I need to sit down."

Youssef's expression shifted immediately to concern. He guided Tom to a mat against the wall. "Breathe. Slowly."

But this episode was worse than the others. Tom's vision started to tunnel. The pressure in his chest was crushing. He gasped for air that wouldn't come.

Nadia appeared with water. Someone else brought a damp cloth for Tom's forehead. Youssef stayed beside him, one hand on Tom's shoulder, steady and calm.

"You are alright," Youssef said quietly. "This will pass. Breathe with me. In through the nose..."

Tom tried to follow the instructions, but his body was rebelling. The cancer was winning. Here, in this abandoned building with these homeless people, Tom was dying.

And somehow, that felt appropriate.

The episode lasted longer than usual, maybe ten minutes. Though it felt like hours. When Tom could finally breathe normally again, he was exhausted and embarrassed.

"I'm sorry," he whispered.

"Why sorry?" Youssef asked. "You are sick. That is not something to apologize for."

"I interrupted—"

"You interrupted nothing." Nadia appeared with a cushion, placing it behind Tom's back. "Rest. We are not going anywhere."

For the next hour, Tom sat against the wall while Youssef's community went about their afternoon. Children played a game with stones. Women talked quietly in the corner. Men dozed in the dim light.

And Tom watched it all, seeing what he'd missed his entire ministry. This was the church.

Not the building. Not the programs. Not the committees and budgets and strategic plans. This. People caring for each other because they had to. Because no one else would. Because that's what you did when you were family.

"How do you do it?" Tom asked Youssef, who'd sat down beside him again.

"Do what?"

"Keep going. When you've lost everything. When the world doesn't care if you live or die. How do you keep going?"

Youssef was quiet for a long moment. "I keep going because I have seen too many people give up. My father gave up. He died of a broken heart. My mother gave up. She followed him into the grave. I refuse to give them that satisfaction."

"Who?"

"Everyone who wants us to disappear. To give up and go away. To stop being an inconvenience." Youssef's jaw was tight. "I keep going because my existence is resistance. My joy is rebellion. My community is victory. They want us to be nothing. Instead, we are everything to each other."

Tom thought about Great Witness. About the declining attendance and the financial struggles and his own exhaustion. They'd been so focused on survival that they'd forgotten to live.

"I think I've been doing it wrong," Tom said.

"Wrong?"

"Ministry. Church. All of it." Tom pointed around the space. "This is what it should look like. Real people helping real people. Not programs and committees. Just... love in action."

Youssef smiled. "Now you are ready."

"Ready for what?"

"To meet my grandmother." Youssef stood and offered Tom his hand. "Can you walk?"

Tom tested his legs. Shaky, but functional. "I think so."

"Good. Because she has been waiting a long time for someone like you."

They walked through the Old City as the afternoon sun began to sink toward the horizon. Tom's legs were unsteady, and Youssef kept a hand on his elbow, steadying him when he stumbled.

"Your grandmother lives in the Old City?" Tom asked.

"Just outside. In East Jerusalem." Youssef guided him through a gate and onto a bus. "It is not far."

The bus wound through narrow streets, eventually stopping in a residential neighborhood. Youssef led Tom to an apartment building. It was old but well-maintained, with flower boxes in the windows.

"She has lived here since 1948," Youssef said, climbing the stairs to the second floor. "After the partition. She was lucky to keep her apartment."

Youssef knocked on a blue door. It opened immediately, as if someone had been waiting.

The woman who answered was ancient—ninety, at least. Possibly older. But her eyes were sharp and alert, taking in Tom with a gaze that seemed to see right through him.

She spoke rapidly in Arabic. Youssef responded, gesturing to Tom.

The grandmother's face broke into a wide smile. She reached out and took both of Tom's hands in hers, speaking again in Arabic, her voice trembling with emotion.

"What's she saying?" Tom asked.

"She says..." Youssef's voice was thick. "She says she has been waiting seventy years for this day. Seventy years for someone like you to come."

The grandmother pulled Tom inside the apartment. It was small but immaculate, with embroidered cushions on low couches and photographs covering every surface. She gestured for him to sit, still speaking rapidly.

"She is very excited," Youssef translated. "She says the scroll has been in our family for almost one hundred generations. Passed from mother to daughter, from grandmother to granddaughter. Waiting for the right person. The one who fulfills the requirements of being deserving of it."

"Requirements? Deserving?" Tom's heart was pounding now.

"She will explain." Youssef sat down beside Tom. "But first, she wants to know... Have you fed the hungry this week?"

Tom thought about the sandwiches shared with Youssef, the bread and cheese given to the community. "Yes."

"Have you given drink to the thirsty?"

The thermos of water at the Garden Tomb. "Yes."

"Have you welcomed the stranger?"

Tom looked around at the apartment, at this grandmother he'd never met, at Youssef, who'd started as a stranger and become... what? A friend? A teacher? "I'm trying to."

"Have you clothed the naked?"

The shirt and thobe from the souk. "Yes."

"Have you visited the sick?"

Tom had spent hours with Youssef's community that day. Had sat with them. Had shared their meal. Had let them care for him when he was sick. "Yes."

"Have you gone to someone imprisoned?"

The interaction with the Israeli police, who had taken Youssef into custody, only to release him to Tom after harassing him.

"Yes, I have."

Youssef translated Tom's answers. The grandmother listened, nodding after each one. Then she stood and walked to a cabinet in the corner.

She opened it and pulled out a wooden box—ancient and worn, held together with leather straps. She carried it to Tom with reverence, as if carrying something sacred.

She spoke again, her voice trembling. Youssef translated.

"She says, 'Nearly two thousand years ago, a woman named Sheerah heard Jesus teach. She wrote down what his words meant to her. They were her fears of what would happen after the next generation took hold of his message.'"

Tom nodded, eyes wide.

"'After her death, a month after writing the scroll, it was given to her cousin's grandmother. Sheerah had one last wish before she died. She asked her cousin to swear an oath that only the person who fulfilled the parable that she heard Jesus preach could receive the scroll.'"

"What parable did she hear Jesus preach?"

"It became known as the Parable of the Sheep and the Goats," Youssef said, looking at his grandmother. "Sheerah insisted that the scroll should be kept safe until someone came who fulfilled the parable not by knowing it but by living it. Living it without knowing they were being tested to see if they were worthy of it."

"But me? I haven't—"

Youssef raised his hand, stopping Tom, then pointed to his grandmother, who was opening the box. Inside, wrapped in linen, was a scroll.

"You have been tested all week," Youssef said quietly. "Every encounter with me was a test. And you passed. Not perfectly. Not always willingly. But you passed."

His grandmother carefully removed the scroll and placed it in Tom's hands.

"Since it was given to her cousin's grandmother more than 1,900 years ago, you are the first person to fulfill Sheerah's requirements. You are the one."

Whatever you have done to the least of these... Tom made no attempt to stop his tears.

"My grandmother says, 'This is yours now. This is what you came to Jerusalem to find.'"

Tom looked down at the ancient parchment in his hands. His hands were shaking. After nearly two thousand years. After nearly one hundred generations. After a week of reluctant sandwich-sharing and grudging water-giving and frustrated clothing-buying...

This.

This was what he'd come to find.

Not the holy places. Not the sacred sites. Not the tourist experiences.

But this. A scroll written by a woman who'd heard Jesus teach. Preserved by people who understood that faith wasn't about belief, but about action. Waiting for someone who would live the parable before receiving the words.

Tom looked at Youssef, his eyes red from crying. "I don't understand."

"You will," Youssef said gently. "Read it. Read Sheerah's fears. Then you will understand everything."

The grandmother spoke again, and this time Tom didn't need translation. Her meaning was clear in her face, in her tears, in the way she touched the scroll one last time before releasing it fully to Tom's care.

This is sacred. This is precious. This changes everything.

And Tom, a dying American pastor from Illinois who'd come to Jerusalem looking for meaning in all the wrong places, finally understood.

He'd been living the greatest pilgrimage of his life without even knowing it.

Not by visiting churches. But by loving people.

Not by worshiping Jesus. But by following him.

Not by seeking holy places. But by becoming one.

CHAPTER ELEVEN

Monday, May 26, 1975
Eden Hotel, Jerusalem
5:30 a.m.

Tom woke in the predawn darkness with yesterday on his mind. The scroll. The grandmother. Youssef's promise that he'd understand when the time came.

But Tom didn't understand. The scroll sat in his suitcase, wrapped in linen—a mystery he couldn't quite grasp. He still didn't feel worthy of such a cherished family gift. What was he supposed to do with it?

More pressing was today's itinerary. Today was the Dead Sea and Masada excursion, the longest tour day of the week. An early departure, a two-hour drive south, hiking in desert heat. Tom's body was already protesting, his breathing labored even while lying still.

He took his morning medication and sat on the edge of the bed, waiting for it to take effect. Through the window, Jerusalem was still dark, but soon the sun would rise, and so would the expectations of his group. It felt strange not to hold those same expectations.

Tom pulled his canvas bag closer and checked the contents. His Thermos, sunglasses, journal, and prescriptions. He should bring the scroll. Keep it with him. But something made him hesitate. It felt too precious to risk in the desert heat.

Finally, he decided to leave it locked in his suitcase. If it had survived two thousand years, it could survive one day in a hotel room.

AT BREAKFAST, THE GROUP BUZZED WITH EXCITEMENT about the Dead Sea. Dr. Bar-El stood at the head of the table, checking his clipboard.

"Today we visit Masada and the Dead Sea," he announced. "The Dead Sea is very hot, very dry. So make sure you have water with you, and drink plenty throughout the day."

Patricia slid into the seat beside Tom. "Still thinking about yesterday?"

Tom nodded. How could he not? The scroll. The grandmother's tears. Youssef's cryptic words about being ready.

But ready for what?

"Are you sure you're up for this?" Patricia asked, concern in her voice. "Masada is serious. The heat, the climbing..."

"I'll be fine," Tom said, though he wasn't sure that was true.

Reverend Hartwell approached their table, his expression hesitant. Since Saturday's confrontation, there'd been a coolness between them. Yet something in Hartwell's face suggested he wanted to change that.

"Brother McGarvey," he said, "might I have a word before we leave?"

Tom followed him to a quiet corner of the dining room. Hartwell cleared his throat, looking uncomfortable.

"I owe you an apology," Hartwell said. "I've been thinking about what you said on Saturday. About Matthew 25. About how Jesus spent his time..." He paused. "You were right. I was so focused on the holy sites that I forgot about holy living."

Tom blinked in surprise. "I appreciate that."

"Margaret pointed out that I was being hypocritical, prioritizing religious tourism over actual Christian charity." Hartwell met Tom's eyes. "I've been in ministry forty years, and somehow I forgot the basics. You reminded me."

"I was reminded myself, Reverend. We're all learning."

Hartwell extended his hand. "Can we start fresh for these last two days? I am truly sorry."

Tom shook his hand. "I'd like that," he said with a smile. Then he let out a slight laugh, thinking about the advice his new friend had given him. "But don't be sorry... let's be better."

The gesture felt significant. A small reconciliation. A reminder that even rigid people could change.

THE VAN WOUND THROUGH THE JUDEAN DESERT, A LANDscape of brown hills and deep ravines. Dr. Bar-El narrated from the front, explaining the geography, the history, and the significance of the region.

Even with all the van windows open, the heat inside kept rising. Tom tried to pay attention but found his mind drifting back to yesterday. To the grandmother's apartment, the wooden box, the scroll wrapped in linen.

To what Youssef had said: *You've been tested all week. Every encounter with me was a test. And you passed.*

But what did passing mean? What was Tom supposed to do now?

The bus arrived at Masada around nine-thirty. The ancient fortress rose from the desert floor like a ship in a sea of sand. Massive, imposing, utterly isolated.

"This is Masada," Dr. Bar-El announced. "Built by Herod the Great. It was the site of the last Jewish resistance against Rome in 73 CE. When the Romans breached the walls, all 960 defenders chose death over slavery." He motioned toward the mountain. "You can take the cable car or hike the Snake Path. I recommend the cable car unless you are very fit."

Tom looked at the winding trail climbing up the mountainside and knew immediately he couldn't do it. His breathing was already labored in the desert heat.

"Cable car," he told Patricia.

Most of the group made the same choice. They rode up in packed cars, tourists from multiple groups heading to the summit. The view from the top was spectacular. The Dead Sea stretching out below, the desert extending in all directions, the ruins of Herod's palace complex spread across the flat summit.

Dr. Bar-El led them through the ruins, explaining the bathhouses, the storerooms, the synagogue, and the mosaic floors still visible after two millennia. Tom tried to appreciate it, tried to absorb the history.

But halfway through the tour, he had to stop. The heat, the altitude, the exertion... it was too much. He found a shaded wall and sat down heavily.

Patricia noticed immediately. "Tom? Are you okay?"

"Just need a minute."

But it was more than that. The pressure in his chest was building again, that familiar warning sign. Tom fumbled for his thermos.

The breathing episode hit hard and fast. One moment he was sitting, the next he was gasping for air that wouldn't come. His vision tunneled. The desert heat pressed in.

Patricia was beside him, calling for help. Dr. Bar-El appeared, then Hartwell, their faces swimming in Tom's distorted vision.

"He needs medical attention," someone said.

"The first aid station is at the bottom," Dr. Bar-El replied, his voice filled with stress. "We've got to get him down. Now."

They half-carried Tom to the cable car. The descent was a blur. At the bottom, an Israeli aid medic, a young woman with efficient hands and kind eyes, waited. She checked his pulse, listened to his breathing, and shone a light in his eyes.

"It looks like hypoxia," she said. "Do you have a medical condition?"

He'd remembered to bring his thermos of water for the day, but forgot to pack the note Dr. Morrison had written him for this very situation. "Cancer," Tom managed. "Lungs."

Understanding crossed her face. "You should not be hiking in this heat. It's very dangerous even for people in good health. You need to rest. You should be drinking water and staying cool. If it gets worse, you should go to the hospital."

Tom nodded, too exhausted to argue.

The group continued without him to the Dead Sea. Dr. Bar-El arranged for Tom to wait in the air-conditioned visitor center. Patricia insisted on staying with him despite his protests.

"I'm not leaving you alone," she said firmly. "End of discussion."

So they sat together in the visitor center cafeteria, where Tom drank water while watching other tourists come and go. He felt like a failure. He'd come all this way and couldn't even manage a simple desert hike.

"Stop it," Patricia said, reading his mind. "This isn't your fault."

"I'm slowing everyone down."

"So what?" She stirred the coffee she bought from one of the vending machines that lined the wall. "Tom, I think you already got what you came here for. Whatever happened with Youssef yesterday, what he told you—that matters more than floating in the Dead Sea."

Tom looked at her sharply. "He told you about the scroll?"

With a look of confusion, Patricia answered him, "No. He didn't say anything about a scroll. But I saw your face when you came back yesterday. You looked... different. Like you'd found something important." She smiled. "Am I right?"

Tom wanted to tell her everything. About the grandmother. About the test. About the scroll wrapped in linen in his suitcase. But he held back. He didn't understand it himself yet. How could he explain it to someone else?

"Maybe," he said finally. "I'm still trying to figure it out."

<hr>

That Evening

THE GROUP RETURNED TO THE HOTEL AROUND SIX-THIRty, sunburned and exhausted. Everyone raved about the Dead

Sea—the floating experience, the mineral-rich water, the surreal feeling of effortless buoyancy.

Tom had missed all of it.

He went straight to his room, took his evening medication, and lay down. His body ached. His lungs ached. Everything ached.

He dozed fitfully, waking to knocking on his door. Tom struggled to sit up, disoriented. The room was dark. He'd slept through dinner again.

"Tom? It's Patricia."

He opened the door. Patricia stood in the hallway with a plate wrapped in a napkin. "You missed dinner. Again. I brought food."

"Thank you." Tom stepped aside to let her in. He turned on the lamp, and Patricia set the plate on the small table.

"How are you feeling?" she asked.

"Better. Tired but better."

They sat together, Tom eating the pita sandwich she'd brought while Patricia watched him with concern.

"What happens tomorrow?" she asked.

"Galilee. The Sea of Galilee, Capernaum, a boat ride. Our last full day before we fly home."

"Can you handle it?"

"I have to." Tom set down the sandwich. "It's where Jesus did most of his ministry. Where he taught. Where..." He trailed off, thinking of Youssef and his grandmother.

"Where what?" Patricia prompted.

Tom shook his head. "Nothing. Just thinking."

"Okay," she said, her head tilted in an almost playful way.

Tom looked at her. Really looked at this woman who, in the course of a week, had become a friend. A confidant. Someone he felt safe sharing things with that he never did before. "I don't know how to explain it," he said. "I came here looking for one thing and stumbled into something I don't understand. But it feels like it's what I was supposed to find all along. Does that even make sense?"

"You want to know what I think?" Patricia asked. "I think your world has been turned upside down. And you're trying to figure out why it happened. Maybe instead of asking *why*, ask *how*. How can you learn from this?"

Her hand was on his knee. He looked into her eyes and saw something special. She didn't just get him, she understood him. And Tom couldn't stop himself from fantasizing about what his life would have been like if they'd met sooner.

The embrace was intimate. What followed next was spontaneous but gentle—an experience of affection and love that Tom had long forgotten. He was too tired and weak for it to turn sexual. But it was special. A moment both had yearned for since their spouses had left them without warning.

It was late when Patricia left his room. Their hug in the hallway outside his door was the kind that directors end their movies with just before the scene fades to black and the credits roll.

Tom went back into his room, sat on the edge of the bed, and closed his eyes, hoping to etch that last scene into his memory. After splashing cold water on his face in the bathroom, he returned to the bed where he'd laid his suitcase. He carefully removed the linen-wrapped bundle and carried it to the desk. He unwrapped it slowly, reverently.

The scroll was smaller than he'd expected. Maybe eighteen inches long when rolled, made of parchment that had yellowed with age but remained intact. The edges were worn, but the writing was still visible.

He unrolled it carefully, squinting at the ancient script in the lamplight. Aramaic, he thought. He'd studied a little of it in seminary, but that was years ago.

Tom pulled out a pen and paper, trying to copy some of the letters, hoping that would trigger his memory. But nothing came. The script was clear but completely incomprehensible.

His stomach churned with frustration. A grandmother had given him this scroll. This precious, ancient scroll that her family had protected for nearly a hundred generations. And he couldn't even read it.

What was he supposed to do with it?

You'll know when the time comes, the grandmother had said through Youssef's translation.

But Tom didn't know. He didn't understand. He'd spent a week chasing after Youssef, missing tour sites, alienating his group, and exhausting his failing body. And for what? A scroll he couldn't read? A message he couldn't access?

Maybe Hartwell had been right. Maybe he had wasted his pilgrimage.

Tom carefully rolled up the scroll and wrapped it back in its linen cloth. Then he lay down on the bed, staring at the ceiling.

Tomorrow was Galilee. Their last day.

And he'd be returning to Stoneford with a scroll he couldn't read, a message he didn't understand, and no idea what he was supposed to do with any of it.

Tuesday, May 27, 1975
7:30 a.m.

TOM WOKE FEELING MARGINALLY BETTER. THE REST HAD helped, though his breathing was still labored. He dressed, took his medications, and forced himself to eat breakfast with the group.

"Today we're heading north to Galilee," Dr. Bar-El announced. "It's a very beautiful area, as you'll see. The Sea of Galilee, with all its historical significance. Then to Capernaum, where Jesus lived. Followed by a boat ride. This is the last full day of the tour, so let's make it one to remember!"

The group murmured agreement, though Tom noticed several people glancing at him with concern. Word had spread about yesterday's episode.

"I'm fine," Tom told Patricia when she sat beside him. "Really."

"You look better," she said. "I hope last night didn't—"

"It did," Tom interrupted. "But in a good way." He smiled. It was the first genuine smile he'd shared in a long time.

Patricia returned a warm smile. "But promise you'll take it easy today. No pushing yourself."

"I won't."

The van left at eight, winding north through increasingly green landscapes. As they entered more fertile regions, Tom felt something shift inside him. This was Galilee. This was where it all began. Where Jesus had lived and taught and gathered his disciples.

Where Sheerah had heard the parable.

Dr. Bar-El narrated as they drove, explaining the geography, the history, and the significance of the region. "Galilee was the breadbasket of ancient Israel, with fertile soil and good water. It was perfect for farming and fishing. Jesus chose this place deliberately, where the poor people lived, not the rich cities."

They arrived at Capernaum around ten o'clock. The ruins were modest. Stone foundations of houses, the remains of a synagogue, and a small church built over what tradition said was Peter's house.

"Jesus lived here most of his ministry," Dr. Bar-El explained. "This was his home base. From here, he traveled through Galilee, teaching and healing."

Tom walked through the ruins slowly, trying to imagine it. Jesus walking these streets. Teaching in that synagogue. Living among fishermen and farmers. Among the poor and overlooked.

Just like Youssef lived in Jerusalem. In abandoned buildings, among the forgotten.

The parallel struck Tom again. Jesus hadn't based himself in Jerusalem, the religious center. He'd chosen Galilee, among ordinary people doing ordinary work. And when he did go to Jerusalem, it was to challenge the religious establishment.

At noon, they boarded a wooden boat for a ride across the Sea of Galilee. The water was calm and blue-green under the midday sun. Other tour boats dotted the lake, all offering the same experience.

Tom stood at the rail, watching the shoreline slip past. Somewhere along these shores, Sheerah had sat. Had listened. Had felt her heart ignite with something that might be found in a scroll.

A scroll preserved for a hundred generations. But a scroll that Tom still didn't know what was written on it.

Why give it to me? Tom thought. *I can't even read it. What good is a message you can't understand?*

The boat docked at a beach on the eastern shore. Dr. Bar-El gave them thirty minutes to explore. Tom bought a cold drink and found a quiet spot near the water.

He pulled out his journal and wrote:

Day 7 - Tuesday

I'm sitting on the shore of the Sea of Galilee. Somewhere near here, Sheerah heard Jesus teach. Heard the Parable of the Sheep and Goats. According to Youssef's grandmother, she wrote about it.

The scroll is in my suitcase. But I can't read it. It's in Aramaic, I think. All my seminary training, and I can't read the one document that might actually matter.

I don't know what I'm supposed to do. Yesterday, I thought the scroll was the point. But maybe I'm missing something. Maybe there's another step I don't see yet.

Tomorrow I go home. Back to Stoneford. Back to dying.

And I'll be bringing a scroll I can't read, a message I don't understand, and no idea what to do with any of it.

Maybe I wasted my pilgrimage after all.

Tom closed the journal and stared out at the water. The tour group was gathering, preparing to reboard the boat. Their last activity in Galilee. Their last moments in the place where it all began.

Tom stood and walked back toward the group, feeling the disappointment settle over him like a shroud.

That Evening
Old City, Jerusalem
6:30 p.m.

THE VAN DROPPED THEM AT THE HOTEL AT FIVE-THIRTY. Dr. Bar-El reminded everyone that tomorrow was departure day. Luggage needed to be outside their doors by seven. The bus to the airport would leave at eight.

Tom didn't go to his room. He grabbed a quick sandwich and headed into the Old City. He had to find Youssef one more time. Had to tell him... what? That he'd failed? That he didn't understand the gift he'd been given?

The evening air was cooler, and the Old City was transitioning from day to night. Tom walked through familiar streets, heading toward the Christian Quarter, toward the places Youssef frequented.

But Youssef wasn't at the fifth station. Wasn't at the abandoned building. Wasn't at Father Mikhail's church.

Tom's worry was rising. He would leave tomorrow morning. He couldn't go without saying goodbye.

He was near the souk where he bought Youssef the thobe when he saw the merchant who sold it. Tom tried to explain he was looking for his friend and asked if the merchant had seen him.

The merchant's face told Tom he didn't understand. And Tom didn't speak Arabic. Just then, another man, dressed in a dirty tunic, tapped Tom on the back. "I speak Arabic. What do you want from this man?"

Tom jumped. A translator! *God has a way of putting people in our path when we're not looking.* Patricia's words rang true. "Hi, I'm sorry. You startled me. I'm looking for a man who frequents this area. I helped him buy a... I don't remember what it's called. But we bought a shirt and a garment from his souk the other day. Can you ask him if he knows where I can find him?"

The two local men spoke to each other, and Tom swore he heard Youssef's name in their exchange. When they finished, Tom's translator said that if the man he was looking for is named Youssef, he can usually be found in the prison on Tuesday nights.

The prison? What would Youssef be doing in prison? Tom was given directions to this prison, described to be a fifteen-minute walk from where they were.

Tom made his way through neighborhoods that reminded him of areas where Great Witness's mission trips were planned. When he got to the place described by the man, confusion set in. The only thing he saw was a dilapidated structure, with sounds of animals barking and crying from behind it.

The sign out front was in both Hebrew and English. It read: Animal Protection Society.

This couldn't be it. This was a pound, not a prison. But it was the only building around that wasn't a house, so Tom went through the makeshift gate into the small office. The smell was a mix of feces and urine, mixed with the distinct odor of dying flesh.

"Excuse me," Tom asked the woman at a folding card table. "I'm looking for my friend. But I think I might be in the wrong place."

"Does your friend have two legs or four?" she asked with a smirk.

"Two. At least that's all I saw on him," Tom replied, trying to match her wit. "His name is Youssef. I was told this is where I could find him. But I was told he's in prison. I think this might be a mistake."

"No mistake. This is the prison. It may say 'Animal Protection Society' out front, but we call it the prison." She motioned to an open door behind her. "You'll see when you go back there."

Tom walked past the table and through the door. The smell almost knocked him over. The scene reminded him of a prison yard he had known during his chaplaincy work before Vietnam. But this was worse.

Cages lined up in no particular order, scattered across the yard. All of them filled with dogs of different sizes and varying states of health. One small tin structure provided shade for the few lucky animals that made it under during the day.

Feces, both dried and fresh, made walking a challenge. A six-foot chain-link fence surrounded the entire compound.

Every sense was overwhelmed. Tom's heart sank.

Then, there, in one of the large cages, he saw Youssef. He was hand-feeding a small dog whose coat was matted with sores.

"Youssef!" Tom shouted over the barking.

Youssef looked up and smiled broadly. "American pastor Tom!" He laid the remaining food on the cement floor of the cage and ran to his friend. "It is good to see you! Come sit. We will talk."

They sat in chairs under a large tree. One man smelling like a kennel, the other trying his best not to vomit.

"They said I would find you in prison. My heart sank when I heard it. I'm relieved to see you're not in prison, but what are you doing here?" Tom asked, bringing his forearm to his face to block the stench.

"This is the prison, my friend. That is what we call it. The sign out front does not describe what happens here." Youssef's eyes revealed a sadness that couldn't be hidden. "These dogs are brought here hungry. Thirsty. Most are sick. All are lonely... they are strangers here. Do you see?"

Everywhere Tom looked, he saw suffering. He saw fear. He saw neglect and abuse. "But why... why are *you* here?"

A smile returned to Youssef's face. "I am here because they need me. I collect scraps thrown out by restaurants and bring them here. It is the best food these dogs will eat. It is not much, but it is something. It is something I can do to ease suffering."

To ease suffering. Tom thought about his own suffering and all he had endured that week. Youssef's actions reminded him that even in suffering, there can be acts of love. Especially in suffering, there *should be* acts of love.

"Youssef. How do you... How do you do it?"

"What do you mean?"

"How do you teach what it means to be the hands and feet of Christ?"

"Ah, yes. Your Jesus. Many people look for their Jesus where they are comfortable. Where they feel safe. Where things look nice. But look around here. Jesus is here. He is with these animals. He can be found in the brutal smell and horrible sounds of this place."

Tom rubbed his head with both hands, hoping to absorb everything Youssef said.

Youssef continued. "Jesus is where thirst and hunger are. Jesus is where loneliness and nakedness need attention. Jesus is where sickness is addressed and where those in prison are suffering. Look around here, Reverend Tom. This is where Jesus is."

"The student becomes the master," Tom whispered.

"Come now. You will help me." Youssef stood and guided Tom from cage to cage, handing food to scared animals in cages. Coming to those caught in their own prisons.

For the rest of the night, Tom worked with Youssef, feeding animals in fear and in pain. He ignored the filth that clung to his shoes and instead focused on tending to the suffering around him. This was the work of Jesus. This was more than just thinking about what he should do or praying for this place to get what it needed. He was doing the work.

By the end of the night, his clothes had absorbed every smell of the shelter. And he couldn't have been happier.

Tom thought of Matthew 25. *I was in prison, and you came to me.* The final requirement. He knew now there were no more tests. This was friendship. Love Working alongside someone who demonstrated that love is more than a feeling.

"Why did you come looking for me?" Youssef asked as they stepped onto the street.

"Because you're my friend," Tom replied simply.

Youssef pulled Tom into a tight embrace. Tom could feel him shaking. "You are a good man, American pastor."

When they separated, Youssef wiped his eyes. "You leave tomorrow?"

"Yes. Early morning."

"Then we honor this moment."

Tom wiped his hands on his pants. "The scroll," he said finally. "I can't read it."

Youssef looked at him. "You tried?"

"It's in Aramaic. I can't understand it." Frustration edged into Tom's voice. "Your grandmother gave me something precious, and I don't even know what it says."

"Then you will find someone who can read it."

"But who? How?"

"You will know when the time comes." Youssef smiled. "This is what my grandmother said, yes? That you would know?"

"But I don't know. That's the problem."

"Not yet. But you will. The scroll found its way to you after two thousand years. It will reveal itself when you are ready."

Tom wanted to argue, wanted to insist that he needed to understand now, before he went home. But something in Youssef's calm certainty made him pause.

Maybe not understanding was part of the lesson. Maybe he wasn't supposed to have all the answers yet.

They stood in silence, watching the stars appear one by one in the darkening sky. Finally, Youssef spoke. "I should go. You need to pack. You need to rest before your journey."

"Thank you. For everything. For the tests. For the teaching. For—"

"For being my brother," Youssef finished. "Because that is what you are now."

They embraced once more. Then Youssef turned and walked away into the shadows of the Old City, his dark blue thobe disappearing.

Tom watched him go, knowing he'd probably never see Youssef again. He would never know what happened to him or his community. He would never be able to repay the gift.

He was surprisingly okay with that. Some gifts weren't meant to be repaid. Only received. And passed on.

Tom walked back to the hotel slowly, savoring his last night in Jerusalem. Tomorrow, he would leave this city and return to Stoneford. But he wouldn't be the same person who'd arrived eight days ago.

That man had been cynical, burned out, dying without purpose. This man was still dying, but he had... something. A scroll he couldn't read. A message he didn't understand. A test he'd passed without knowing what it meant.

And maybe that was enough for now.

Tom's alarm went off while the city was still dark. He got up, showered, and carefully packed his belongings. The scroll went in his carry-on bag, wrapped in its linen cloth, protected by his extra clothes.

He couldn't read it. Didn't understand it. Had no idea what to do with it.

But it was precious. That much he knew. And he would guard it until he figured out what came next.

Downstairs, the group gathered for a quick breakfast. Everyone was processing the week, already nostalgic.

"I can't believe it's over," Mrs. Thompson said. "It went by so fast."

"But what a week," her husband added. "I'll never forget it."

Tom caught Patricia's eye. She gave him a questioning look. *Did you figure it out?* He shook his head slightly. *Not yet.*

Dr. Bar-El checked his clipboard one last time. "The bus leaves in fifteen minutes. Please check you have passports, tickets, and all your belongings. The flight to New York is at eleven."

Tom finished his coffee and went back to his room for one last look. The room where he'd written in his journal. Where he'd tried and failed to read the scroll. Where he'd wrestled with disappointment and confusion.

He grabbed his carry-on and headed downstairs.

The bus wound through Jerusalem's streets one last time. Tom pressed his face to the window, trying to memorize the scene. The stone walls. The golden dome. The narrow alleys. The people beginning their day.

Somewhere in the Old City, Youssef was waking up, starting another day of survival—living the kingdom of God without calling it that.

Remember us, he'd said.

I will, Tom had promised. *I won't forget.*

At the airport, the group checked in and, one by one, said goodbye to Dr. Bar-El. Tom was the last in line. "Thank you, Dr. Bar-El, for sharing your insights with us. It was truly a memorable trip."

"Reverend McGarvey, it has been my pleasure." Dr. Bar-El grabbed hold of Tom's shoulders. "I've been doing this for many years now, and I've seen many tourists pass through searching for something," he said, pointing to the airport exit.

"But I have never seen a transformation like I've seen in you. I can see it."

Tom felt the weight of his clothes hanging on his thinning frame. They used to fit perfectly. Before he got sick. *Was this the transformation Dr. Bar-El saw?*

"Thank you," Tom managed. "But I really don't know what I experienced. I came searching for something. I found something. I'm just not sure what it is."

"Whatever you found," Dr. Bar-El said, "promise me… promise yourself that you'll remember its sacredness."

"I will."

Tom clutched his bag tightly as he moved through security, hyperaware of the scroll inside.

The flight to New York was long and uneventful. Tom slept fitfully, dreaming of desert heat, ancient stones, and a scroll covered in words he couldn't understand.

In New York, they all had a layover before flights to their various home cities. Tom and Patricia found a quiet corner near their gate.

"You still haven't figured it out," she observed.

"No." Tom set his carry-on on the seat beside him. "Dr. Bar-El said he saw a transformation in me this week. I don't know about that."

"I do," Patricia said, sharing another warm smile. "Sometimes we can't see what others see in us."

"All I see is a scroll that's supposed to be important. But I can't read it. Don't know what it says. Don't know what I'm supposed to do with it."

"Maybe that's the lesson," Patricia said gently. "That you don't always get immediate answers. That sometimes you have to sit with mystery."

"I don't have time to sit with mystery," Tom said, frustration spilling out. "I have six months to live. Probably less. I thought this scroll would give me answers. Instead, it's just another question I can't answer."

Patricia was quiet for a moment. "Who's waiting for you in Stoneford?"

"Kayla. The young seminarian I told you about."

"The one covering for you?"

"Yes."

"Maybe she can help," Patricia suggested. "Maybe you're not supposed to figure this out alone."

Tom considered that. Kayla, with her fire and passion. Her research on early Christianity. Her belief that the church needed to change.

Maybe Patricia was right. Maybe he wasn't supposed to understand the scroll alone.

"I'll talk to her when I get back," Tom said.

Patricia pulled out a business card and wrote her phone number on the back. "Call me when you figure it out. When you need support. I'd like to be there if you need me."

Tom took the card. "Thank you. For everything."

They sat together until their flights were called—Patricia to Florida, Tom to Chicago. They hugged goodbye, two strangers who'd become dear friends in just one week.

Tom's flights were smooth. Shortly after nine p.m., he was driving his El Camino south toward Stoneford.

The scroll sat in his bag on the passenger seat. Ancient. Precious. Incomprehensible.

He pulled into his driveway just after midnight. The house was dark, exactly as he'd left it. Tom grabbed his bags and let himself inside.

Home. He was home.

Tom set down his luggage and walked through the house, turning on lights, checking that everything was as he'd left it. Then he went to his den and carefully placed the scroll on his desk.

Tomorrow, he would call Kayla. Tomorrow, they would look at it together. Tomorrow, they would try to understand what he'd been given.

But tonight, Tom pulled out his journal and wrote one final entry:

I'm home. The pilgrimage is over.

But I don't feel the way I thought I would. I don't have answers. I don't have clarity. I have a scroll I can't read and a message I don't understand.

I spent a week in Jerusalem. Missed important tour sites to help a homeless man. Exhausted myself. Alienated people. All for this scroll.

And I can't even read it.

Was it worth it? I don't know. Maybe I wasted my last healthy days chasing after something I'll never understand.

Or maybe, and I'm holding onto this maybe, maybe not understanding is part of the journey. Maybe I'm supposed to need help. Maybe that's what Youssef kept trying to teach me. That I can't do everything alone.

Tomorrow I'll call Kayla. Tomorrow we'll look at the scroll together. Tomorrow we'll try to figure out what I was given and why.

But tonight, I just feel let down. Like I traveled halfway around the world and came back empty-handed.

Please God, let there be more to this than I can see right now.

Tom closed the journal and stared at the scroll on his desk. Wrapped in ancient linen. Covered in words he couldn't read. A gift he didn't understand.

Tomorrow, everything might become clear. Or tomorrow might bring only more confusion.

Either way, Tom was home. And whatever came next, he wouldn't face it alone.

Kayla would help him. He was sure of that much at least.

He turned off the desk lamp and went to bed, too tired to think anymore, too confused to hope, too stubborn to give up.

The scroll sat in the darkness, waiting.

Just as it had waited for two thousand years. A few more days wouldn't matter.

PART THREE
Back in Stoneford

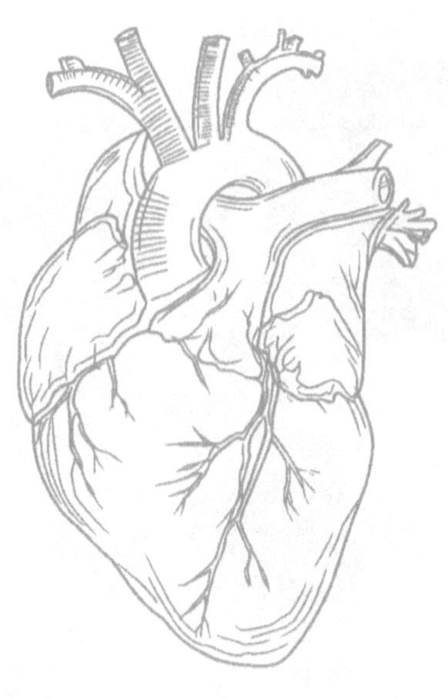

CHAPTER
TWELVE

Thursday, May 29, 1975
Stoneford, Illinois
8:30 a.m.

Tom sat at his kitchen table, staring at the phone. He'd been home for less than eight hours, had unpacked, showered, and slept in his own bed. And now, in the morning light streaming through the windows, he had to make a decision.

Call Kayla. Ask for help. Admit he couldn't do this alone.

His hand hovered over the receiver, his ego and pride conspiring against him. He could figure it out himself. Find a library book on Aramaic, work through it methodically, and decode the scroll without bothering anyone. But that was the old Tom, the one who'd left for Jerusalem more than a week ago.

The new Tom, the one who'd learned to accept help and let people carry his burdens—that Tom knew what he had to do.

He picked up the phone and dialed the church office.

"Great Witness Community Church, this is Kayla."

"Kayla. It's Tom. I'm back."

"Tom!" The joy in her voice was immediate. "You're home! How was... How are you feeling? When did you get in?"

"Late. After midnight. I'm okay." Tom paused, trying to find the right words. "Kayla, I need to ask you something. Can you come to my house? There's something I need to show you. Something important."

The line went quiet for a moment. Then, "Is everything alright?"

"I don't know yet. That's why I need your help."

"I'll be there in twenty minutes."

<hr>

Tom used those twenty minutes to make coffee and set up his den. He placed the scroll on his desk, still wrapped in its linen cloth. He pulled out the notes he'd made, his failed attempts to copy the Aramaic letters and to make sense of the ancient script.

The doorbell rang. He opened the door to find Kayla standing on his porch, her canvas bag slung over one shoulder, wearing jeans and an unclaimed Great Witness T-shirt from last year's vacation Bible school. She looked so young, so full of energy, that Tom felt suddenly ancient in comparison.

"Hi," she said, studying his face. "You look... different."

"Different how?"

"I don't know. Thinner, definitely. But also..." She tilted her head. "Lighter, somehow. Like you're carrying less weight than when you left."

Tom stepped aside to let her in. "That's an interesting observation, considering I came back with more questions than I left with."

They walked to his den. Kayla set down her bag and looked around at the books lining the walls, the sermon notes scattered across the desk, and the photograph of Tom and Sheldon in Vietnam.

"I've never been in your house before," she said. "It's very... you."

"Is that good or bad?"

"It's honest." Kayla turned toward the desk. "So what did you need to show me?"

Tom picked up the linen-wrapped bundle. "Before I show you this, I need to tell you what happened in Jerusalem. It's going to sound strange. Possibly insane. But I need you to hear me out."

"Okay." Kayla sat in the chair facing his desk. "I'm listening."

For the next thirty minutes, Tom told her everything. About Youssef. About the tests he didn't know he was taking. About the grandmother and the wooden box. About the scroll that had been waiting for someone to fulfill the Parable of the Sheep and Goats. He shared his frustration at not being able to read it.

Kayla listened without interrupting, practicing the ministry of presence she had been perfecting. Her expression shifted from curiosity to wonder, then to something like awe as Tom recounted his journey.

When he finished, she remained quiet for a long moment. "Show me."

Tom carefully unwrapped the scroll and placed it on the desk between them.

Kayla leaned forward, her eyes widening. "Tom. This is... this looks ancient. Like, actually ancient. Not reproduction, not replica." She reached down and touched the scroll. "This is real parchment." She looked up at him. "Do you understand what you're holding?"

"I think so. I'm not sure. That's why I called you."

Kayla stood, bending to examine the scroll without touching it. "The script is definitely Aramaic. Tom, if what you're telling me is true... if this was really written by someone who heard Jesus teach, this is..." She straightened, running her hands through her hair. "This is the most significant archaeological find in modern history. Can you read it?"

"I tried. My Aramaic is... I wish I'd paid more attention in seminary," he admitted with a shrug. "I can make out a few letters and a word here and there. But no, I can't read it."

She shook her head. "We need an expert. Someone who specializes in first-century Aramaic. Someone fluent in it."

Tom felt his stomach sink. "Where would we find someone like that?"

Kayla was quiet for a moment, thinking. Then her face lit up. "Dr. Feldman. Susan Feldman. She was one of my professors. Taught a course on Ancient Near Eastern languages. I heard she's the department chair at the University of Chicago now. She's brilliant and specializes in exactly this kind of thing."

"Would she help us?"

"Are you kidding? If I told her what you have here, she'd drive down today." Kayla pulled out her notebook and began scribbling. "But, Tom, I don't think we should let this out of our hands. It's too precious. Too important. If something happened to it..."

"Then we go to her."

Kayla looked up, concern flickering in her eyes. "Chicago? You just got back from there."

"It's only three hours." Tom started to search for his keys. "We could drive up today, have her translate it, and drive back tonight."

"You should be resting."

"I've rested since I got home." Tom felt a surge of energy. "Besides, I don't think I could rest even if I wanted to. Not knowing what this says."

Kayla studied him for a moment, then nodded. "Okay. Let me call her. If she's available, we go."

DR. SUSAN FELDMAN WAS AVAILABLE. MORE THAN AVAILable. She was thrilled.

"An Aramaic scroll from the first century?" Her voice crackled with excitement over the phone. "Written by a woman who heard Jesus teach? Kayla, if this is authentic, this is extraordinary. Bring it to me. Today. I'll clear my afternoon."

Kayla's excitement matched her former professor's. Until, "Kayla, I have to caution you not to get too excited. Don't get your hopes up. There were a lot of forgeries floating around in the second and third centuries. I won't be able to authenticate the date of it, but I will be able to tell you if it's real."

It didn't matter. By noon, she was with Tom in his El Camino, heading north on I-55 toward Chicago. The scroll sat safely in a briefcase between them, carefully wrapped, precious cargo that might change everything.

The drive gave them time to talk. Kayla updated him on the past two weeks. The services she'd led, the pastoral care visits she'd made, and the veterans program she'd started organizing. Tom shared more about his experiences in Jerusalem. The conversations with Patricia, Reverend Hartwell's apology, and Father Mikhail's tiny church serving just twenty families.

"It sounds like you learned more on the streets than in the holy places," Kayla remarked.

"That's exactly right." Tom kept his eyes on the road. "I went looking for God in ancient stones. I found God in the face of a homeless man and in the stench of a dog pound."

"That's very Matthew 25 of you."

"That's the thing, Kayla. I didn't realize that's what was happening. I wasn't trying to fulfill some biblical requirement—I was just..."

"Helping someone who needed help?" Kayla finished his thought.

"Exactly! Apparently, that's what the whole test was about. Living the parable without knowing you're living it. I still can't believe no one fulfilled those requirements before me. Youssef's grandmother said nearly 100 generations."

Kayla fell silent for nearly a mile. Then, "That's beautiful. And terrifying."

"Why terrifying?"

"Because it means most of us are failing. We know the parable. We've heard it hundreds of times. But we're not living it. We're just... worshiping. Praying. Going through religious motions." She looked at Tom. "That's what your sermon on Acts was about, wasn't it? Before you left. These who have turned the world upside down."

"Yes."

"And now you have a scroll that might prove you were right. That the early Christians understood something we've forgotten. That following Jesus is about doing, not just believing."

Tom nodded. "If it says what I think it says. If Sheerah wrote what Youssef's grandmother claimed she wrote."

"We'll know soon enough."

They drove in silence for a while, the Illinois farmland rolling past on either side of the highway. Tom noticed his breathing grow more labored as they drove—a combination of the exertion of the trip, stress, and the cancer slowly doing its work. He took one of his pills without mentioning it to Kayla.

"Are you okay?" she asked.

"Fine. Just tired."

"You should have let me drive."

"I'm fine, Kayla." Tom softened his tone. "Really. I need to do this. I need to see this through."

THEY ARRIVED AT THE UNIVERSITY OF CHICAGO CAMPUS around three o'clock. Dr. Feldman's office was in the Divinity School, an imposing Gothic building that resembled a cathedral more than an academic facility. Kayla and Tom navigated hallways lined with portraits of distinguished scholars and theologians, finally stopping at an office door marked "Dr. Susan Feldman, Department Chairperson, Ancient Languages."

Kayla knocked.

"Come in!"

Dr. Feldman was a woman in her fifties with salt-and-pepper hair pulled back in a bun and reading glasses perched on her nose. Her office was a mess. Books stacked on every surface, papers covering her desk, and a blackboard filled with Hebrew letters and grammatical notes.

"Kayla!" Dr. Feldman stood and embraced her former student. "It's so good to see you! And this must be Reverend McGarvey." She extended her hand to Tom. "Susan Feldman. Kayla tells me you might have something extraordinary to show me."

"That depends on your definition of extraordinary," Tom said, shaking her hand. "But yes, I think I do."

"Well, don't keep me in suspense." Dr. Feldman cleared a space on her desk, pushing aside stacks of papers. "Let's see it."

Tom opened the briefcase and carefully removed the linen-wrapped bundle. He placed it on the desk and slowly unwrapped the scroll.

Dr. Feldman's eyes lit up. She leaned forward, looking over the parchment with the intensity of someone who could read history in the fibers themselves.

"May I?" she asked, her hand hovering over the scroll.

"Of course."

Dr. Feldman gently touched the edge of the parchment, feeling its texture before pulling out a magnifying glass to examine the script closely.

"The parchment is authentic," she said after a moment. "Definitely first century, possibly earlier. The script is Aramaic... Galilean dialect, based on the letter forms. The ink is carbon-based, which is correct for the period." She looked up at Tom. "Where did you get this?"

"Jerusalem. From a family that's been protecting it for nearly a hundred generations."

Dr. Feldman set down the magnifying glass. "Reverend McGarvey, do you understand what you have here? If this is what Kayla says it is, if this is truly a first-century account written by someone who heard Jesus teach, this is..." She paused, searching for words. "This is unprecedented. We have no original New Testament documents from the first century. None. Everything we have is copies of copies, fragments from the second or third century at the earliest. This would be the only eyewitness account in existence."

Tom felt his heart pound in his chest. "Can you translate it?"

"I can. It will take a few minutes. Aramaic is complex, and I want to be precise. But yes, I can translate it." Dr. Feldman looked at both of them. "This is going to change your lives. You know that, right?"

"We're counting on it," Kayla said softly.

DR. FELDMAN WORKED AT HER DESK WHILE TOM AND Kayla sat in chairs against the wall. She filled a legal pad with notes, writing slowly, occasionally muttering to herself in Hebrew. She'd read a phrase aloud, testing it, revising it, and getting the English just right.

Tom watched Dr. Feldman work, feeling time stretch out. This was it. The moment he'd been waiting for since the grandmother had placed the scroll in his hands. Soon he would know what Sheerah had written. Soon he would understand what he'd been given.

And soon he would have to decide what to do with it.

Finally, after what felt like hours, Dr. Feldman set down her pencil. "I think I have it. And I think it's as accurate as anyone could be. The Aramaic is clear, but there are always nuances that don't translate perfectly into English."

She picked up the legal pad and looked at Tom and Kayla. "Are you ready?"

Tom nodded, heart racing, anticipation coursing through him.

I, Sheerah, a woman of no standing in the eyes of men but seen by God, write these things not because I am certain but because I am afraid.

I fear what we began will not remain as we lived it.

I fear that those who did not walk beside him will reshape him into someone he never was.

I followed him. I heard him.

On a hill near the olive trees. Yeshua was asked what must be done to inherit the kingdom when the son of man comes.

He spoke in a parable, saying all nations will be called to account. The King will separate them, just as a shepherd separates the sheep from the goats.

He will place the sheep at his right hand and the goats at his left hand.

The king will tell those on his right to inherit the kingdom that is prepared for them.

I was hungry and you gave me food.

I was thirsty and you gave me drink.

I was a stranger and you welcomed me.

I was naked and you clothed me.

I was sick and you visited me.

I was in prison and you came to me.

The righteous on the right will not understand and will ask when did they see the king hungry and give food? Or thirsty and give drink? Or as a stranger and be welcomed? Or naked and be clothed? Or sick and be visited? Or in prison and come to him?

The king will answer them.
Truly I say to you, as you did it to one of the least of these my brothers, you did it to me.

The goats on his left will be told they are not welcome in the kingdom.
The king will tell them he was hungry, and they did not give him food. He was thirsty and they did not give him drink. He was a stranger and they did not welcome him. He was naked, and they did not clothe him. He was sick and they did not visit him. He was in prison, and they did not come to him.

And they will not understand.
The king will answer them.
Truly I say to you, as you did not do for the least of these, you did not do it for me.

The king will announce that the righteous have earned eternal life.

I heard him again. I was there. On the large peak by the sea.

Yeshua spoke of the poor as if they were blessed, not cursed.
Yeshua called the peacemakers the children of God.
Yeshua said the meek would inherit everything.

I now fear.

I fear that the powerful will not allow such a kingdom to rise.

I fear that one day, people will speak more about him than live like him.

They will praise his name but ignore his way.
They will build temples in his honor, but not open their doors to the hungry.

They will make their own concepts of reward and punishment.
I fear they will take up judgment of others instead of justice for everyone.

I fear they will make belief more important than mercy.
I fear they will debate who he was instead of remembering what he did.

He told us to act. To feed, to welcome, to forgive, to love even our enemies.
But I fear they will replace action with prayer and love with rules.

He said we would be known by our love.
But I fear they will become known by their boundaries.

I fear that those who suffer will once again be left outside the gates.
That the widow, the leper, the Samaritan, the child, the beggar, and all he touched will be forgotten in favor of those who lecture, not those who serve.

I fear that his message to those who have nothing will be stolen by those who have much.

I fear his example to the oppressed will be stolen by the powerful and used as a weapon against those it was intended for.

I fear one day nations will look beyond his humility by making him a king to be worshipped.
I fear that future generations will worship Yeshua more than follow his way.

I fear that men will rise who never knew him but will claim his authority.
I fear they will write down what must be believed and punish those who question it.

I write these things because I believe.

I believe he meant it. Every word.
I believe he was not trying to start a new way of praying but a rebellion of compassion.

He was not for power but mercy.
He was not seeking revenge but forgiveness.
He was not creating boundaries but hospitality.
He was not interested in rules but justice.
He did not want assessments of people. He asked us to love them. All of them.

He is gone from us, killed by the ones in power he spoke against.

I have not seen any of the miracles that are now being talked about him. But I have witnessed change in people who heard his message.

Even the sick who will surely die, no matter how much we pray. They, too, have been blessed by his love.

If you read this, whoever you are, wherever in Judea you are.

Remember that the kingdom he spoke of was not power but presence.

Not creed but kindness.
Not prayer but action.

We turned the world upside down not by our beliefs but by how we loved.

If you carry anything forward carry this.

Dr. Feldman set down the legal pad. The office was silent.

Tom sat very still, his hands gripped together in his lap. Kayla had tears streaming down her face.

"That's it," Dr. Feldman said quietly. "That's what she wrote."

Tom couldn't speak. His throat was too tight. His chest ached—not from the cancer, but from something else. Something that felt like grief and hope twisted together.

"Reverend McGarvey?" Dr. Feldman's voice was gentle. "Are you alright?"

Tom stood abruptly. "Excuse me. I need... I need a minute."

He walked out of the office, down the hallway, and into the early evening air. The campus was mostly empty now, just a few students walking to the library. Tom found a bench near the Divinity School entrance and sat down heavily.

I was hungry and you gave me food.

He thought about the countless times he'd prayed for the hungry. The food drives at church. The canned goods collected and distributed. The meals served on holidays. But how often had he actually sat with a hungry person? Shared his own food? Made sure they left satisfied?

I was thirsty and you gave me drink.

Thermoses of water given reluctantly to Youssef. Never to the homeless people in nearby Springfield. He'd driven past them, averted his eyes, and told himself the church programs were enough.

I was a stranger and you welcomed me.

How many strangers had walked through Great Witness's doors? And how often had Tom been too busy with sermons and committees to really welcome them? To sit with them? To make them family?

I was naked and you clothed me.

One thobe and one shirt bought for Youssef. How many opportunities had he missed in Stoneford? How many coat drives had felt more like obligation than love?

I was sick and you visited me.

Hospital visits as a pastor, yes. But how often had he really been present? How often had he practiced the ministry of presence he'd preached about? Or had he been going through the motions, checking boxes, fulfilling duties?

I was in prison and you came to me.

He'd never truly visited anyone in prison. Only to fulfill his chaplaincy requirements.

Tom put his head in his hands.

Sheerah's words echoed in his mind. Two of her fears punching him in the gut.

I fear one day nations will look beyond his humility by making him a king to be worshiped. I fear that future generations will worship Yeshua more than follow his way.

And...

I fear they will praise his name but ignore his way. They will build temples in his honor but not open their doors to the hungry.

She'd been right. She'd seen it coming two thousand years ago, and she'd been exactly right.

And Tom had been one of them. One of the goats. Worshiping Jesus. Praying about problems. Building programs. But not actually doing what Jesus did.

For years. Years! He'd been the chaplain who prayed instead of acting. The pastor who organized food drives instead of feeding people himself. The minister who preached about love but didn't practice it.

He'd been a goat pretending to be a sheep.

The realization was devastating.

"Tom?"

He looked up. Kayla stood a few feet away, her expression worried.

"I'm sorry," Tom said, his voice rough. "I just... I needed a minute."

"Take all the time you need." Kayla sat down beside him. "That was intense."

"Sheerah was right." Tom stared at the ground. "Everything she feared came true. We did exactly what she was afraid we'd do. We turned following Jesus into worshiping Christ. We built buildings and created programs and argued about doctrine. But we stopped doing what he actually did."

"Some of us stopped," Kayla said gently. "But not all of us."

"I stopped. I've been stopping for years." Tom looked at her. "Do you know how many hospital visits I've done where I was just going through the motions? How many times I prayed for someone instead of actually helping them? How many homeless people I've driven past without stopping?"

"You stopped for Youssef."

"Only after a lot of resistance. After being forced to. And even then, I gave grudgingly at first." Tom shook his head. "I've been a pastor for years, Kayla. Years of ministry. And I just now learned what it actually means."

"Then you learned." Kayla's voice was firm. "That's what matters. You went to Jerusalem looking for answers, and you found them. Now you get to do something about it."

Tom wanted to believe her. But the significance of his failure pressed down on him like a physical weight.

"Sheerah wrote that scroll to preserve not just the words of Jesus but how those words stirred people to act. She ended it by asking whoever reads it to carry forward the love she and all the apostles shared—radical love that got them accused of turning the world upside down."

Tom stopped to catch his breath. "She wrote it for someone who fed the hungry because hunger demanded it. Who welcomed strangers because love required it. I'm not that person, Kayla. I'm the person she was warning about. The one who worships but doesn't follow."

"You *were* that person," Kayla corrected. "Past tense. But you're not anymore."

"How do you know?"

"Because you helped Youssef. Because you chose him over the holy sites. Because you used your privilege to help him when he was about to be arrested. Because you worked with him in that filthy pound." Kayla turned to face him fully. "Tom, you passed the test. Youssef's grandmother wouldn't have given you the scroll if you hadn't. You lived the parable. Maybe not perfectly, maybe not at first, but you did it."

Tom thought about that. About the week in Jerusalem. About each encounter with Youssef—the water, the food, the clothes, the community, the sick care, the intervention with police, the makeshift dog shelter.

I was hungry and you gave me food.
I was thirsty and you gave me drink.
I was a stranger and you welcomed me.
I was naked and you clothed me.
I was sick and you visited me.
I was in prison and you came to me.

All six. He'd done all six. Not because he was trying to pass a test. Not because he was trying to be righteous. But because Youssef needed help, and Tom had helped.

"That's what Sheerah meant," Tom said slowly. "Living it without knowing it. As a natural response to need."

"Exactly."

"But I only learned that because of Youssef. Because he kept showing up and forcing me to choose. If he hadn't..." Tom trailed off.

"If he hadn't, you wouldn't have the scroll," Kayla finished. "But he did. And you do. And now you get to share what you learned."

Tom looked at her. "Share it how?"

"That's what we need to figure out." Kayla stood and extended her hand. "Come on. Dr. Feldman is probably wondering if we're okay. And we need to talk about what comes next."

Tom took her hand and let her pull him up. His legs felt unsteady, his breathing labored. But Kayla's grip was firm, and something in her certainty gave him strength.

They walked back into the Divinity School together.

<hr>

DR. FELDMAN WAS STILL IN HER OFFICE, MAKING CAREFUL notes on the translation. She looked up when they entered.

"Better?" she asked Tom.

"Getting there." Tom sat down, and Kayla took the seat beside him. "Dr. Feldman, what do we do with this? The scroll, the translation. What happens now?"

Dr. Feldman set down her pen. "That depends on what you want to happen. If you want to keep this private, you can. It's yours. No one else has to know it exists."

"But that's not what Sheerah intended," Kayla said. "She wrote it to be shared. To remind people what following Jesus actually means."

"True." Dr. Feldman looked at them both. "But if you share this, if you go public with it, you need to understand what you're getting into. This scroll will challenge everything the church has become. Everything the institutional church values. It will threaten power structures, theological positions, and entire denominations."

"Good," Tom said.

Dr. Feldman raised her eyebrows. "You say that now. But when you're facing opposition from church leaders, from denominational authorities, from people who think you're trying to destroy Christianity... will you still think it's good?"

Tom thought about Sheerah. A woman with no standing, who'd written words that would wait two thousand years to be heard. Taking a risk that most people wouldn't even consider.

"Yes," he said. "I'll still think it's good."

"Then you need to authenticate it first," Dr. Feldman said. "Before you share it publicly, you need proof that it's genuine. Otherwise, people will dismiss it as a forgery or a hoax."

"How do we authenticate it?"

"Carbon dating on the parchment. Analysis of the ink. Comparison of the script to other first-century documents. It will take time and money, but it can be done." Dr. Feldman looked at Tom seriously. "I can help with that. I have colleagues who specialize in this kind of authentication. But you need to be prepared—the process will take weeks, maybe months."

Tom felt his chest tighten. "I don't have months."

The words hung in the air. Dr. Feldman's expression shifted to one of understanding.

"The cancer," she said gently. "Kayla mentioned you were sick."

"Six months. Probably less. I'm already..." Tom gestured vaguely at himself. "I'm already running out of time."

Dr. Feldman was quiet for a moment. "We'll work fast. I'll call in favors and expedite the testing. But Reverend McGarvey, you need to understand—even if the scroll is authenticated tomorrow, sharing it won't be quick or easy. The church doesn't change overnight. And from what Sheerah wrote, the church doesn't particularly want to change at all."

"So what do I do?" Tom heard the frustration in his voice. "I have this scroll, this message, and only months to share it. How do I make that matter?"

"You start small," Kayla said. "You start with Great Witness. You preach this message. You show people the scroll. You challenge them to actually follow Jesus instead of just worshiping him."

"And if they reject it?"

"Then you try the next church. And the next. And you write about it. You tell everyone who will listen." Kayla's voice was fierce now. "Tom, you're dying. You don't have time to be careful or diplomatic or worried about offending people. But you have time to tell the truth."

Dr. Feldman smiled. "I like her. She's right, you know. You have nothing to lose. Use that."

Tom looked at the scroll on Dr. Feldman's desk. Ancient parchment with words that might change everything. Or might change nothing. He didn't know which.

But he knew he had to try.

"Okay," he said. "Let's authenticate it. Let's see what happens."

"Good." Dr. Feldman picked up the scroll carefully. "I'll start the process first thing tomorrow. I'll need to keep the scroll here for testing. Is that alright?"

Tom's instinct was to say no. To grab the scroll and protect it. But that instinct was the old Tom again. The one who couldn't let go, couldn't trust, and couldn't accept help.

The new Tom replied, "Yes. Keep it as long as you need to. Just... take care of it."

"I will treat it like the treasure it is," Dr. Feldman promised. "And I'll make sure my colleague in the archaeology department gets me an airtight artifact container to keep it in. It needs to be preserved. This parchment is beyond fragile."

"I appreciate that," Tom said.

"I'll call you as soon as I have results."

"That's great. But I need to do one thing before we leave. I need to write it down myself. The words. Her words. I need to see them in my own handwriting. May I borrow your pen?"

Dr. Feldman flipped to a clean sheet of paper and smiled, understanding why he needed to do this. "Here," she said, handing Tom her pen. "Have a go at it."

<hr>

The Drive Home
8:30 p.m.

Tom and Kayla left Chicago well after dinnertime, the city lights receding behind them as they headed south. The briefcase sat between them, the scroll swapped out with two sheets of yellow-lined paper filled with Sheerah's words in Tom's handwriting.

"Are you okay?" Kayla asked after they'd been driving for twenty minutes.

"Honestly? I don't know." Tom kept his eyes on the road. "I feel like I just looked at a reflection and didn't recognize myself."

"What do you mean?"

"For years—my entire ministry—I thought I was doing it right. I thought I was being faithful. Preaching sermons, leading worship... running programs. I thought that was what being a pastor meant." Tom paused. "But Sheerah's words... they showed me what I've been missing. What I've been avoiding. I've been worshiping Christ but not following Jesus."

"You're following him now."

"Am I? Or am I just realizing how far behind I've fallen?" Tom's grip tightened on the steering wheel. "Sheerah feared that the church would forget to feed the hungry. That we'd build buildings instead of helping people. That we'd argue about doctrine instead of practicing love. And she was right. We did all of it. I did all of it."

"Then change it," Kayla said simply. "You can't undo the past. But you can change the future. That's what Sheerah's words can do. They remind people what matters. To call them back to following Jesus instead of just worshiping him."

Tom thought about Great Witness. About declining attendance and financial struggles, and the slow death. "What if they don't want to hear it?"

"Then we find people who do." Kayla's voice was steady. "Tom, the church is starting to die because we've forgotten how to live. We've turned following Jesus into a Sunday morning routine. We pray for the hungry but don't feed them. We sing about love but don't practice it. We talk about being radical disciples while living comfortable, safe lives."

"You sound like Sheerah."

"I hope so. She understood something we've forgotten. That the kingdom of God is here, now, in our actions. Not someday in heaven. Not in our prayers and worship. But in how we treat the least of these."

Tom drove in silence for a few miles, processing everything. The highway stretched out ahead of them, mostly empty now. Farmland on either side, growing darker and quieter.

"I'm scared," Tom admitted finally.

"Of dying?"

"Of wasting whatever time I have left. Of having this scroll, this message, and not knowing how to share it. Of trying to change the church and failing."

"You might fail," Kayla said. "Probably will, actually. The church has been ignoring this message for two thousand years. We're not going to fix that in a few months."

"Then why try?"

"Because Sheerah tried. Because Youssef tried. Because Jesus tried. And because even if we fail, even if nobody listens, at least we'll have told the truth." Kayla looked at him. "Besides, maybe failure isn't the point. Maybe the point is just faithfulness. Being faithful to the message, whether it changes anything or not."

Tom thought about that. About Sheerah writing words that would wait two thousand years. About the grandmother protecting the scroll her whole life. About Youssef living the kingdom of God in an abandoned building with fourteen other outcasts.

They hadn't succeeded in changing the world. But they'd been faithful.

Maybe that was enough.

"When I get home," Tom said slowly, "I'm going to preach on this. Maybe not on the scroll, but I will preach on Sheerah's words, on what I learned in Jerusalem. I'm going to challenge Great Witness to actually follow Jesus instead of just showing up on Sundays."

"And if they don't like it?"

"Then I'll have been faithful." Tom glanced at Kayla. "Will you help me? I can't do this alone."

"Of course I'll help you. That's what partners do."

"Partners." Tom liked the sound of that. "Not mentor and student?"

"Not anymore. We're in this together now. Partners in whatever comes next."

They drove the rest of the way in comfortable silence, each lost in their own thoughts. Tom's mind was already working on the sermon he would preach. The words he would use. The challenge he would issue.

Love is a verb meant to be lived. And shared.

That's what Sheerah had called for. That's what the earliest Christians had done. And maybe, just maybe, that's what Tom could do in whatever time he had left.

Not alone. But with Kayla. With Dr. Feldman. With whoever else would join them in this impossible mission.

They pulled into Stoneford just after eleven. After Kayla left, Tom sat in his den. But his house didn't feel quite as empty anymore. Because now he had a purpose. Now he had a message. Now he had a mission.

And he had only months to see it through.

Tom pulled out his journal and began to write.

Today I learned what was written on the scroll. Today I heard Sheerah's words. Words she wrote two thousand years ago. Her fears were a warning that the church would forget what matters. That we would worship instead of follow. That we would pray instead of act.

She was right. About all of it.

And I had a look in the mirror and saw myself clearly for the first time. I saw that I've been one of the goats pretending to be a sheep. Praying for the hungry but not feeding them. Singing about love but not practicing it. Worshipping Jesus but not following him.

It was devastating. It still is.

But Kayla reminded me that I passed the test. That I lived the parable in Jerusalem, even if I didn't understand what I was doing. That I'm not the person I was two weeks ago.

She's right. I'm not.

I'm someone who knows the truth now. Someone who has Sheerah's words. Someone who has less than six months to share this message before I die.

So that's what I'm going to do. I'm going to preach on Sheerah's words. I'm going to challenge Great Witness to actually follow Jesus. I'm going to turn my remaining time into something that matters.

I'll probably fail. The church has been ignoring this message for two thousand years. But at least I'll have tried. At least I'll have been faithful.

Sheerah wrote her scroll as a woman whose voice would be forgotten. As a witness who wouldn't be remembered. But she wrote it anyway, because the truth mattered more than who spoke it.

I understand that now. I understand what it means to speak truth even when no one wants to hear it. To be faithful even when success seems impossible.

Tomorrow I start working on the sermon. Tomorrow, Kayla and I start planning how to share this message.

Tomorrow, the real work begins.

But tonight, I just feel grateful. Grateful to Sheerah for her courage. Grateful to Youssef for his teaching. Grateful to Kayla for her partnership. Grateful to Dr. Feldman for her help.

And grateful for whatever time I have left to do something that matters.

Tom closed the journal and sat in the darkness of his den for a long time. Tomorrow would bring new challenges, new opposition, and new struggles.

But tonight, he had a purpose. He had a mission. He had Sheerah's words echoing in his mind.

We turned the world upside down not by our beliefs but by how we loved. If you carry anything forward carry this.

Tom smiled in the darkness.

"Let's give it a try," he whispered.

And somewhere in the ancient past, maybe Sheerah smiled too.

CHAPTER THIRTEEN

Monday, June 9, 1975
Tom's Kitchen
7:30 a.m.

Tom sat at his kitchen table, his sermon notes spread before him like a battle plan. The yellow legal pad was covered in crossed-out lines, circled phrases, and arrows connecting thoughts. In the center, underlined three times: Matthew 25:31-46. The Parable of the Sheep and the Goats.

It had been nearly two weeks since Chicago, since hearing Sheerah's words. Nearly two weeks of waiting for Dr. Feldman to authenticate the scroll.

And in those two weeks, Tom had lost six more pounds he couldn't afford to lose.

He looked down at his hands resting on the table. The veins stood out prominently now, the skin loose. He rubbed his ring finger, a habit since his wife divorced him. He imagined how loose his wedding band would be now.

The phone rang. Tom let it ring three times before answering, using those seconds to steady his voice, to hide the rasp that had developed in his chest. "Hello?"

"Tom! It's Susan. Susan Feldman."

Tom sat up straighter. "Dr. Feldman. Do you have news?"

"I do. And it's good news. The carbon dating came back this morning." She paused, and Tom could hear the smile in her voice. "Tom, the preliminary results are as definitive as I've ever seen. The parchment is authentic. Early first century, somewhere between 20 and 50 CE. The ink analysis confirms it's carbon-based, consistent with the same timeframe. I'm told they were able to narrow the dating of the ink to 30 to 35 CE."

"That's..." Tom stopped to catch his breath.

"And my colleague in paleography examined the script. It's genuine Galilean Aramaic, written by someone with limited formal education."

Tom closed his eyes. "So, it's real."

"It's real. What you have is a first-century document written by someone who likely heard Jesus teach. Tom, do you understand what this means? This is the earliest Christian document in existence. Nothing even comes close."

"How long until you have the full authentication report?"

"Another week, maybe two. They're being extremely thorough. But Tom, these preliminary results are solid. You can move forward with confidence. This is legitimate."

After they hung up, Tom sat in the silence of his kitchen. The scroll was real. Sheerah was real. Everything Youssef had told him was true.

Now he just had to convince Great Witness Community Church to care.

Tuesday, June 10, 1975
Church Office
2:30 p.m.

KAYLA LOOKED UP FROM HER DESK WHEN SHE HEARD THE outer office door open. She'd been working on the bulletin for Sunday's service—the last bulletin she'd prepare under the old format. Next week, there would be no service. Just community service.

If Tom lived that long.

Randolph Wescott walked into the office without knocking. He had been voted in as the new board president after Howard Beckner abruptly resigned a little more than a week ago.

"Miss Andersen. Is Reverend McGarvey available?"

"He's at home today, Mr. Wescott. Not feeling well."

"I see." Wescott's expression suggested he saw quite a lot. "Perhaps you can help me, then. Reverend McGarvey, on his own, combined this week's services into one large service. Can you explain that?"

"I'm afraid I can't." She could, but Kayla wasn't about to violate Tom's trust. "That was Tom's decision. But I'm sure he had his reasons."

"*Tom's* decision? I'm sure you're referring to *Reverend* McGarvey. It was Reverend McGarvey's decision. But it wasn't his decision to make. He needs to understand something. As do you, Miss Andersen." Wescott stepped closer to Kayla. "Mr. Beckner is no longer involved with the board, so *Reverend* McGarvey now answers to me. And I'll report to the rest of the board what they need to know."

"I understand."

"Another thing. Have I heard correctly that Reverend McGarvey is going to preach on a passage that's not in the lectionary?"

Kayla kept her voice neutral. "Tom... Reverend McGarvey... felt called to preach on Matthew 25. The Parable of the Sheep and Goats."

"I'm familiar with the passage." Wescott's tone suggested he was familiar with much more than that. "I'm also hearing rumors about his plans for the following Sunday. Something about canceling the service entirely?"

"Not canceling. Redirecting. Tom believes—"

"I know what Reverend McGarvey believes." Wescott looked around the office. "Miss Andersen, you're young. You're almost through with your seminary education. So let me share something I've learned in my years of church leadership. Change can be good. But radical change destroys churches. It divides congregations. It drives away the faithful members who've supported this church for decades."

"Or maybe it reminds people what the church is supposed to be about."

Wescott's eyes narrowed. "I understand Reverend McGarvey has been something of a mentor to you. That's admirable. But he's dying. He'll be gone in a few months. But this church will still be here. And those of us who remain will have to deal with the damage he causes."

Kayla felt her jaw tighten. "Tom isn't causing damage. He's trying to save—"

"That's what every revolutionary thinks." Wescott straightened. "Tell Reverend McGarvey I'll be calling on him.

Tomorrow morning. Ten o'clock. I trust he'll be well enough to receive visitors?"

"I'll let him know."

After Wescott left, Kayla sat very still, her hands clenched on her desk. She knew that tone. That dismissive, patronizing tone that men like Wescott used when they wanted you to know your place.

She picked up the phone and dialed Tom's number.

Wednesday, June 11, 1975
Tom's House
10:00 a.m.

TOM WAS DRESSED AND WAITING WHEN WESCOTT AR-rived at ten. He had taken extra medication that morning, determined not to show weakness. But he couldn't hide the weight loss or the shadows under his eyes.

They sat in Tom's den. Tom behind his desk, Wescott in the chair facing him. Like a meeting between a boss and an employee being called on the carpet.

"Randolph. Would you like coffee?"

"No, thank you. I won't take much of your time. I know you're not well." Wescott settled into his chair, crossing his legs. "Tom, I'll be direct. I'm concerned about the direction you're taking the church. This sermon you're planning, this... community service idea."

"It's not community service. It's following the teachings of Jesus. What concerns you about it?"

"Everything concerns me about it. You're planning to preach on a passage that's not in the lectionary. You're telling people not to come to church the following Sunday. You're essentially saying that worship isn't important, that gathering as a community of believers doesn't matter."

"That's not what I'm saying at all."

"Then what are you saying?"

Tom leaned forward, ignoring the pain in his chest. "I'm saying we've forgotten what following Jesus actually means. We've turned Christianity into a Sunday morning routine. We show up, we sing, we pray, we go home. But Jesus didn't call us to show up on Sundays. He called us to feed the hungry, welcome strangers, and visit the sick. To actually do the work, not just pray about it."

"We have programs for that. The food pantry, community outreach—"

"Programs aren't enough." Tom's voice grew stronger. "Randolph, I went to Jerusalem. I met a man who's been living Matthew 25 every single day. Not because he's religious. Not because he's trying to earn salvation. But because people need help. That's what Jesus taught. That's what the early church practiced. And we've lost it."

Wescott was quiet for a moment. "I heard you brought something back from Jerusalem. Some kind of religious artifact?"

Tom's stomach tightened. "Where did you hear that?"

"We're a small church, Tom. People talk. Especially when their pastor starts acting erratically." Wescott leaned forward. "Is it real? This artifact or whatever it is?"

"It's with archeologists now. I've been told it looks promising."

"What are you trying to say?"

Tom held Wescott's gaze. "What I'm trying to say is exactly what I've been trying to tell you. That we've lost our way. That we've turned following Jesus into worshiping Christ. That we've replaced action with prayer and love with rules."

"That's heresy."

"That's history." Tom stopped, unsure how much he wanted Wescott to know. "I believe... I firmly believe that there are accounts of those who heard Jesus teach that weren't included in the canon of scripture. Who saw what the early church was supposed to be before we turned it into an institution."

Wescott stood. "Tom, I'm going to be very clear with you. I... I mean, the board has serious concerns about your fitness to lead this church. Your judgment has been questionable since you returned from your trip. This obsession with social justice, this dismissal of traditional worship, this reliance on some unverified ancient relic—"

"You needn't be concerned with its authenticity. I know it's real. And I know what I need to do."

"—it's starting to cause division in the congregation," Wescott finished. "People are concerned. Especially those who've financially supported this church for decades. We can't afford to lose faithful members."

"Then let them leave." Tom stood as well, his legs unsteady but his voice firm. "If they're more concerned about comfortable pews than hungry people, they've already left. They just don't know it yet."

Wescott's face shifted, veins showing in his forehead. "You're making a terrible mistake, Tom. And you're dragging that young woman down with you. Miss Andersen has a promising future in ministry. But if she continues following your radical agenda, she'll destroy her career before it starts."

"Kayla makes her own decisions."

"Does she? Or is she simply following a dying man's delusions?" Wescott moved toward the door, then stopped. "Tom, I'm asking you, as a brother in Christ, as someone who's known you since you got here, don't preach this sermon. Don't cancel next Sunday's service." His voice softened. "Step back. Let Kayla lead worship. Take the time you have left to rest, to heal your relationships, and to make peace with God."

"I am at peace with God, Randolph. For the first time in years, I actually am."

"Then you're deceiving yourself." Wescott opened the door. "The board will be watching on Sunday. And I promise you, we will do whatever is necessary to protect this church from damage."

After Wescott left, Tom sat down heavily in his chair. His hands were shaking. His chest ached. He fumbled for his medication and took another pill.

The phone rang. Patricia's voice was warm when he answered.

"Tom? I've been thinking about you. How are you holding up?"

"Just had a visit from the new board president. He's threatened to remove me if I preach what I plan on Sunday."

"Can he do that?"

"He can try. The board has that authority if they claim I'm unfit for ministry."

"And are you? Fit, I mean?"

Tom looked at his hands, still shaking. At the medication bottles lined up on his desk. At his reflection in the window. Gaunt, exhausted, dying.

"Honestly? No. I'm not fit. I can barely make it through the day. But Patricia, I have to do this. I have to preach this sermon. If I don't, if I back down now, then everything that happened in Jerusalem was for nothing."

"Then preach it. But Tom, promise me something. Promise me you'll take care of yourself. Don't kill yourself trying to save a church that might not want to be saved."

After they hung up, Tom returned to his sermon notes. The words swam on the page, but he forced himself to focus. To write. To prepare.

Sunday was four days away.

Thursday, June 12, 1975
Great Witness Community Church
7:45 p.m.

KAYLA WAS LOCKING UP THE CHURCH OFFICE WHEN SHE heard voices from the sanctuary. She walked quietly down the hallway and stood at the door, listening.

Inside, Randolph Wescott sat in the front pew with the other board members. Kayla recognized them: Harold Peterson, the retired banker, and Carolyn Foster, a longtime Sunday school teacher. They sat between Eleanor Pritchard and Bob Matthews. Frank Delacroix, who owned the largest farm in the county, sat in the pew behind them.

"—can't let him do this," Peterson was saying. "My family has been members of this church for three generations. We don't need some dying pastor telling us we've been doing Christianity wrong."

"He's not saying that," Eleanor protested weakly.

"That's exactly what he's saying." Wescott's voice was measured, controlled. "He's claiming that traditional worship is meaningless. That our programs aren't enough. That we need to abandon everything we've built and start over with some radical social gospel agenda."

"Maybe he has a point," Eleanor tried again. "Jesus did say to feed the hungry—"

"We feed the hungry. We have a food pantry. We support missions." Wescott stood. "What Tom is proposing isn't ministry. It's political activism dressed up as theology. And it will destroy this church."

"So what do we do?" Bob asked.

"We wait until next Sunday. We listen to this sermon. And then we make a decision about Reverend Tom McGarvey's fitness to continue in ministry."

"And the girl?" Peterson asked. "The seminary student?"

"Miss Andersen will be returning to her seminary." Wescott's voice hushed, as if he might not want anyone else, or even God, to hear it. "Effective immediately after next Sunday's service."

Kayla felt her stomach drop.

"We can't do that," Eleanor said. "Just... dismiss her?"

"We can end her externship," Wescott answered. "We'll frame it as a mutual decision that our theological differences make it impossible to continue the relationship. We'll offer her a positive reference for another placement. But she can't stay here. Not if she's supporting Tom's agenda."

"What if Tom refuses to resign?" Frank asked.

Wescott was quiet for a moment. "Then we'll remove him. For his own good, of course. His health is clearly affecting his judgment. It would be cruel to let him continue when he's obviously not capable of fulfilling his duties."

Kayla backed away from the door quietly. Her heart was pounding. They were planning to get rid of her. To remove

Tom. And they thought they were doing it for the good of the church.

She got to her car and sat in the fading daylight, trying to breathe. She should warn Tom. Should tell him what she'd heard.

But would it change anything? Would he back down?

No. She knew he wouldn't. Tom was going to preach that sermon even if it cost him everything.

The question was, was she willing to stand with him?

Friday, June 13, 1975
Tom's House
3:00 p.m.

TOM WOKE FROM A NAP TO FIND KAYLA SITTING IN HIS den, reading his sermon notes.

"How long have you been here?" His voice was rough.

"About twenty minutes. I used my key. You didn't answer when I knocked." Tom had given her the key just in case... he didn't answer his phone one day.

She set down the legal pad. "Tom, we need to talk."

He pulled himself upright on the couch, trying to shake off the fog. "What's wrong?"

Kayla told him about the conversation she'd overheard. About the board's plans to remove her. About their intention to declare Tom too sick to continue as pastor.

When she finished, Tom was quiet for a long time.

"I'm sorry," he said finally. "This is my fault. If I'd just—"

"Don't." Kayla's voice was sharp. "Don't apologize for doing the right thing. Don't apologize for preaching the truth.

Don't apologize for trying to wake up a church that's been asleep for decades."

"But your career—"

"My career doesn't matter. Not compared to this. Not compared to what you're trying to do." She moved to sit beside him. "Tom, I've spent the last three years learning theology, studying Greek and Hebrew, and memorizing systematic doctrine. And you know what I've realized? None of it matters if we're not actually living what Jesus taught. You're the first person who's shown me what that looks like."

"I showed you a homeless man in Jerusalem. And a dog pound."

"You showed me what love looks like when it's a verb. You showed me what faith looks like when it's action instead of belief. You showed me what following Jesus actually means." Kayla's eyes were fierce. "So no, I'm not backing down. I'm not leaving. And I'm standing with you on Sunday, no matter what happens."

Tom felt tears burn behind his eyes. "They could destroy you."

"Maybe. Or maybe we'll start something that can't be destroyed. Something that matters more than our careers or our reputations or our comfort." She stood. "Your sermon. Is it finished?"

"Almost."

"Finish it. I'll handle everything else. The bulletin, the arrangements for next Sunday's community service, and the phone calls. You focus on the sermon."

"Kayla—"

"Partners, remember? That's what we said. So let me be your partner. Let me carry some of this weight."

After she left, Tom returned to his desk. His hands were steadier now. His breathing easier. Not because his body was healing; it wasn't. But because he wasn't alone anymore.

He picked up his pen and continued writing.

———

Saturday, June 14, 1975
Tom's Den
11:00 p.m.

TOM READ THROUGH THE SERMON ONE FINAL TIME. EIGHT pages, single-spaced. Maybe twenty minutes if he could make it that long without his breathing giving out.

He thought about Sheerah, writing her scroll two thousand years ago. Knowing she might never be heard. Knowing powerful people would resist her message. Writing it anyway, because the truth mattered more than the reception.

He thought about Youssef, living Matthew 25 in the streets of Jerusalem. Not seeking recognition or reward. Just helping those who needed help.

He thought about Kayla, risking her entire future to stand beside a dying pastor nobody would remember in six months.

The phone rang. Dr. Feldman.

"Tom, I wanted to call before tomorrow. To tell you that the full authentication report will be ready next week. But I also wanted to tell you..." She paused. "I've spent thirty years studying ancient texts. And in all that time, I've never encountered anything like Sheerah's scroll. The clarity, the urgency, the way she captures both her faith and her fears. Tom, this document is going to change how we understand early Christianity."

"If anyone listens."

"They'll listen. Maybe not at first. Maybe not the people you most want to reach. But eventually, they'll listen. Truth has a way of outlasting opposition."

After hanging up, Tom placed his sermon in a folder. Tomorrow morning, he would stand in that pulpit one last time. Would challenge his congregation to actually follow Jesus instead of just worshiping him. Would invite them to live Matthew 25 instead of just reading it.

Would some walk out? Would some demand his removal? Would some call it heresy?

Maybe. But maybe... just maybe one or two would hear it. Would understand. Would change.

That would be enough.

Tom took his evening medication and went to bed early. He needed rest. Needed strength. Tomorrow was going to be the most important Sunday of his life.

His last sermon. He was going to make it count.

Sunday, June 15, 1975
Tom's House
7:30 a.m.

TOM STOOD IN FRONT OF HIS BATHROOM MIRROR, TRYING to knot his tie. His hands shook so badly he gave up after the third attempt. He settled for leaving his collar open, covering it with his best suit jacket, which now hung on him like a thrift store bargain.

The face staring back at him was barely recognizable. Hollowed cheeks. Dark circles under his eyes. Skin with a grayish pallor. He looked like a man who should be in a hospital bed, not a pulpit.

Maybe Wescott was right. Maybe he wasn't fit for ministry anymore.

Tom splashed cold water on his face and dried it with a towel. Then he picked up his sermon folder and walked to the kitchen, where Kayla was waiting.

She'd let herself in with her key, made coffee, and arranged his medication on the table beside a glass of water.

"You look terrible," she said.

"Thank you."

"I mean it, Tom. Are you sure you can do this?"

He sat down heavily, took his medications, and drank the coffee she'd poured. "I have to."

"You don't have to. We could reschedule. Give you another week to rest."

"There is no other week, Kayla. We both know that." He looked at her. "Did you sleep?"

"Not much. Did you?"

"Some."

They sat in silence for a few minutes, drinking coffee, not talking about what was coming.

Finally, Kayla stood. "We should go. People will start arriving soon."

Tom picked up his sermon folder. His hand was steady now. Not because his body was stronger. But because his purpose was clear.

They drove to the church together in Kayla's Plymouth Valiant. The parking lot was already half full.

Inside, the sanctuary was buzzing with conversation. Tom could feel the tension as soon as he walked through the door. People stopped talking when they saw him. Eyes followed him as he walked down the side aisle toward his small office behind the sanctuary.

Randolph Wescott was standing near the front pew, surrounded by the other board members. His expression was measured. A man preparing to do what he thought needed to be done in the best interests of the church.

Eleanor Pritchard caught Tom's eye and gave him a small, sad smile. At least someone still saw him as human.

In the office, Tom hung up his jacket and tried one more time to fix his tie. His hands shook worse now. Kayla reached over and tied it for him without a word.

"Thank you."

"Don't thank me yet. Thank me after you survive this." She straightened his collar. "Tom, no matter what happens out there, I want you to know... you've changed my life. You've shown me what ministry is supposed to be. And I'm grateful."

"I haven't done anything."

"You've done everything." She kissed his cheek and wiped off the smudge of her lipstick. "Now go preach."

Great Witness Community Church Sanctuary
10:00 a.m.

TOM STOOD AT THE DOOR TO THE SANCTUARY, LISTENING to the organ prelude. Kayla had helped Tom choose the hymns: "Love Divine, All Loves Excelling" for the opening and "Forth in Thy Name, O Lord, I Go" for the closing. Two of the most traditional hymns sung in the church. Tom wanted to honor tradition for this last service.

The sanctuary was packed. Tom couldn't remember the last time they'd had this many people. Were they here to support him? Or to witness his downfall?

He stepped into the center aisle, walking slowly toward the front, feeling every eye on him. The weight of their judgment, expectations, and fear pressed down.

He climbed the three steps to the pulpit and looked out at the congregation. Wescott in the second pew, arms crossed. Helen Morrison, who had called this week with her concerns. Mr. and Mrs. Johnson, with whom he had different conversations throughout the week.

In the back row, he saw a group of young people he didn't recognize. College-aged, most with long hair and wearing peace buttons. They appeared uncomfortable, but they were present, nonetheless.

The row opposite them had men, mostly in their twenties, a few in their early thirties. All were wearing tattered olive drab field jackets.

Kayla sat in the front pew, her expression fierce with loyalty. Tom looked at her and motioned with his eyes to the group in the back. Kayla nodded with a smile. She'd started it—this was the beginning of the veteran's project he wanted to get up and running.

Tom gripped the edges of the pulpit. Felt the wood solid under his hands. Took a breath that rattled in his chest.

"Please stand for the opening hymn," he said.

His voice was weak, but it carried.

The organ began to play.

Tom prepared to preach the most important sermon of his life.

CHAPTER
FOURTEEN

The organ's final notes faded. The congregation settled into their pews. Tom stood at the pulpit, his hands gripping the wooden edges to keep them steady. He looked out at the faces before him. Some curious, some concerned, some already cynical about whatever he might say.

Kayla sat in the front pew this morning, her expression fierce and loyal. Ready.

Tom took a breath that rattled in his chest. Then he began.

"Before I share with you what I believe God has placed on my heart to share today, I want to address some rumors that have been circulating." His voice was weak at first, but it carried. "Yes, I have terminal cancer. The doctors have given me six months, probably less. I'm grateful for the time I have left."

A ripple of murmurs moved through the sanctuary. Some tapped others on the shoulder, confirming what they'd just heard. Some bowed their heads in prayer.

"Yes, I recently returned home from a tour of the Holy Land. And yes, something happened there that changed me.

Changed how I see my faith. Changed how I understand what it means to follow Jesus."

More murmuring. Wescott shifted in his pew, arms still crossed. Other board members gently elbowed each other. Tom looked away from them.

"And yes, I believe changes need to happen in this church. Not because I think we're bad people. But because I think we've forgotten what we're supposed to be."

Tom paused, letting the words settle. Then he asked the question that would begin everything.

"How many of you consider yourselves Christians?"

Nearly every hand went up. A few people looked confused by the question.

"That's what I thought. That's what I would have said before I left for the Holy Land." Tom gripped the pulpit tighter. "But I want to ask you something else. Have you ever really considered what it means to be a Christian? Not the creeds we recite. Not the promises we made when we joined the church. And certainly not what we learned in Sunday school as children. But as adults, with our full understanding, what does it actually mean to be a Christian?"

He let the silence stretch. Let them think about it. Then he dropped the bomb.

"Because I've come to realize something. My identity is no longer that of a Christian."

Gasps erupted throughout the sanctuary. Someone in the back stood up. Wescott leaned forward, his face darkening.

Tom raised his hand, asking for quiet. "Let me explain. I now see myself as a follower of Jesus. And there's a difference. A crucial difference that we've lost over the centuries."

"This is heresy," Harold Peterson called out from the second-row pew.

"Is it?" Tom's voice grew stronger. "Or is it what we were always supposed to be? Christianity, as it exists today in too many places, emphasizes worshiping Christ more than following the teachings of Jesus. We've turned a movement into a monument. We've replaced action with adoration. We've made Jesus into someone to be revered rather than someone to be followed."

More people shifted uncomfortably. Some whispered to their neighbors. A few heads that nodded in agreement didn't escape Tom's eyes.

"What if we stopped concerning ourselves with being Christians... with having the right beliefs, reciting the right creeds, defending the right doctrines... and focused instead on actually doing what Jesus asked his followers to do? The church would become what it was always meant to be."

Tom could see he was losing some of them. But he had to continue. Had to push through.

"Now that I've got your attention, let me ask you another question. What is love?"

The congregation stared at him, uncertain where he was going. He waited a full ten seconds, literally counting down in his head, letting the silence do the work.

"We use that word constantly. I love my wife—" Tom stopped and corrected himself. "I loved my wife. I love chocolate cake. I love watching the Cubs play. We love our children. We love God. But what does that word actually mean?"

He leaned forward. "Here's what I've learned. Love is more than a feeling. When we say we love someone because of how they make us feel, is that really love? Or is that something else? Something more... selfish?"

Tom saw a few more people nodding, following his logic.

"Let me put it this way. We say we love a good steak, right?" A few chuckles rippled through the crowd. "But we love the steak because of how it tastes, how it makes us feel when we eat it. Not because we actually love the cow. Because if we really loved that steak, if we truly, deeply loved it, we wouldn't kill it. We wouldn't butcher it, slice it up, season it, and cook it on the grill. That's not love!"

More nervous laughter. But Tom could see them getting it.

"The world doesn't need steak love. It doesn't need the kind of love that's all about how something makes us feel. The world needs people-love. The kind of love that's so radical, so reckless, so completely upside down that it risks everything. The kind of love that's a verb, not just a feeling."

Tom paused to catch his breath. His chest was tight, but he pushed on.

"Jesus lived that kind of love. He taught that kind of love. And he asked those who claim to follow him to share that kind of love. Not just feel it. Not just pray about it. But do it."

He opened his Bible to Matthew 25.

"Most of you know this parable. The Parable of the Sheep and the Goats. But I want us to hear it differently today. Not as a story about the future. But as a mirror showing us who we are right now."

Tom read the passage slowly, letting each requirement sink in. Hungry. Thirsty. Stranger. Naked. Sick. Imprisoned.

When he finished, he set down the Bible.

"In Jerusalem, I met a man. His name is Youssef. He's homeless. Lives in an abandoned building with fourteen other people. And he showed me what it means to actually live this parable. Not preach about it. Not organize programs about it. But live it. Every single day."

Tom could feel the tension building in the sanctuary.

"And it made me realize something painful. I've been a pastor for years. More than ten years of ministry now. And I've been worshiping Christ while ignoring Jesus. I've been praying for the hungry instead of feeding them. I've been organizing mission trips instead of helping the people right here in Stoneford who need help. I've been one of the goats pretending to be a sheep."

"Pastor McGarvey—" Wescott stood up, his expression dark. "I think you need to—"

"Please, Randolph. Let me finish." Tom's voice was firm. "I need to ask us some hard questions. And I need us to be honest about the answers."

He took a breath and began asking the questions that had been burning in his heart since Chicago. The questions that Sheerah had asked two thousand years ago.

"Are we, as a church, speaking more about Jesus or living like him?"

Silence.

"Are we more focused on honoring Jesus with our beautiful buildings or opening our doors to the hungry people who walk past them every day?"

A man in the middle section stood up and walked out. Then another one.

Tom continued.

"Are we more focused on judging others than we are on seeking justice for the lost, the last, the least, and the lonely?"

More people stood. Wescott was among them now, his face red with barely contained anger.

"Are we more willing to debate our beliefs and doctrines than we are to remember what Jesus actually did?"

"This is unconscionable!" Peterson called out. "We don't have to sit here and be insulted!"

But Tom kept going, his voice growing stronger even as his body grew weaker.

"Do we prioritize prayer over action? Rules over love? Are we known by our love or by our boundaries? Do we build walls to protect ourselves from those who suffer? Do we listen to preachers instead of serving others?"

Half the congregation was standing now. Some heading for the doors. Some frozen in place, conflicted.

Tom's vision started to blur, but he pressed on.

"Jesus's message... his message of radical love, justice, mercy, hospitality, and forgiveness... was meant for those who have nothing. For the oppressed. For the suffering. But we've hijacked it. We, the comfortable and powerful, have stolen his message and used it as a weapon against the very people it was meant to help."

"Enough!" Wescott shouted. He looked behind him and addressed everyone. "Reverend McGarvey is clearly not well. Tom, let's not continue—"

"No, Randolph." Tom's voice cut through the commotion. "Let me finish. Please."

Something in his tone, maybe the desperation, maybe his visible deterioration, made Wescott pause. He didn't sit down, but didn't leave either.

Tom looked at the remaining congregation. Maybe half were still seated. The veterans hadn't moved. The college kids leaned forward, listening intently. Eleanor Pritchard was crying quietly. Mr. and Mrs. Johnson sat together, holding hands.

"In Jerusalem, I learned something that broke my heart. Christianity went from what to do and how to act, to what to believe and how to think. In just 300 years, everything changed. We turned a movement of action into a religion of belief. We made knowing the right answers more important than doing the right things."

Tom could barely see now. His chest felt like it was being crushed. But he had to finish.

"Jesus didn't start a new religion. He started a rebellion. A rebellion of compassion, not prayer chains. A demonstration of mercy, not a thirst for power. He practiced forgiveness, not revenge. He created hospitality, not boundaries. He was interested in justice, not rules. He didn't want us to assess people. He asked us to love them. All of them."

He gripped the pulpit, his knuckles white.

"The kingdom Jesus spoke of was not power, but presence. Not creeds, but kindness. Not prayer, but action. Those who followed these principles after his death were accused of turning the world upside down. That's how radical this love is. And it didn't have to stop two thousand years ago."

Tom looked directly at the veterans in the back row. Then at the college students. Then at Kayla.

"We all have it in us to love so recklessly that we, too, might be accused of turning things upside down. But it won't happen in here. It can't happen inside the safe confines of this building. The church must go out into the community and do what Jesus called us to do."

Here it comes, Tom thought. The moment that would change everything or destroy everything.

"That's why we're not going to have a church service here next Sunday."

The remaining congregation erupted into chaos. Voices overlapping, questions shouted, Wescott moving toward the pulpit.

Tom raised his voice over the uproar. "We're going out into our community to do what needs to be done. We're going where people are hungry and thirsty. We're going to welcome strangers. We're going to visit the sick and the imprisoned. We're going to make this church a church of action, not just words."

"You can't do this!" Wescott had reached the steps to the pulpit. "You don't have the authority—"

"Kayla has a list." Tom spoke directly to those still listening. "She has locations, times, and places where we're needed. There are boxes of index cards at the back of the sanctuary. Each card has a location and time. Take one as you leave. Next Sunday, instead of going to church, we will be the church."

"This is madness!" Peterson shouted.

But Tom wasn't finished.

"For those concerned that this isn't real church, don't worry. We'll gather later in the day. We'll share our experiences. We'll sing. We'll pray. Mr. and Mrs. Johnson have offered us the use of their old barn for our first Vespers."

He looked at the Johnsons, who smiled with encouragement.

"Some of you may have read about it in the newspaper. We know it's been used by homeless people as a shelter. It's not in good shape. There's no air conditioning. And yes, we might encounter homeless people there. People who smell. People who are dirty. People who are uncomfortable to be around."

Tom's voice dropped to a whisper, but somehow it carried throughout the sanctuary.

"And that's okay. I've learned that Jesus is found in exactly those kinds of places, in exactly those kinds of conditions." He had to stop momentarily to clear phlegm from his throat. "And we'd all be foolish not to look for Jesus in the faces there."

He looked out at what remained of his congregation. Some were crying. Some were angry. Some were confused. But some, a precious few, looked like they understood.

We turned the world upside down not by our beliefs but by how we loved. If you carry anything forward, carry this.

Tom released his grip on the pulpit.

And collapsed.

THE FALL SEEMED TO HAPPEN IN SLOW MOTION. TOM'S knees buckled. His hand slipped from the wooden edge. His body crumpled, hitting the platform hard.

Kayla was on her feet instantly, running toward the pulpit. So were several others. One of the veterans from the back row moved with surprising speed, his medic training kicking in.

"Call an ambulance!" Kayla shouted.

"I'll do it!" Eleanor Pritchard was already moving toward the church office.

Wescott stood frozen at the base of the pulpit stairs, his anger transformed into something that looked like shock. Or maybe guilt.

The veteran, whose name was Danny something, knelt beside Tom, checking his pulse and breathing. "He's alive. But his breathing is bad. Real bad."

Kayla cradled Tom's head in her lap. His eyes fluttered open, confused.

"Did I... finish?" His voice was barely audible.

"You finished." Kayla's tears fell onto his face. "You said everything."

"Good." Tom's eyes closed again. "That's good."

The sanctuary was in flux. Emotions ranged from fear to confusion and from concern to alienation. Many moved forward. Some to help, most just to catch a glimpse of their soon-to-be-former pastor lying on the floor.

The veterans formed a protective circle. The college students stood nearby, uncertain how to help but unwilling to leave. Mr. and Mrs. Johnson stood hand in hand, their weathered farmer faces creased with concern.

And Randolph Wescott stood apart from everyone, staring at the man who'd just torn his church in half.

The ambulance arrived within minutes. EMTs rushed in with equipment, asking questions that Danny answered with practiced efficiency. They got him on a gurney and placed an oxygen tube in his nose. His right eye, where it bounced off the podium on his way to the floor, was already red and swollen.

"I'm riding with him," Kayla said. Not asking but stating.

One of the EMTs nodded. "Are you family?"

"Close enough."

They wheeled Tom out through the sanctuary, past the hard wooden pews and scattered bulletins, past the boxes of index cards that some had taken and many had ignored. Kayla looked back one last time.

Wescott was still standing there. Alone in the center aisle. Looking smaller than he had an hour ago.

In the ambulance, Tom drifted in and out of consciousness. Kayla held his hand, feeling how thin his fingers had become and how loose his skin was over the bones.

"Kayla," he whispered.

"I'm here."

"The scroll. Tell them... about Sheerah."

"I will. I promise."

"The veterans. Did you see them? They stayed."

"They stayed. A lot of people stayed, Tom. Not everyone left."

He smiled weakly. "That's enough. One or two. That's all it takes to start a revolution."

His breathing grew more labored.

The EMT adjusted the oxygen and made notes. "We're almost there," she said to Kayla. "County Memorial. Three minutes."

Tom's eyes opened again. "Patricia. Should call her. Her number's in my wallet."

The alert EMT reached into Tom's pocket and handed the wallet to Kayla. "I will," she said, wiping tears from her eyes. "I'll call her from the hospital."

"And the Johnsons. Thank them for the barn."

"Tom, stop. Save your strength."

But he kept talking, his voice growing fainter. "Sermon. How was it?"

Kayla laughed through her tears. "You want sermon feedback? Now?"

"Old habits."

"It was perfect. Terrifying and beautiful and perfect. You said everything that needed to be said."

"Some walked out."

"Some will always walk out. And walk away. But some will stay. Some did stay. And they heard you, Tom. Really heard you."

He squeezed her hand. Or tried to. His grip was weak. "Turning the world upside down."

"Turning the world upside down," Kayla repeated.

The ambulance pulled into the emergency bay. Doors opened. Voices shouting medical terminology. The gurney being pulled out, wheels locking, movement.

Kayla tried to follow, but a nurse stopped her. "Are you family?"

"No, but—"

"Then you'll need to wait in the waiting room. Someone will update you as soon as we know anything."

"Please, I'm all he has."

The nurse's expression softened. "I understand. But right now, the best thing you can do is let us work. I promise, we'll keep you informed."

And then Tom was gone, wheeled through double doors that swung shut behind him.

Kayla stood alone in the emergency room hallway, still wearing her church clothes, her hands shaking, her mind replaying the sermon.

If you carry anything forward, carry this.

She walked to the waiting room. Sat down in an uncomfortable plastic chair. And began to wait.

AN HOUR PASSED. THEN TWO. OTHER PEOPLE CAME AND went. Emergencies that were resolved, families reunited, bad news delivered.

But no one came to talk to Kayla about Tom.

She found a payphone and called Patricia in Florida. The conversation was brief and painful. Patricia promised to catch the first flight she could. Told Kayla to be strong. To have faith.

Kayla wanted to scream that faith wasn't the problem. That she had faith. What she needed was for Tom to be okay.

But he wasn't going to be okay. They both knew it.

She returned to the waiting room, finding the others who had arrived. Danny the veteran, still wearing his field jacket. Two of the college students. Eleanor Pritchard. Mr. and Mrs. Johnson.

"Any news?" Eleanor asked.

Kayla shook her head. "Not yet."

They sat together in silence. Strangers brought together by a sermon that had torn a church apart and maybe, just maybe, planted the seeds for something new.

Finally, after nearly three hours, a doctor emerged. He was young, maybe forty. His face was carefully neutral in that way doctors learn when the news isn't good.

"Are you here for Thomas McGarvey?"

They all stood. Kayla stepped forward. "I am. We are. How is he?"

The doctor gestured for them to sit. He pulled up a chair, which Kayla knew was a bad sign. Doctors who had good news usually delivered it standing up.

"Mr. McGarvey is stable for now. But his condition is critical. The cancer has progressed significantly. There's fluid building up in his lungs, which is making it difficult for him to breathe. We're providing oxygen and medication to keep him comfortable, but..."

He paused, choosing his words carefully.

"But what?" Kayla demanded.

"But given the advanced stage of his illness and the stress his body endured today, I need to be honest with you. Mr. McGarvey is dying. It might not be tonight. It could be a few days. But it's no longer a matter of months. Or even weeks."

Kayla felt the world tilt. She felt Mrs. Johnson's hands steadying her.

"Can I see him?" Her voice sounded far away to her own ears.

"Soon. We're getting him settled in a room. It'll be about thirty minutes. But yes, you can see him. All of you can, if you keep the visits short."

After the doctor left, Kayla sat very still. The others shared condolences, offered support, and asked if she needed anything.

But what she needed was impossible.

She needed Tom to live long enough to see his vision become reality. To see the church transformed. To know that his sermon hadn't been in vain.

She needed more time.

But time was the one thing they'd run out of.

Room 537. That's where they'd put him.

Kayla stood outside the door, bracing herself. The others waited in the hallway, giving her privacy for this first visit.

She pushed open the door.

Tom looked tiny in the hospital bed. Tubes and wires connected him to machines that beeped and hummed. An oxygen mask covered his nose and mouth. His eyes were closed.

Kayla pulled a chair close to the bed and sat down. She took his hand, careful of the IV line.

"Tom? It's me. It's Kayla."

His eyes opened slowly. He tried to speak, but the oxygen mask muffled his words.

She leaned closer. "Don't try to talk. Just rest."

But Tom was shaking his head. He pulled the mask down just enough to speak. "How many?"

"How many what?"

"How many... index cards... were taken?"

Kayla felt tears spill down her cheeks. The man was dying, and he wanted to know about index cards.

"I don't know. I'll find out. But Tom, it doesn't matter right now. Just rest. Please."

"It matters." His voice was barely a whisper. "Has to matter."

"It does. It will. I promise you, it will matter."

He seemed satisfied with that. His eyes closed again. His breathing, even with the oxygen, sounded like grinding stones.

Kayla sat with him as afternoon faded into evening. Other visitors came and went.

Patricia called again from the airport. Dr. Feldman called the nurses' station, asking for updates.

But Tom mostly slept. And when he was awake, he seemed to be somewhere else. Somewhere beyond the hospital room. Beyond Stoneford. Beyond even Jerusalem.

Maybe he was already seeing what came next.

As darkness fell outside the hospital window, Kayla finally let herself acknowledge the truth.

This was the end.

Tom's last sermon had been exactly that—his last sermon.

And next week, when the church was supposed to be sent out for community service, for Vespers in a barn with homeless people, they'd be gathering without him.

If they gathered at all.

The church had split. The board would likely remove Tom from ministry officially, though the point would be moot. Kayla herself was already terminated, even if the paperwork wasn't finished yet.

Everything Tom had tried to build had collapsed in a single morning.

All was lost.

Kayla lay her head on the edge of Tom's bed and finally let herself cry. not quiet, dignified tears. But deep, wrenching sobs that shook her whole body.

Tom's hand moved weakly to rest on her head. A blessing. Or maybe just comfort.

"Not lost," he whispered. "Just beginning."

But Kayla couldn't believe that.

Not yet.

CHAPTER
FIFTEEN

Monday, June 16, 1975
County Memorial Hospital - Room 537
Morning

Kayla woke with her head on the edge of Tom's hospital bed. Her neck ached, and her back screamed. The chair she'd slept in, the fitful dozing she'd managed, had left her stiff and disoriented.

Morning light filtered through the venetian blinds, casting stripes across Tom's face. He looked worse than yesterday. His skin had taken on a grayish hue, stretched tight over his cheekbones. The oxygen mask fogged and cleared with each labored breath.

Kayla stretched carefully, trying not to disturb the IV line and monitor wires that connected Tom to machines that beeped. She'd been here all night. Had been here since yesterday morning when the ambulance brought him in.

Almost twenty-four hours now.

A nurse came in, the same one from last night. "You should go home. Get some real sleep."

"I'm fine."

"You're not fine," the nurse said in a tone more like a concerned mother than a healthcare worker. "And you're not helping him by wearing yourself out." The nurse checked Tom's vitals and made notes on her clipboard. "He's stable. Comfortable. The medication is keeping him from being in pain."

"When will he wake up?"

The nurse's expression shifted to the carefully neutral sympathy that medical professionals learn. "I don't know that he will. Not today, anyway. The doctor said his body is shutting down. It's a matter of time now."

Kayla already knew that. But hearing it stated so plainly made it real in a way it hadn't been before.

"You have visitors in the waiting room," the nurse added. "They've been there since seven."

Kayla stood, her legs unsteady. "Who?"

"An older woman. Said she flew in from Florida. And a few others."

Patricia. Of course, Patricia had come.

Kayla looked back at Tom one more time before leaving the room. His chest rose and fell in a mechanical rhythm: breath in, breath out, pause too long, breath in again. She wanted to memorize that rhythm, to hold onto it for when it stopped.

THE WAITING ROOM WAS FULLER THAN KAYLA EXPECTED. Patricia sat near the window, looking exhausted. Eleanor Pritchard was there with her husband. Mr. and Mrs. Johnson sat together, holding hands. And in the corner were three veterans in field jackets, Danny and two others whose names Kayla didn't know yet.

Patricia stood when she saw Kayla. They embraced with only a few words of introduction to each other. Patricia smelled like airplane air and perfume, and something that reminded Kayla of Tom.

"How is he?" Patricia asked.

"Dying." The word came out flat, factual. Kayla was too tired for euphemisms.

"Can I see him?"

"Of course. Room 537."

After Patricia left, Kayla sank into a chair. The others looked at her with expressions that ranged from pity to determination.

"We wanted to be here," Eleanor said. "In case... you needed anything."

"Or in case Tom woke up," Mr. Johnson added. "Wanted to tell him the barn is ready for next Sunday."

Next Sunday. The Vespers service. The community outreach. Tom's vision.

"I don't know if that's still happening," Kayla said quietly.

Danny, the vet, leaned forward. "Why wouldn't it be?"

"Because Tom is dying. Because the church—" She stopped, realizing she still wasn't formally notified. "The church is going to let me go. I'm sure it will be this week."

Silence.

"What?" Eleanor's voice was sharp with anger. "They're getting rid of you? While Tom is in the hospital?"

"It'll be a 'separation agreement.' I'm sure it will be very professional. Very polite. It'll talk about theological differences." Kayla heard the bitterness in her own voice. "They've been planning it since before the sermon."

"That's reprehensible," Eleanor said.

"That's the church," Danny said. "Sorry, but it is. They protect the institution, not the people."

Mrs. Johnson pulled an envelope from her purse. "This came to our house this morning. It was in our mailbox. I think... I think you should read it."

Kayla took the envelope. The Johnsons' names were written on the front in careful handwriting. Inside was a single sheet of paper—a letter from the board to the congregation.

The letter was dated today, so it couldn't have made it to the post office to be delivered this early. Someone had placed it inside their mailbox.

Kayla's hands shook as she read:

The board of elders, under the new leadership of Randolph Wescott, has determined that it is in the best interest of Great Witness Community Church and its congregation to sever our relationship with Kayla Andersen and offer her a separation agreement effective immediately. This allows her to return to her seminary without any negative reporting regarding her time with our church. This also allows Kayla to finish her externship with another church where her theology and Christology are more in line with each other.

As brothers and sisters in Christ, we recognize that some differences are too great to overcome, and the best course of action is to part ways. Although we surely did pray for her discernment, it has become obvious that her free will has overridden what God wants ordained.

Everyone can rest assured that the board of elders will be praying very hard for a suitable replacement for Rev. McGarvey, a replacement that embodies the traditions of this church and takes the sacred scripture and its creeds and doctrines seriously.

Kayla read it twice. Then a third time. The words blurred.

"Her free will has overridden what God wants ordained," she repeated. "They're saying God doesn't want me in ministry. They're saying I'm going against God's will."

Eleanor took the letter from Kayla's shaking hands, read it, and her face flushed red. "This is spiritual abuse. They're using God as a weapon against you."

"They're scared," Danny said. "Tom challenged everything they built their identity on. And you stood with him. So they're eliminating the threat."

"I'm not a threat." Kayla's voice broke. "I'm just a seminary student who believed in a dying pastor's vision."

"You are a threat," Mrs. Johnson said gently. "Because you might actually change things. And they can't allow that."

Kayla stood abruptly. She couldn't sit here anymore. Couldn't breathe in this waiting room with kind people and their righteous anger.

"I need to get some air."

She walked out before anyone could stop her.

Later that Afternoon

Patricia found Kayla in the hospital cafeteria, staring at a cup of coffee she hadn't touched.

"Tom's still sleeping," Patricia said, sitting down across from her. "But the nurse says he's comfortable."

Kayla nodded but didn't speak.

"Eleanor told me about the letter. About what they did to you."

"I don't want to talk about it."

"Okay." Patricia sipped her own coffee. "Then let's talk about Tom. Tell me about the sermon. I want to hear what he said."

So Kayla told her. About the "I'm not a Christian, I'm a follower of Jesus" moment. About the steak-love metaphor. About the questions that made people walk out. About Tom pushing through even as his body failed. About the announcement of next Sunday's plan. About his collapse.

When she finished, Patricia had tears in her eyes.

"He did it," Patricia said. "He actually did it. He spoke the truth, cost be damned."

"And it cost him everything. The church split. Half the congregation walked out. The board is removing him from ministry officially, though that hardly matters now. They dumped me. And Tom..." Kayla's voice cracked. "Tom is dying without knowing if any of it mattered."

"It mattered."

"How? How did it matter? He tore the church apart for a vision that's dying with him."

Patricia reached across the table and took Kayla's hand. "You don't see it yet because you're too close to it. But I saw those people in the waiting room. The veterans. The farmer and his wife. Eleanor. They're not there because Tom failed. They're there because he succeeded. He changed them. He showed them what following Jesus actually looks like. And that can't be undone."

"But next Sunday—"

"Will happen or it won't. But either way, Tom spoke the truth. And some people heard it. That's all a prophet can do, Kayla. Speak the truth and trust that someone, somewhere, will hear it."

Kayla wanted to believe that. But sitting in this sterile cafeteria, holding a cup of cold coffee, watching people move through their normal days while Tom died upstairs, she couldn't find the faith for it.

* * *

Tuesday, June 17, 1975
Morning

TOM WOKE BRIEFLY AROUND NINE IN THE MORNING. His eyes opened slowly, confused about where he was. Kayla was beside him instantly.

"Tom? Can you hear me?"

His hand moved weakly toward the oxygen mask. She helped him lower it slightly.

"Kayla..." His voice was barely a whisper. "How long?"

"Two days since the sermon. You've been here since Sunday afternoon."

He tried to sit up and failed. "Sunday. Next Sunday. Did you—"

"Don't worry about that right now. Just rest."

But Tom was shaking his head, agitated. "Vietnam," he said. "Need to tell you. About Vietnam."

Kayla pulled her chair closer. "Okay. I'm listening."

Tom's breathing was labored, each word an effort. "The medic. I told you... the soldier died. But I didn't tell you... my fault."

"Tom, you don't have to—"

"Let me finish. Please." His eyes were desperate. "Combat situation. Soldier was wounded. Paulson, the medic, asked me... to hand him medication. Two vials. Looked the same. I grabbed... the wrong one. Gave him... the wrong medication."

Kayla felt her breathing quicken.

"Soldier died. Minutes later. Because I gave Paulson... wrong medicine. My fault. All my fault." Tom's face contorted. "I killed him, Kayla. Killed him because I wasn't paying attention. Because I was scared. Because I failed."

Tears were running down Tom's face, into the oxygen mask, making it foggy.

"I've been trying... to make up for it. My whole life. Trying to save enough people... to balance it out. But it's never enough. Never..."

Kayla took his hand and held it tight. "Tom, listen to me. It was a mistake in an impossible situation. A terrifying situation. You were in a war zone, trying to help. And yes, someone died. But Tom, you've spent your whole life trying to make amends. And look what you started now. You got to live Matthew 25."

"Not enough," Tom whispered.

"It is enough. Tom, it has to be enough. At some point, you have to forgive yourself. At some point, you have to accept that you're human. That you make mistakes. That you can't save everyone."

"But I could have helped to save him."

"Maybe. Maybe not. You'll never know. But what I do know is that you've saved other people. You saved me, Tom. You showed me what ministry is supposed to be. You showed Youssef's community what kindness looks like. You showed Great Witness that following Jesus means more than worship services."

Tom's eyes were closing. The effort of talking had exhausted him.

"You've already made amends, Tom. You've already been forgiven. Now you need to forgive yourself. You deserve the same grace you show others."

His hand squeezed hers weakly. "Thank you," he breathed. Then he slept again.

Afternoon

THE PHONE AT THE NURSES' STATION RANG AROUND TWO o'clock. A nurse found Kayla in the waiting room.

"There's a call for you. A Dr. Feldman from the University of Chicago."

Kayla took the call at the desk, her heart pounding.

"Kayla, it's Susan Feldman. I wanted to call you directly with the news. The full authentication is complete. Every test confirms it. The scroll is genuine first-century Aramaic, dated to approximately 30–35 CE. The parchment, the ink, the script—everything is authentic. This is the earliest Christian document in existence."

Kayla closed her eyes. "Thank you for letting me know."

"There's more. I've shared the findings with colleagues at Princeton and Oxford. They're already calling it the most significant archaeological discovery of the century. Kayla, this changes everything. This confirms that women were part of Jesus's ministry. That the early church was different than what we've believed. This is—"

"Tom is dying," Kayla interrupted. "He's unconscious most of the time. He doesn't know that it's been authenticated. He won't live to see anyone care about it."

Silence on the line.

"I'm so sorry," Dr. Feldman said finally.

"He's going to die thinking he split his church apart and did it without ever seeing that scroll again."

"Kayla, even if Tom doesn't see it, his legacy will live on. Sheerah's words will live on. The truth will outlast all of us."

"It's not fair." After hanging up, Kayla returned to Tom's room. He was still sleeping, his breathing more labored than before. She sat beside him and took his hand.

"It's real, Tom," she whispered. "The scroll is authenticated. Sheerah was real. Everything you believed is true."

His hand twitched slightly in hers. Maybe he heard. Maybe he didn't.

Either way, the truth was confirmed.

Dinnertime

A soft knock at the door woke Kayla from the chair in Tom's room. She was confused, thinking she had only dozed off for a few minutes.

"Kayla, may I come in?"

It was Dr. Feldman, who had driven all afternoon to get to the hospital, holding a cylinder-shaped container. She nodded to Kayla. "I brought it. I had to get it here in time. I mean, before Tom..." Her voice trailed off as she walked to Tom's bed.

"Oh, Tom," she said, handing the tube to Kayla as she reached for Tom's hand.

Kayla hugged the tube to her chest. Knowing what it held—the weight of history and hope—was the only sense of comfort she felt in the last 36 hours. "Thank you, Dr. Feldman. I know you understand what this means to him."

"Kayla, I can't stay. I have to head back. But I had to make sure you have this now. You have my number. Call me when…"

"I will."

Those were the hardest two words Kayla spoke all day.

Wednesday, June 18, 1975
Morning

TOM BARELY WOKE ON WEDNESDAY. WHEN HE DID, HIS eyes unfocused, looking at something Kayla couldn't see. The doctor said this was normal. That he was transitioning. That it wouldn't be long now.

Kayla knew what she needed to do.

She placed the cylinder containing the scroll in Tom's hand. Then retrieved the translation of it from her bag, the pages Tom had copied in Dr. Feldman's office. She pulled her chair close to Tom's bed and began to read.

"I, Sheerah, a woman of no standing in the eyes of men, but seen by God, write these things not because I am certain but because I am afraid."

Tom's breathing changed slightly. Not much. But enough to tell her he was listening.

She read slowly, letting each word settle. Read about Sheerah hearing Jesus teach the Parable of the Sheep and the Goats. Read about her fears—that people would speak more about

Jesus than live like him, that temples would be built while doors stayed closed to the hungry, that belief would become more important than mercy.

When she reached the ending, her voice broke.

"We turned the world upside down not by our beliefs but by how we loved. If you carry anything forward, carry this."

Tom's eyes opened. For the first time in days, they were clear. Focused. Present.

He tried to speak but couldn't. So he just smiled.

And Kayla knew he'd heard every word.

Afternoon

THE VETERANS CAME TO VISIT. ALL OF THEM THIS TIME. Not just Danny but the others who'd been at the sermon. Seven men in total, ranging from early twenties to mid-thirties. All wearing their field jackets like armor.

They stood around Tom's bed in a loose circle. Tom was awake but barely responsive. His eyes followed them, but he couldn't speak anymore.

Danny stepped forward. "Sir, we wanted you to know. We're doing it. Next Sunday. The community service. The Vespers at the barn. All of it. We're in."

One of the other vets, a kid who couldn't have been more than twenty-three, spoke up. "You asked what prayer ever changed in your first sermon. Well, you changed something. You showed us that faith is supposed to look like something. Supposed to do something. So we're going to do it."

Tom's hand moved slightly on the bed. Kayla took it, and he squeezed with what little strength he had left.

The veterans stood there for a long time, not saying much. Just being present. Being witnesses.

Finally, they filed out one by one. Each pausing to touch Tom's hand or shoulder. A benediction. A promise.

When they were gone, Eleanor arrived with her husband. Then the Johnsons. Then two of the college kids from the sermon. Then Patricia.

Tom's room became a revolving door of people he'd touched. People he'd changed. People who wanted him to know he hadn't failed.

Evening

THE SUN WAS SETTING OUTSIDE THE HOSPITAL WINDOW, painting the room in orange and gold. Patricia had gone to get something to eat. The other visitors had left. It was just Kayla and Tom now.

Tom's breathing had changed again. Each breath came with more difficulty. The pauses between breaths grew longer.

He was dying. And they both knew it.

Kayla leaned close to his ear. "Tom, I need to tell you something. The church split. Half the congregation left. The board got rid of me. They say my theology doesn't align with theirs. Your replacement will be someone who takes doctrine seriously."

She swallowed hard.

"It looks like we failed. Like everything you tried to do collapsed. But Tom, the veterans are still coming. Eleanor is still coming. The Johnsons are still coming. The people who heard you aren't going to let your vision die."

Tom's eyes opened. His hand moved weakly, gesturing for her to come closer.

She leaned in until her ear was nearly touching his mouth.

"Promise me." His voice was barely a breath. "Next Sunday. Do it anyway."

Tears streamed down Kayla's face. "I promise."

"Not because of me. Because it's right."

"I promise, Tom. I'll do it."

His hand relaxed in hers. His eyes closed. But she could see a small smile on his lips.

<hr>

Thursday, June 19, 1975
Dawn

Kayla woke to the sound of the heart monitor flatlining.

One moment, she was dozing in the chair, holding Tom's hand. The next, the machine was sounding its single continuous note.

Nurses rushed in. They looked up at the monitor. One pressed her fingers against the side of Tom's neck.

But Kayla already knew.

Tom was gone.

His hand was still warm in hers. His face peaceful, finally free of pain. The oxygen mask had been removed at some point during the night, and he looked younger without it. More like the Tom from the photograph with Sheldon in Vietnam. Before everything went wrong.

A stethoscope was held to Tom's chest for a full minute. Nothing.

Tom McGarvey was dead.

Patricia appeared at some point. Kayla didn't remember her arriving. Didn't remember leaving Tom's room. Didn't remember walking to the waiting room.

But suddenly she was there, sitting in a chair with Patricia beside her. And the world had tilted sideways.

"He's gone," Kayla heard herself say.

"I know, honey. I know."

"He died before seeing if it mattered. If any of it mattered."

"It mattered. It all mattered."

But Kayla couldn't believe that. Not yet. Not sitting in this waiting room. Not with the words of the letter from the board echoing in her mind: *her free will has overridden what God wants ordained.*

The church had fired her. Tom was dead.

The scroll was authenticated, but who would care? Some academics, maybe. But would it change anything? Would it transform the church? Would it make people actually follow Jesus instead of just worshiping Christ?

Probably not.

Everything they'd tried to do had collapsed in a single week.

Tom had given his final sermon. Torn the church apart. Announced a radical vision.

And then died before seeing if anyone would follow through.

Kayla sat in that waiting room as morning light filtered through the windows. Sat as other people came and went with their emergencies and their normal problems. Sat as life continued all around her while her world had stopped.

Eleanor arrived. Then the Johnsons. Then Danny and the other veterans. Then the college kids. All of them wanting to say goodbye. To offer condolences. To promise they'd still show up on Sunday.

But Kayla couldn't process their words. Couldn't feel their compassion. Couldn't believe their promises.

All she could feel was the absence.

Tom was gone.

And with him, maybe, went any chance of the church changing. Any hope of Sheerah's message being heard. Any possibility of turning the world upside down.

It was over.

All of it was over.

Late Morning

KAYLA STOOD OUTSIDE THE HOSPITAL ENTRANCE, THE June sun warm on her face. Patricia had offered to make arrangements with the funeral home. The others had slowly dispersed. And Kayla was alone again.

She looked up at the hospital. Room 537. The fifth floor. Where Tom had visited Gladys Peterson months earlier, and where he had just spent his final days. Where he'd confessed about Vietnam. Where he'd smiled when she read Sheerah's words. Where he'd made her promise to do it anyway.

Do what anyway? Show up at community service locations with a handful of people? Hold a Vespers service in a barn for the few who cared? Pretend that any of it mattered when the institutional church would just keep doing what it had always done?

Kayla got in her car. The same car they'd ridden in together, planning how to change the church. She gripped the steering wheel but didn't start the engine.

The scroll sat on her passenger seat in its protective case. Authenticated. Confirmed. Real.

But Tom would never know that it mattered. Would never see scholars studying it. Would never witness the possibility of transformational faith because of Sheerah's words.

He'd died not knowing.

Kayla finally turned the key. The engine coughed to life. She pulled out of the parking lot without looking back.

Room 537 was already being cleaned for the next patient. The next crisis. The next death. Life moved on.

But Kayla felt stuck in this moment. This terrible, dark moment where everything they'd worked for had died with Tom.

She drove home in silence. Parked in front of her apartment. Sat there for a long time.

The Dark Night of the Soul wasn't a metaphor anymore.

It was Thursday morning, June 19, 1975.

And Kayla had never felt more alone.

CHAPTER
SIXTEEN

Kayla stood in Tom's house, surrounded by the remnants of his life. Oxygen tanks and equipment he refused to hook up, too proud to admit he needed them. A walker that remained folded in the corner, unused. Rows of medication bottles lined up on his desk like soldiers awaiting a deployment that would never come. And the hospital bed that had been delivered two weeks ago but was never slept in because Tom collapsed before he could come home.

Patricia had helped her pack everything up yesterday, sorting through Tom's clothes, books, and papers, boxing up a lifetime reduced to cardboard and tape.

The medical equipment needed to go back to the hospital. They'd called asking for it. Other patients needed it.

Kayla loaded the oxygen equipment into her trunk. The walker was in the back seat, and the unused medications were in a bag for disposal. She drove to County Memorial Hospital in silence.

She pulled into the parking lot and sat there for a moment, engine running.

Room 537 was up there. The fifth floor. The window she'd stared out of for four days while Tom lay dying.

Someone else was probably in that room now. It might be someone else dying. Someone else's loved ones keeping vigil, drinking bad coffee, dozing in uncomfortable chairs.

Life moves on. "Life always moves on," Tom would say, usually with a smile that meant he knew something about loss that he couldn't quite put into words.

Kayla turned off the engine and carried the equipment inside. A nurse at the desk checked everything off a list, thanked her efficiently, and that was it. Tom's medical equipment returned. Task complete.

She walked back to her car slowly, feeling the warm June sun on her shoulders. She got in and gripped the steering wheel.

Tomorrow was Sunday. The community service. The Vespers at the Johnsons' barn. Tom's vision that she'd promised to carry out.

But could she? Should she?

The church had fired her. Tom was dead. Maybe it was time to just... let it go. Go back to seminary. Finish her externship somewhere else. Forget about Great Witness and its radical dying pastor and his impossible dream.

But Tom's last words echoed in her mind: "Promise me. Next Sunday. Do it anyway."

Kayla started the car and drove away from the hospital, leaving Room 537 and its pain behind.

She had one more day to decide.

Sunday, June 22, 1975
Morning
Various Locations Around Stoneford

KAYLA WOKE AT DAWN WITH A KNOT IN HER STOMACH. Today. She had to decide today.

She'd made the calls yesterday. Confirmed the locations with the shelters, the soup kitchen, and the nursing home. Eleanor had the master list. Danny had recruited more veterans. The Johnsons were busy preparing the barn, transforming a space that smelled like decades of farm work into something that could hold a church service.

But Kayla still didn't know if she could go through with it.

At 7:30 a.m., her phone rang.

"Kayla? It's Eleanor. I'm at the homeless shelter. There are about fifteen people here already. Should we start?"

Kayla closed her eyes. This was it. The moment of decision.

"Yes," she heard herself say. "Start."

BY EIGHT O'CLOCK, SHE WAS AT THE SHELTER HERSELF, and Eleanor was right—people had shown up. They were waiting to be fed, along with two of the college kids from the sermon and a few families she didn't recognize. Carolyn Foster was there, expertly cracking eggs for scrambling. She and Eleanor were the only board members to support this cause.

They served breakfast to thirty-seven homeless people that morning. Scrambled eggs, toast, coffee in paper cups, orange juice in plastic cups. Nothing fancy. But it was food. It was presence. It was Matthew 25 in action.

At the nursing home, Barbara Pritchard led a group of eight people visiting residents who never got visitors. Reading to them from books in large print. Playing cards. Just sitting with them.

At the county jail, Danny and two other veterans who'd done time themselves sat with inmates. They listened without fixing. Offered no judgment, no empty promises. Just presence.

It was messy. It was small. It was imperfect.

But it was real.

And Kayla, standing in that homeless shelter watching a church board member smile while she served eggs to a man who smelled like he hadn't bathed in weeks, finally understood what Tom had been trying to show them.

This was church. This was following Jesus. This was love as a verb.

That Evening
The Johnsons' Barn
6:00 p.m.

KAYLA ARRIVED AT THE BARN AN HOUR EARLY TO HELP set up. Patricia was with the Johnsons, working all day. Cleaning and arranging folding chairs borrowed from a neighboring church, not Great Witness, which had refused.

The barn still smelled like hay and animals and decades of farm life. But it was... beautiful, somehow. Honest. Real.

"We left it a little rough around the edges," Mr. Johnson said, gesturing at the worn wood and cobwebs in the rafters. "Seemed like that's what Tom would have wanted."

Mrs. Johnson was arranging wildflowers in Mason jars. Black-eyed Susans, Queen Anne's lace, and purple coneflowers picked from the fields around the barn brought in color and life. "We invited some of the homeless folks who've been using this place as shelter. Hope that's okay."

"It's perfect," Kayla said. "It's exactly what Tom wanted."

Eleanor arrived next, carrying a battery-powered record player and a small box of records wrapped in a dish towel. "Found these at the church. Thought we could sing along if we don't have an organist." Her smile was conspiratorial, like they were getting away with something.

Then the veterans. Then the college kids with their long hair and new faith. Then families from this morning's community outreach. Then people Kayla had never seen before—neighbors who'd heard about it over fences and coffee, and community members curious about this different kind of church.

A young couple hung by the barn entrance, their two daughters at their mother's leg. The woman's eyes scanned the space, taking in the bales, the wildflowers in Mason jars... the hodgepodge of people. As if trying to decide if they were in the right place.

Kayla approached them with a big smile and an outstretched hand. "Hi, I'm Kayla. You're here for the service?"

The woman's grip was tentative yet grateful. "Is this... Is this the service that Reverend Tom started?"

"It sure is. Did you know him?"

"We met once." The woman's voice caught in her throat. "It was in the hospital. I was visiting my daughter and husband. Reverend Tom was..." She paused, searching for the right words. "He was an answer to our prayers."

Kayla searched her memory, trying to place them. Tom had never mentioned visiting a mother in the hospital. But then he had probably done a lot of things he never mentioned. "Well, he never said anything to me about that visit, but I'm sure he'd be glad you're here."

A small voice popped up from knee-height. "Mommy, tell her about the unicorn!"

The youngest daughter, maybe five, with pigtails and grass-stained knees, dug into her pocket with the fierce concentration only children possess. She pulled out a purple stuffed unicorn, slightly worn. Clearly beloved.

"Reverend Tom gave me this." She held it up like a trophy. "We were at the elevator. Me and Mommy. He gave me this, and then we went down to see my sister." She pointed to the older girl, maybe seven, who was much shyer than her younger sister.

"This is Charlotte," the woman said. "And that's her sister, Alysia. I'm Maria, and this is my husband, Pete. Reverend Tom helped me in ways he probably didn't know. He helped all of us. We wanted to come to honor him."

Maria told the story. Her fear at the hospital, her daughter and husband both on different floors. How Tom's purple unicorn and his simple presence changed her fear into hope. "We had to come," Maria said, looking down at her daughters. "To say thank you."

"We're glad you're here, Charlotte and Alysia." Kayla's smile was broad and genuine. "And thank you for bringing your mommy and daddy with you! Please, make yourselves comfortable."

A short while later, a car pulled up and a man in his forties got out. Trim beard, glasses, wearing slacks and a collared shirt, but no clerical collar.

Kayla had to look twice.

"Rabbi Levine?" she called out.

He turned, smiled, and walked over with the gait of someone comfortable in his own skin. "Kayla. I'm so sorry I didn't make it in time. I tried, but—"

"You're here now. That's what matters." She embraced him. "Thank you for coming."

"Tom was my best friend for two years in hell. Of course I came." Sheldon looked around at the barn, at the gathering people, at the unlikely congregation forming. "So this is what he was building. A church in a barn."

"With a Jewish rabbi helping," Kayla said with a small smile. "Tom would love that."

"Just like Vietnam," Sheldon said, his voice filled with memory, loss, and perhaps joy. "The Protestant chaplain and the rabbi serving side by side. Our commanding officer used to joke that we were the most ecumenical company in the whole damn war."

More people kept arriving as the sun lowered toward the horizon. By seven o'clock, there were maybe forty people crammed into the barn. Some sitting on folding chairs that wobbled on the uneven dirt floor. Some standing along the walls. Some sitting on hay bales. A few homeless people lingered near the back, unsure if they were really welcome, despite Mrs. Johnson's invitation.

Kayla made a point of greeting them specifically. "Please sit up front. You're our guests of honor."

At 7:15, Kayla stood at the front of the barn. No pulpit, no altar, no platform to elevate her above the crowd. Just her, standing on the dirt floor, looking out at this impossible gathering.

Movement at the barn entrance caught her eye. Dr. Morrison. The man who signed Tom's death certificate early in the week was there to witness the birth of his radical dream. He slipped through the door with the practiced invisibility of someone used to hospital corridors. He found a seat in the shadowed back corner, a wealthy physician sitting on a hay bale among farmworkers and homeless men.

Their eyes met. Dr. Morrison nodded with a smile, a signal that even in death, Tom's vision was about to be realized.

Kayla took a breath and began.

"Welcome," she said. Her voice cracked. She cleared her throat and started again. "Welcome to our first Vespers service. I'm Kayla Andersen. For those who don't know me, I was Tom McGarvey's intern at Great Witness Community Church. Until they fired me last Monday."

A ripple of murmurs went through the barn.

Kayla turned and looked behind her at a bale of hay on the dirt floor. Resting on top of it was a cylinder—the protective case that held a sacred scroll. Almost two thousand years old. Written by a woman who had fears that came true. A woman who'd been right about it all.

Tom's scroll. Tom's gift. Tom's burden and blessing.

Tom McGarvey may not have been able to physically be at his first Vespers, but Kayla made sure his spirit was. The scroll sat there as a witness, a reminder of why they were all here.

"I'm not telling you that for sympathy. I'm telling you that because it's important to be honest. Tom taught me that. He taught me a lot in the short time I knew him. But the most important thing he taught me was that following Jesus isn't about having the right beliefs or saying the right prayers. It's about doing the right things. It's about love as a verb, not just a feeling."

She looked around at the diverse crowd. Veterans and farmers. College kids with peace buttons and retirees who'd spent their lives in this community. Church members and people who'd never set foot in a church. Homeless people and business owners. A physician. A rabbi. And a young child with a purple unicorn. All of them here because of Tom.

"This morning, many of you served in our community. You fed hungry people. You visited people who are sick. You sat with people in jail. You welcomed strangers. And tonight, we're gathering to share what we experienced. To sing together. To pray together. To be church together."

Kayla paused, her heart pounding against her ribs, recalling how Tom had described him. "Before we begin, I want to invite someone to speak: Reverend Edward Hartwell. He traveled to Jerusalem with Tom in May, and he has something he'd like to share."

Hartwell stood from his seat next to his wife, Margaret. He looked different from how Tom described him weeks ago. Less rigid, more human. He walked to the front slowly, and when he turned to face the crowd, Kayla could see tears already gathering in his eyes.

"I didn't come here tonight to preach," Hartwell began, his voice thick with emotion. "I came to confess."

The barn went absolutely silent.

"When I first met Tom McGarvey in Jerusalem, I judged him. Thought he was wasting his pilgrimage. Missing the important sites. Prioritizing some homeless man over the Church of the Holy Sepulchre, over the Via Dolorosa, over everything we'd paid good money to see."

Hartwell took a breath.

"But if I'm honest...and Tom taught me I need to be honest...I was envious. Tom had something I didn't. A connection to what we were all supposed to be experiencing. A genuineness I'd lost somewhere along the way. And I responded to that envy with criticism. With judgment. With attempts to control him."

He looked around the barn.

"Our group visited all the holy sites. We walked where Jesus walked. We saw the Church of the Holy Sepulchre. We prayed at the Western Wall. We floated in the Dead Sea. And it was magnificent. I felt something. We all did. It was intense, emotional, and powerful."

Hartwell's voice dropped.

"But when I got home? That feeling faded. Within a week, I was back to my normal life, my normal faith, my normal church. The intensity of Jerusalem became just a memory. A nice experience. A story to tell over coffee after Sunday worship."

He paused, letting that sink in, hoping they would see their own lives reflected in his words.

"Tom missed those sites. He spent his time with a homeless man named Youssef instead. Helped him. Fed him. Welcomed him. Bought him clothes. Sat with him in a dog pound feeding stray animals. Things that seemed, to me, like a waste of precious time in the Holy Land."

Hartwell's eyes glistened.

"But when Tom came home, he didn't come home the same. What he experienced didn't fade. It didn't become just a nice memory. It transformed him, changed everything about how he understood his faith, his ministry, and his purpose. And it stayed with him until his final breath."

Someone in the crowd said, "Amen."

"I asked Patricia to keep me updated about Tom. I saw the chemistry between them in Jerusalem and asked her to report back on how Tom was doing. Because I needed to know if what I saw in him was real. If his transformation would last. Or if he'd fade back to normal like the rest of us."

He smiled sadly.

"Every update Patricia gave me confirmed it. Tom was living differently. Preaching differently. Challenging his congregation. Starting a veterans program. Planning this—" he gestured around the barn, "—this radical experiment in actually following Jesus instead of just worshiping him. I was both inspired and terrified because if Tom was right about what following Jesus meant, then I'd been wrong for decades."

The barn was so quiet Kayla could hear hay rustling as someone shifted in their seat.

"Our tour guide in Jerusalem was Dr. Rami Bar-El. He's not a Christian. He's led tours of Jerusalem for more than a decade. Hundreds and hundreds of pilgrims. On our last day, he pulled me aside and said something I'll never forget."

Hartwell's voice broke.

"He said, 'In all my years, I've taken countless people through this city, and I've never seen anyone change like your friend Tom. Whatever he found here, it was real.'"

Hartwell wiped his eyes with the back of his hand, not ashamed.

"That's when I knew. Tom found what we were all looking for. He just found it in a place we refused to look—in the face of someone who needed help. In the mess of actual human need. In the discomfort of getting down in the dirt and doing the work instead of just praying about it."

He looked directly at Kayla, his expression raw with honesty.

"Tom asked in his final sermon 'Are we speaking more about Jesus or living like him?' I've been speaking about Jesus for thirty years. Tom lived like him for one week in Jerusalem and never stopped. He turned his world upside down. And he invited all of us to do the same."

Hartwell turned to face the full congregation. His body language shifted from confession to challenge.

"So I'm here tonight to mourn Tom and to confess that he was right and I was wrong. And to ask myself, and to ask all of you, are we willing to be transformed? Or do we just want to feel religious?"

Silence.

Then Hartwell smiled, gesturing around the barn.

"This place smells like animals. It's uncomfortable. The chairs are wobbly. There are people here I wouldn't normally worship with. And Tom would say that's exactly where Jesus is. Not in the beautiful sanctuaries with cushioned pews and air-conditioning. Not in the comfortable spaces where everyone looks like us and thinks like us and believes like us. But here. In the mess. In the discomfort. In the places where hungry people are fed and strangers are welcomed and everyone is treated like they belong."

He looked up at the rafters, the cobwebs, the rough wood.

"That's where Tom found Jesus in Jerusalem. In a dog pound. In an abandoned building. In the face of a homeless man nobody else would help. And that's where we might find him, too. If we're willing to look."

Hartwell returned to his seat next to Margaret, who wrapped her arms around him and let the tears that were still on his cheeks dampen her shoulder. No one spoke. No one moved. The moment hung in suspended sacredness.

Then, slowly, someone started clapping. One person. Then another. Then more.

It built into applause that filled the barn, echoing off the rafters, mixing with the sounds of people crying, laughing, saying "Amen," "Thank you," and "Yes."

Kayla stood, wiping her own tears. "Thank you, Reverend Hartwell, for your honesty. For your courage."

She took a breath that steadied her.

"Let's sing. We don't have an organ. We don't have a choir. But we have voices. And I think that's enough."

Eleanor started the record player. The crackly sound filled the barn. And forty voices, most of them off-key, all of them sincere, sang together.

After the hymn, Kayla invited people to share stories from the morning's service. A shy teenager with acne talked about serving eggs at the shelter, moved to tears recounting a man who thanked him. Barbara Pritchard cried as she described sitting with a woman at the nursing home who hadn't had a visitor in three years. Danny shared about sitting with inmates who just needed someone to listen without judging.

One of the homeless men stood up, hesitant, like he wasn't sure if he had permission to speak. "I been sleeping in this barn for months. Never thought I'd be sitting here with all you folks, being treated like I matter. Whoever said Jesus is with the poor, I think they was right."

More stories. More tears. More laughter that bubbled up from joy too big to contain.

They sang again. Then once more.

Sheldon, the Jewish rabbi, stood up. "I'm not Christian, but Tom was my brother. And what do I see happening here tonight? This is what faith is supposed to look like. Not separation, not judgment, not boundaries. But people coming together to help people who need help."

Someone said, "Amen, Rabbi."

"Tom and I shared our beliefs and our traditions during our time together in Vietnam. I'd like to honor our friendship by sharing what I imagine Tom would agree with. It comes from the Torah. I didn't bring mine with me, so I'll spare you a religious reading. But please let me paraphrase what I see this community building."

Sheldon held out his arms in a welcoming manner, embracing the whole barn, the whole unlikely congregation.

"From the Book of Deuteronomy. It goes something like this... When you come upon someone who is in trouble or needs help... Someone hungry or thirsty, or sick or a stranger, perhaps... When you share this land that God has given you together... Don't look the other way, pretending not to see him."

He brought his arms across his chest, holding his words close.

"Give freely to anyone in need. Do it with spontaneity. Be generous always—with open hands and open hearts. Give to your neighbors who are hurting, who are hungry, thirsty, and strangers. Give to those who are sick, naked, and imprisoned. Give to your poor. God will bless you for it."

Sheldon dropped his hands and nodded. "If this is what following Jesus means, then I'm honored to be part of it." His eyes glistened. "Shalom."

There was quiet, but only for a brief moment.

One of the vets went first. "Shalom!"

Then a teenager. "Shalom!"

Hartwell stood. "Shalom!"

Then everyone joined in, a chorus rising to the rafters: "Shalom! Shalom!"

The service lasted well over an hour. No one seemed to want to leave. People lingered, talking, crying, hugging strangers. The veterans stood in a circle, arms around each other. The college kids sat on hay bales, processing what they'd experienced. Eleanor and Hartwell talked quietly in a corner, two people from different churches finding common ground.

As the service came to a close, Kayla asked Eleanor to put one more record on the record player.

"This was Tom's favorite song. He played it *all the time*. I thought I got sick of hearing it. Until..." Her voice cracked. "Until his death." She reached over and touched the scroll's cylinder.

"Now I can't hear it enough."

Kayla nodded at Eleanor, who dropped the needle on the record. Kayla motioned for everyone to stand. She took a hand of each of the Johnsons, who were standing on either side of her. Everyone took that as a cue, and the entirety of this new congregation held hands.

The music started. The Youngbloods' "Get Together." Kayla led everyone in singing, her voice breaking on the words Tom had loved so much.

Hugs were shared when the song ended—tight hugs, genuine hugs, hugs between people who, an hour ago, had been strangers. Then slowly, reluctantly, people began to drift away, thanking the Johnsons with handshakes and embraces. Thanking Kayla with eyes that said more than words could. Promising to come back next Sunday.

"So, we're doing this again?" someone asked.

Kayla heard herself say, "Yes. We're doing this again."

Patricia was the last to leave. She hugged Kayla tightly. "Tom would have loved this." She turned around, taking it all in one last time—the hay-strewn floor, the wildflowers beginning to wilt in their jars, and the folding chairs everywhere. "He really would have loved this."

She had to get back to her hotel and pack. She had a plane to catch in the morning, back to Florida, back to her life. "Kayla, you kept your word to Tom. Promise me you'll keep your word to yourself, too."

"I will. Not because of Tom, but because it's right."

"It mattered." Patricia's voice was fierce. "It all mattered."

They shared one final hug, each letting tears flow—tears of sorrow and tears of joy.

Later That Night
The Empty Barn
10:00 p.m.

KAYLA WAS ALONE NOW. EVERYONE HAD GONE HOME TO their normal lives that would never be quite normal again. The folding chairs were scattered everywhere. The battery-powered record player sat silent in the corner. The sun was setting fast.

She sat on a hay bale, exhausted. Overwhelmed. Changed.

Tom had been right. About all of it.

This wasn't a failure. It was a beginning.

The church had split, the board had fired her, and Tom had died before seeing if his vision would take root in soil that had been hard and dry for so long.

But forty people had shown up tonight. Forty people who'd served their community that morning. Forty people willing to try something different, to risk being uncomfortable. To turn their world upside down.

That wasn't failure. That was a seed planted. That was a revolution beginning.

Kayla looked around the barn, breathing it all in. She smelled the hay, animals, and earth. Felt the presence of what had happened here tonight. Something sacred in something ordinary.

She clutched the scroll's protective cylinder against her chest. This two-thousand-year-old testimony had cost Tom everything. She let herself sink onto the hay. The barn's dirt was cool against her legs. The hay prickled through her jeans.

She'd lie here for a moment. Just a few minutes to let the adrenaline drain away. Her eyes grew heavy. The barn smelled like earth, animals, lingering wildflowers, and something else. Something indefinable that might be called grace.

Just a few minutes...

THE BARN FADED IN AND OUT. KAYLA WASN'T SURE IF SHE was dreaming or remembering, or thinking. Time stretched and compressed like her old Slinky toy. She was here, lying on hay. She was in Tom's hospital room, holding his hand. She was driving to Chicago, discussing theology. She was reading Sheerah's scroll aloud while Tom smiled with his eyes closed.

Her mind drifted through questions like wind through corn. Where had Tom's story really begun?

"Transformation lives in doubt," Tom had told her once, leaning back in his office chair, looking like he'd discovered something precious. "Not having the answers is okay. It's a good thing."

It all started with an ancient scroll, a dying pastor, and a homeless man. They conspired to start a revolution of compassion.

And like the scroll, without anyone caring enough to preserve it, it would become just another nice story. The institutional church would grind it down, sanitize it, make it safe, put it in a liturgy, and forget what it cost.

Still... where did Tom's story really begin? What set all this in motion? A doubting pastor questioning prayer and faith, leaving the hospital bedside of a woman whose husband had just died? When did the change begin for Tom?

"Following Jesus wasn't about having the beliefs," she heard Tom say, his voice echoing through the half-space of half-consciousness. "It was about doing the right things. It was about love as a verb. It was about turning the world upside down."

And that revolution started with one person willing to tell the truth. Even if it cost him everything.

Tom was right. He was right because Youssef was right. Youssef was right because the scroll led him to righteousness. A homeless man got it right. The church had gotten it wrong—

for nearly a hundred generations, for nearly two thousand years.

Outside, the June night sky had lightened to dawn without Kayla noticing. Birds started singing their morning songs. The farm came to life around her.

Kayla opened her eyes. The scroll was tucked under her arm, protected even in sleep. A soft blanket covered her. Another blanket was folded as a pillow under her head. Mrs. Johnson had seen to it that Kayla, who spent the night asleep in a smelly barn, was at least warm and comfortable.

Her worn Revised Standard Version Bible was barely visible next to her leg under the hay and dirt. Kayla held it in her hands, hands that were tired but confident. A torn white piece of paper with the initials TM written on it poked out farther than the other bookmarks she used. And although she didn't need to read the verse to know where it was marked, she opened to that page anyway and read it aloud to herself, her voice hoarse from sleep and singing.

From the Book of Acts: "These men who have turned the world upside down have come here also—"

Kayla had lost count of the number of times Tom, *TM*, told her it was now her time to risk being accused of the same. The gift he was given in the Holy Land was now hers.

Kayla remembered the first time she walked into Tom's office. Nervous, idealistic, certain she knew what ministry should look like. Now there were so many things she wished they could have discussed. Those opportunities were gone, closed like the cover of a finished book. But Tom's gifts to her—his mentorship, his friendship, and the scroll—they were all still here with her. And, as the title of the book that verse came from suggests, it was time to act.

Kayla reached into her canvas bag, fumbling through its contents. More legal pads and at least a dozen pens filled the bottom of the bag. She reached for a pen, her fingers brushing against her Remington portable typewriter that she bought when she entered seminary. Instead of a pen, she grabbed her set of car keys.

She held them up, watching them catch the morning light streaming through the barn's weathered boards. And suddenly she was back in Tom's El Camino, driving home from Chicago, windows down, Tom cranking "Get Together" on his eight-track stereo.

"In your hands," Tom had said, tapping the steering wheel to the beat, his face more alive than she'd seen in weeks, "you really do hold the keys to both love and fear. The song says it. You just have to decide which one you're going to unlock."

Kayla looked at her car keys. Then at the typewriter in her bag.

"Keys," she whispered. Then louder, with dawning realization... "Keys!"

Even just one key was enough to unlock love and fear. Kayla reached back into her bag and pulled out her typewriter. She placed it on the hay bale in front of her, kneeling on the dirt floor, using the bale as a desk. It had a whole lot of keys.

She opened the lid. The typewriter paper she'd shoved inside the case after she brought it home from the store would work just fine.

She fed the paper behind the roller, her fingers hovering over the keys. These weren't the same keys Tom had talked about, the ones that could unlock both love and fear. These keys could create. Share. Transform.

The title and subtitle came to her immediately, fully formed: "SHEERAH'S TESTIMONY: What the Church Got Right and What the Church Got Wrong."

Then, in a structure that reeked of manure, damp hay, earth, and grace, Kayla began typing her story. Her own sacred scroll. It would be a story of how a man who dared to risk everything learned what love can transform when it's a verb instead of a feeling.

It would help ensure that his legacy would be remembered.

It would be a story that would risk accusations of turning things upside down, beginning with a doubting pastor who had just left the hospital room of a beloved parishioner, questioning what prayer had ever changed.

It was a story that was just beginning.

Chapter One's first sentence appeared slowly, one letter at a time:

Tom stood at the elevator, waiting for the doors to open, unaware of the young mother and daughter who walked up behind him—

The End

THE JUDGEMENT OF THE NATIONS

Matthew 25:31-46
"The Parable of the Sheep and the Goats"

"WHEN THE SON OF MAN COMES IN HIS GLORY, AND ALL the angels with him, then he will sit on his glorious throne. Before him will be gathered all the nations, and he will separate them one from another as a shepherd separates the sheep from the goats, and he will place the sheep at his right hand, but the goats at the left.

Then the king will say to those at his right hand, 'Come, O blessed of my Father, inherit the kingdom prepared for you from the foundation of the world; for I was hungry and you gave me food, I was thirsty and you gave me drink, I was a stranger and you welcomed me, I was naked and you clothed me, I was sick and you visited me, I was in prison and you came to me.'

Then the righteous will answer him, 'Lord, when did we see thee hungry and feed thee, or thirsty and give thee drink? And when did we see thee a stranger and welcome thee, or naked and clothe thee? And when did we see thee sick or in prison and visit thee?'

And the King will answer them, 'Truly, I say to you, as you did it to one of the least of these my brethren, you did it to me.'

Then he will say to those at his left hand, 'Depart from me, you cursed, into the eternal fire prepared for the devil and his angels; for I was hungry and you gave me no food, I was thirsty and you gave me no drink, I was a stranger and you did not welcome me, naked and you did not clothe me, sick and in prison and you did not visit me.'

Then they also will answer, 'Lord, when did we see thee hungry or thirsty or a stranger or naked or sick or in prison, and did not minister to thee?

Then he will answer them, 'Truly I say to you, as you did it not to one of the least of these, you did it not to me.'

And they will go away into eternal punishment, but the righteous into eternal life."

RECOMMENDED READING

For a free downloadable discussion guide for *The Peasant's Scroll*, visit RustyWilliams-Author.com.

IF YOU'VE GAINED ANYTHING FROM THIS BOOK, YOU should know this: This story came about because of the wonderful people—many of them scholars—who did the hard work before I typed the first word. These individuals have devoted a significant portion of their lives to the academic study of the holy texts.

Please consider supporting them by reading their books. Here is just a short list:

- *Saving Jesus from the Church: How to Stop Worshiping Christ and Start Following Jesus*
  — Robin R. Meyers, 2010, HarperOne.

- *Lost Scriptures: Books That Did Not Make It Into the New Testament*
  — Bart D. Ehrman, 2005, Oxford University Press, U.S.A.

- *The Bible Says So: What We Get Right (And Wrong) About Scripture's Most Controversial Issues*
— Dan McClellan, 2025, Macmillan US.

- *Why Christianity Must Change or Die: A Bishop Speaks to Believers in Exile*
— John Shelby Spong, 2001, HarperOne.

AUTHOR'S NOTE

Dear Reader,

Now that the final words of *The Peasant's Scroll* have been written (or have they?), I want to take a moment to share my gratitude with you.

This book is the result of years of research and would not exist without the support of so many people, beginning with my wife, Elissa. Elissa's encouragement and gentle nudges helped give me the confidence needed to begin this project. She listened to my ideas and my struggles, patiently reading every chapter as they were completed and offering her supportive feedback. I am forever grateful for her love, understanding, and especially her presence in my life.

My gratitude extends to those in the field of academic biblical research. Their decades of studies into the historical accuracy of the sacred texts are inspiring. They have forged and continue to forge a path for all who benefit from their findings. Some of these scholars have even personally answered my questions so that this book could represent the historical Jesus's mandate as recorded in *The Parable of the Sheep and the Goats*.

And, of course, my editor, Ita, who inspired me to bring this work to publication. Her attention to detail and suggestions made this book what it is today. More than anything, I am grateful for her friendship.

The Twelve-Week Book Group has been there for me and with me for what seems like forever. Their belief in me is what pushed me past the imposter syndrome I fought throughout the writing process, and I am thankful for each one of them.

And, most importantly, you—the reader—who chose to spend precious hours of your life immersed in the journey of Tom McGarvey.

Although Tom's journey here was brief, the actual journey of writing this book took more than three years. In those three years, I learned a lot about myself through Tom. Now you know what Tom knew about me and what I knew about Tom.

So, thank you. Thank you for accompanying Tom (and me) on his journey through the time he had left, where he experienced a transformational faith because he chose to feed the hungry, give drink to the thirsty, welcome the stranger, clothe the naked, and visit the sick and imprisoned.

May we all, when given the opportunity, choose to do the same.

With gratitude,
Rusty
January 2026

"Never doubt that a small group of thoughtful, committed citizens can change the world. Indeed, it is the only thing that ever has."

— Margaret Mead

OTHER BOOKS BY RUSTY WILLIAMS

- *Moral Fractures, 2025, The Barefoot Ministries.*
- *Finding Gratitude in Hope: How Humor, Optimism, Patience, and Empathy Can Help Us Accept What We Find Unacceptable, 2023, The Barefoot Ministries.*
- *Cranial Constipation: Proven Ways to Let Go of Sh!tty Thoughts and Cr@ppy Ideas, 2023, The Barefoot Ministries.*
- *G-Pa Has Stinky Feet, 2023, The Barefoot Ministries.*
- *What We Learned From Fostering Dogs: One Family's Journal of Pee, Poop, Heartache, and Unconditional Love, 2022, The Barefoot Ministries.*
- *The Living Eulogy Journal: A Year of Sharing Gratitude and Becoming Happier, 2021, The Barefoot Ministries.*
- *Doubt On Trial: An Agnostic Minister's Case For Questioning The Bible, 2021, The Barefoot Ministries.*
- *Doubt On Trial – Jury Notes: Journaling Your Thoughts During Doubt's Testimony, 2022, The Barefoot Ministries.*

To learn about all the author's books, follow this link:
RustyWilliams-Author.com

ABOUT THE AUTHOR

READERS OFTEN ASK HOW MUCH OF AN AUTHOR'S LIFE finds its way into their stories. In my case, the answer is simple: You'll discover pieces of me scattered throughout every chapter.

Even so, a few details might help fill in the picture.

I entered the Christian ministry in 2008 after completing a Master of Divinity in Pastoral Counseling, and later a Doctor of Ministry focused on church development. My early years in ministry were spent serving a small community church as a youth minister—a role I cherished until a spinal cord tumor in 2009 forced a major shift in my life's direction. Since then, writing and the practices of mindfulness and self-hypnosis have become central to my healing and daily rhythm.

Service has been the throughline of my adult life. Before the pulpit or the pen, there were "sirens and streetlights." I became the youngest certified paramedic in my state—right out of high school—and then spent twenty-five years in law enforcement, retiring as a detective. Along the way, I taught at the state level, served on professional boards, and traveled the country presenting workshops. I also built a practice as a clinical hypnotist and hosted a national weekly radio show.

Of all the roles I've held, none come close to the joy of being a grandfather, the father of two incredible men, a father-in-law to their extraordinary wives, and the husband of Elissa—the love of my life. Navigating disability has meant gravity and I have had our disagreements, and my family has lifted me up, both physically and emotionally, more times than I could ever repay. Their presence is my greatest blessing.

When we're not chasing possibilities together, Elissa and I spend our time with our pets and savor the quieter moments of this winding journey.

I'd love to connect with you. I'm active on Facebook, where I post regularly and share Sunday sermonettes. You can find me there as *Rusty Williams, Author*, and you're welcome to visit my website at RustyWilliams-Author.com.

If Tom's story resonated with you, I would be incredibly grateful if you would leave a review of *The Peasant's Scroll* on your preferred platform. Sharing your thoughts on this work of historical fiction helps other readers discover it.